Brit vs Scot

Want to know how the
Brit vs. Scot crossover
event began?

Check out these lead-up
books (in order):

One Hot Crush
(Hot Brits, Book 3)

Irresistible in a Kilt
(Hot Scots, Book 8)

One Hot Escape
(Hot Brits, Book 4)

Natural Satisfaction
(Au Naturel Trilogy, Book 3)

And don't miss these
follow-up books!

Devastating in a Kilt
(Hot Scots, Book 9)

One Hot Rumor
(Hot Brits, Book 5)

Praise for Anna Durand's Books

"*Brit vs. Scot* was a whole lot of fun to read! [Anna Durand] did an excellent job of keeping me guessing about what was going to happen next [and] developing her characters. As a man, I sympathized with Grey Dixon. Sometimes he messes up royally, and that's part of what makes him an appealing character. [...] Another charming aspect of Brit vs. Scot is its British and Scottish terminology. [...] I recommend *Brit vs. Scot* to rom-com fans."
Joe Wisinski, Readers' Favorite

"Wow! I'm so happy I picked up [*Natural Passion*]. [...] Refreshing, funny, and sexy, with a unique twist on a vacation spot. [...] Another author to add to my favorites list, and I can't wait for Ollie and Mara's story in *Natural Impulse*."
Sharon Clayton, The Eclectic Review

"Durand's Hot Scots series has been loads of fun to read, and this newest installment in the series is no exception. [...] The author's action-packed and suspenseful plot keeps the reader on their toes, and the grown-up sizzle never disappoints."
Jack Magnus, Readers' Favorite

" I loved the slow-burn, should we-shouldn't we, what's right, dilemma and desire that built and built until the steam had to escape. [*One Hot Chance*] is equal parts fun, steam, and moral quandary. [...] I am in love with Chance and his brothers already."
MaryLou Hoffman, Page Princess blog

"[*Lethal in a Kilt* is] full of hot sex, adventure, and so much laughter. I found myself laughing-out-loud at the antics of the Witches of Ballachulish (Logan's sisters) and the hilarious flirting and sexy banter between Serena and Logan. [...] Recommend highly! "
Sharon Clayton, The Eclectic Review

"I loved the Scottish in Ian and the strength of Rae, but the love of one little girl makes [*Notorious in a Kilt*] something to behold."
Coffee Time Romance

"I have enjoyed this whole series, but Emery and Rory [from *Scandalous in a Kilt*] have stolen my heart and are now my favorites!"
The Romance Reviews

Other Books by Anna Durand

One Hot Chance (Hot Brits, Book One)
One Hot Roomie (Hot Brits, Book Two)
One Hot Crush (Hot Brits, Book Three)
The Dixon Brothers Trilogy (Hot Brits, Books 1-3)
One Hot Escape (Hot Brits, Book Four)
One Hot Rumor (Hot Brits, Book Five)
Natural Passion (Au Naturel Trilogy, Book One)
Natural Impulse (Au Naturel Trilogy, Book Two)
Natural Satisfaction (Au Naturel Trilogy, Book Three)
Dangerous in a Kilt (Hot Scots, Book One)
Wicked in a Kilt (Hot Scots, Book Two)
Scandalous in a Kilt (Hot Scots, Book Three)
The MacTaggart Brothers Trilogy (Hot Scots, Books 1-3)
Gift-Wrapped in a Kilt (Hot Scots, Book Four)
Notorious in a Kilt (Hot Scots, Book Five)
Insatiable in a Kilt (Hot Scots, Book Six)
Lethal in a Kilt (Hot Scots, Book Seven)
Irresistible in a Kilt (Hot Scots, Book Eight)
Devastating in a Kilt (Hot Scots, Book Nine)
Lachlan in a Kilt (The Ballachulish Trilogy, Book One)
Fired Up (standalone romance)
The Outlands Shifter (standalone romance)
The Mortal Falls (Undercover Elementals, Book One)
The Mortal Fires (Undercover Elementals, Book Two)
The Mortal Tempest (Undercover Elementals, Book Three)
The Janusite Trilogy (Undercover Elementals, Books 1-3)
Obsidian Hunger (Undercover Elementals, Book Four)
Willpower (Psychic Crossroads, Book One)
Intuition (Psychic Crossroads, Book Two)
Kinetic (Psychic Crossroads, Book Three)
Passion Never Dies: The Complete Reborn Series

Brit vs Scot

A Hot Brits / Hot Scots / Au Naturel Crossover Book

ANNA DURAND

JACOBSVILLE BOOKS · MARIETTA, OHIO

BRIT VS. SCOT

ISBN: 978-1-949406-49-8 (paperback)
ISBN: 978-1-949406-50-4 (ebook)
ISBN: 978-1-949406-51-1 (audiobook)
Library of Congress Control Number: 2020923294

Manufactured in the United States.

Jacobsville Books
www.JacobsvilleBooks.com

Publisher's Cataloging-in-Publication Data
provided by Five Rainbows Cataloging Services

Names: Durand, Anna, author.
Title: Brit vs. Scot : a Hot Brits/Hot Scots/Au Naturel crossover book / Anna
     Durand.
Description: Marietta, OH : Jacobsville Books, 2021.
Identifiers: LCCN 2020923294 (print) | ISBN 978-1-949406-49-8 (paperback) | ISBN
     978-1-949406-50-4 (ebook) | ISBN 978-1-949406-51-1 (audiobook)
Subjects: LCSH: British--Fiction. | Scots--Fiction. | Americans--Fiction. | Triangles
     (Interpersonal relations)--Fiction. | Man-woman relationships--Fiction. | Romance
     fiction. | BISAC: FICTION / Romance / Romantic Comedy. | FICTION /
     Romance / Contemporary. | FICTION / Romance / New Adult. | GSAFD: Love
     stories.
Classification: LCC PS3604.U724 B75 2021 (print) | LCC PS3604.U724 (eb-
     ook) | DDC 813.6--dc23.

Chapter One

Grey

I HAVE THE WORST LUCK ON EARTH. IF I FLEW TO MARS, I'm sure my bad luck would outdo all those little green men and women over there too. How else would I end up with a brother who's insane and impossible to understand, not to mention a best friend who's the sexiest woman on earth but who has no interest in me whatsoever? No sexual interest, that is. She never forgets to share all the details of her love life with me.

So yes, I have monumentally bad luck.

Jessica O'Connor has done this to me. She drives me barmy, but I can't help the fact that I love her. I'm *in* love with her, have been for years, but she sees me as her asexual best friend, the mate she shares all her innermost thoughts with even when I'd rather not hear them. Do I seem asexual? I have no idea. I love sex, but apparently, I'm bloody awful at it.

That's why Jess lost interest. It's why all the women I shag lose interest.

My brother doesn't make matters any easier. He's determined to "help" me with my problems and ensure I win Jessica's heart. It's rubbish. He's off his trolley and bloody irritating. I have no say in any of it, though. Alex will do whatever he thinks is best, which will most likely wind up being something that humiliates and emasculates me even more than I've already done on my own.

Today, I'm sitting in the backseat of a taxicab with my best friend beside me, heading toward a mysterious destination. My half-brother, Alex Thorne, is getting married here in America, despite the fact he lives in Scotland now with his fiancée, Catriona MacTaggart. His adoptive parents have moved there too, but they're as British as Alex and I are. My brother has refused to tell me what sort of destination he and Cat have chosen for their wedding. He even threatened to blindfold me and Jessica during the cab ride to wherever we're going, but I put my foot down.

"No, Alex, absolutely no way," I'd said yesterday when he mentioned the idea. "If you try to blindfold me, I will tell Cat that you called her brother Rory a Cro-Magnon relic of the ice age who needs to thaw his shriveled, frozen bollocks in his wife's mouth."

"I was joking when I said that," Alex told me, smirking like he loves to do. "Everyone knows that. I was joking about the blindfold too. Mostly."

"The MacTaggarts all think you're barmy, and I agree."

"Don't be so provincial, Grey. If you want to shag Jessica again, and do it right this time, you need to loosen up and develop a sense of humor."

The conversation had devolved after that. Alex insists I have no sense of humor, but I have got one. Jess loves my jokes. She might treat me like a eunuch, but a eunuch that she loves.

As a mate. Only a mate.

Bloody hell.

I glance at Jessica. Her eyes always entrance me, the way they're blue but with golden rims around the pupils. Her dark-chocolate hair glistens, and I wish I could brush my fingers through it.

She's gazing out the side window, smiling while she takes in the scenery.

Trees, that's the scenery. Loads of ruddy trees. I like nature—honestly, I do—but being ferried through the forests of Oregon in a cab driven by a strange man who leers at us in the rearview mirror is not my idea of a good time.

Jessica bounces on the seat, grinning and pointing at something in the sky. "Look! A bald eagle!"

She aims her excited expression at me.

My heart stutters whenever she looks at me that way, so full of joy and excitement. She's been talking about this trip for weeks, ever since Alex ordered me to invite Jess to come along. Why does she have to be so beautiful and adorable? It makes me long to kiss her, but she doesn't want that.

"Did you see it?" she asks.

What had she been on about a second ago? I was too busy staring at her lips to notice. "See what?"

"The bald eagle." She gives my shoulder a halfhearted shove. "Pay attention, Grey. Daydreaming about your computer stuff is not allowed this week, remember?"

I was daydreaming about her, not "computer stuff," but there's no point in telling her that. Instead, I say, "Sorry. I'll stop thinking, I promise."

That's not much of a sacrifice since my brain shuts down every time she smiles. And Alex did command me not to do any work while I'm here in Oregon. He vowed to smash my computer with a sledgehammer if I brought it with me. I did bring it, of course, but I've hidden it in my largest bag with my clothes. Unless Alex rifles through my bag, he won't know I've brought my forbidden laptop.

"Oh!" Jessica cries out, scooting closer to me so she can lean over my body to see out the window on my side. Her breasts brush against my chest, and she lays a hand on my thigh, much too close to my groin. Her attention is riveted to the view outside. "What is that? I think it might be a turkey, but I can't see it very well with the trees in the way."

"Should I burn down the forest to give you a better view?"

"No, silly."

I'm enjoying the view of her cleavage a bit too much. Why did she have to wear a low-cut T-shirt? The way she's leaning over forces me to stare at the slopes of her lush breasts. All right, maybe I'm not forced to do it. But I'm only a man, you know. I can't help that my eyes veer to her chest when those tits are dangling right in front of me.

And the part of me that I least want to hear from right now is clamoring for my attention.

Shifting in my seat, I grimace at the heaviness growing in my, ah, nether regions. Fine, it's my testicles. And it's Jessica's fault I'm getting randy against my will.

No, it's my fault. I won't blame her. She's sexy as hell, but I should have the willpower not to get aroused by her. I'm the one who cocked up sex, which convinced her I'm a eunuch.

Her hand on my thigh slips, and it brushes against my dick.

I choke on my own saliva.

Jessica pulls away from the window, sitting inches away from me. She combs her fingers through my hair while I try to stop coughing. "Oh Greybee, are you okay?"

"Fine, yes."

Christ, why does she have to call me that embarrassing nickname when other people are around? Greybee is a contraction of "Grey baby," though she decided to spell it with two E's at the end for reasons I don't even try to understand. She insists on using that pet name in emails, usually accompanied by emojis of hugs and mouths blowing kisses. I might enjoy her affectionate, if silly, name for me if we were a couple. But it's bloody humiliating to have her call me that in front of the macho MacTaggart men—or in front of the leering cab driver in the front seat.

And of course, Jessica used that name in front of my brother. And of course, Alex now calls me Greybee whenever he wants to harass me.

"Almost there," the driver says, leering at us again. "Bet you can't wait to join the other weirdos. I hear it's a real freak-a-palooza out there this week."

"Jessica is not a freak," I announce. "She's a lovely person."

The lovely woman in question laughs and pinches my cheek. "You're so sweet, Greybee."

"Could you please call me Grey while we're at this wedding-week extravaganza?" I'm positive my brother will turn it into a true extravaganza with all sorts of crazy activities. If he tries to rope me into a round of Highland games with his Scots mates, I will murder him. With my bare hands. And I won't feel bad about it at all.

Jess leans her head against my shoulder, snuggling up to me.

I need to kiss her, so badly. I need to shag her too, even more badly, but I can never, ever do that again.

Unless I somehow, by a genuine miracle from heaven, become brilliant at sex.

The driver turns down a gravel driveway, passing through an open metal gate. I glimpse a sign on the gate, but I don't have a chance to read it. Jessica's body nestled against mine is distracting me from everything else in the universe.

A few minutes later, we pass through another open gate. The trees thin out, revealing a big clearing that houses various buildings of various sizes and what looks like a large lawn with a volleyball net set up in the middle of it. Other cars are parked behind the largest building and behind a smaller house. The MacTaggarts will be here along with my cousins and our mates, the Hunters. So will Alex and his fiancée, Cat, along with Alex's adoptive parents.

My chest aches, but not because of Jessica. Alex has parents. I don't, not anymore, not really. Alex and I share the same birth mother, but she's in prison. I don't count her as my mother, anyway. I grew up with only my father, and he's gone now. I've known my brother for only about four months, so we're still getting to know each other.

I wish Dad were here. He'd know what to do about...everything. Selwyn Dixon always had the right answer to every question.

Jessica kisses my cheek. "Stop thinking sad thoughts about your dad. This is a time to be happy. Your brother is getting married."

"How did you know what I was thinking about?"

"Because I know you." She touches the spot between my eyebrows. "And I know that crinkly-between-the-eyes look you get when you're thinking about your dad. Selwyn would want you to be happy."

Jessica and I have known each other since university, so she knew my father. He loved her and used to tell me, often, that I should marry her. Dad passed away five years ago, and I wouldn't have survived that without Jess. Honestly, I'm not sad about it anymore, not most of the time, but my life has been turned upside down over the past few months—finding out I have a half-brother, meeting his Scottish fiancée and his soon-to-be in-laws who are the barmiest bunch of Scots I've ever met. I like them, but I don't feel like I belong...anywhere.

Except with Jessica.

The driver stops the cab near the smaller house. "You're here. Enjoy the freak fest."

I get out first, then help Jessica out. She stumbles into me, crushing those beautiful breasts against my chest, but quickly pulls away. Her gaze swivels left and right while she takes in our surroundings.

The cab's boot pops open. Our driver climbs out to retrieve our bags and drops them on the ground. He gets back in the taxi and leans his head out the window, leering at us again. "The freaks in charge will take real good care of you, I'm sure."

I give the man a tip, though considering his rather disturbing attitude, I don't think he's earned it. Etiquette requires I give him one anyway.

As the driver turns the taxicab around and rolls down the driveway, Alex walks out of the little house, followed by two people I've never seen before. The woman has strawberry-blonde hair, and the man has dark hair that's longish and full of wild curls. He has an outrageously muscular body, so I'm sure all the women in attendance at this event will drool over him.

I am not jealous. I'm stating a fact, that's all.

"There you are," Alex says, clapping me on the shoulder. "Took you bloody long enough to get here."

"Our flight got delayed during the stopover in Des Moines, where I picked up Jessica. I texted you."

"Yes, I know. Whenever you text me, I'm amazed anew at how carefully you compose your messages. Perfect grammar, perfect punctuation, complete sentences."

He's smirking, which lets me know he's teasing me. Alex has the most bizarre sense of humor.

"It's cute," Jessica says. "Grey cares about using proper English. Mostly. I mean, you Brits do have a strange idea of what proper English is."

Alex raises his eyebrows, his lips twitching up at the corners. "We invented the language, love. It's you Americans who have deformed it beyond recognition."

I snort. "Not as much as the Scots have."

"You might have a point there." He leans in, his hand still on my shoulder. "But don't tell Catriona I said that."

I roll my eyes.

Jessica is smiling. She thinks Alex is, to quote her verbatim, "hot, weird, hilarious, and unique."

Why can't she describe me that way? Oh bugger. Now I'm whining in my thoughts about how Jess doesn't want me. *Grow a pair, mate, or you'll never convince her to want you.* Since I've had years to make that happen and have failed at every attempt, I'm not likely to change my luck this week.

Jessica is glancing around again, boosting up onto her tiptoes for a better look. "What is this place? Grey doesn't even know, and I'm getting curiouser and curiouser."

Alex hooks his thumbs in his waistband and rocks back on his heels. To the strawberry-blonde woman, he says, "Why don't you explain it to them, Eve?"

"Sure, but we should introduce ourselves first." The woman offers me her hand. "I'm Eve Silva, and the sexy beast beside me is my husband, Val. We own the resort."

I shake her hand. "It's a pleasure to meet you."

Val steps up and shakes my hand, then both Eve and Val shake Jessica's hand.

"Now that the introductions are over," Eve says, "you must be dying to know what sort of place your brother has brought you to. He insisted on secrecy. But I'll let Val explain."

"Thank you, Eve," the so-called sexy beast says. He has an accent, but I can't quite place it. Val crosses his arms over his chest and smiles. "Welcome to Au Naturel Naturist Resort."

"Naturist?" I say, not at all sure what that means.

"Yes." Val waves an arm in a sweeping gesture, indicating our surroundings. "You are guests at a nudist resort. Clothing is optional, though, so you don't need to go nude unless you want to."

My jaw goes slack, and for a few seconds, I can't form a single coherent thought. "My brother brought us to a nudist camp?"

Alex clucks his tongue. "Don't be such a prude, Grey. You can keep your kit on, but maybe you'll embrace the naturist lifestyle. You never know."

He rotates his eyes toward Jessica and tips his head in her direction, lifting his brows.

Oh no, he had better not be plotting what I think he's plotting. The last thing on earth that I need is my brother meddling in my life. Well, any more than he already has. It's too late to nip it in the bud.

"There's one more thing," Alex says. He clamps a hand on my shoulder. "Domhnall Sterling is here."

All the blood gushes out of my body as an icy chill sweeps through my veins. My eyes must be bulging, and though my mouth opens, I can't generate any sound.

Jessica's eyes flare wide too. "What is he doing here? How do you know my ex-fiancé?"

Oh yes, I have worse luck than anyone in the universe.

Chapter Two

Jessica

OH. MY. GOD. HOW DID THIS HAPPEN? I BROKE UP WITH Domhnall months ago, but he shows up here at the wedding of my best friend's brother. How did he even know I'd be here? I certainly never told him.

"I don't know Domhnall," Alex Thorne says. "He showed up a few hours ago and said he's your fiancé. I know that's not true, since Grey told me you ended the engagement, but I thought you should sort things with him."

"Uh, yeah. Sure." I can't think of anything else to say. Can't think, period. Why did Domhnall follow me here? If he wants me back, he can screw that idea. "I'll talk to him. I'm sorry he butted in on your special week."

"Oh, I've handled much worse invasions than this."

I've heard the stories about Alex—from Alex. So I know he's been through some crazy stuff. That includes being kidnapped by his birth parents earlier this year, though an Australian bad guy orchestrated that whole affair. Alex's adoptive parents are here somewhere, and I'm looking forward to meeting them. Grey says they're lovely people. Though he and Alex share the same biological mother, Alex considers his real mom to be the woman who actually raised him, his adoptive mother, Imogen Bennett.

Grey and Alex's birth mother is a con artist. Or she used to be. Now she lives inside a prison in Inverness, Scotland. Poor Greybee. He deserves a loving mom, not a criminal who abandoned him when he was six weeks old.

"Jessica doesn't need to talk to Domhnall," Grey announces.

His overprotective instincts can be sweet, but right now, he's stepping over a line.

"That's my decision," I say. "And I think I'd better talk to Domhnall. Convince him to scram before he turns Alex and Catriona's wedding into a reenactment of the Battle of Bannockburn."

Grey swerves his gorgeous caramel eyes toward me, and a muscle jumps in his jaw. "Why did you use Bannockburn as your example of the disaster ahead of us? The Scots won that."

"It was just a metaphor."

Why is he prickly about that? Sheesh. Domhnall taught me about Scottish history. What's the big deal? Grey has been behaving...not quite like himself lately.

I blame his big brother.

Yeah, I have zero evidence Alex is to blame, but he's a convenient scapegoat. I like Alex, but Grey has changed since meeting his half-brother, though I can't figure out why. They might share DNA and the same smoky-brown hair color, but otherwise, they seem like complete opposites.

"How did Domhnall know I'd be here?" I ask.

Alex shrugs. "He came with your friend Carly."

"What? Oh, she's getting an earful for sure."

"Carly is an invited guest, and he's her... What do they call it? Her plus one. That seems odd since he claims to be engaged to you, but then, Scots rarely make sense."

Before I can speak, a woman's voice calls out from behind Grey and his brother. "Alex Thorne, quit your havering. Haven't I told you insulting my people is not allowed?"

A pretty woman with chestnut hair walks out from behind the men. She stops beside Alex, hands on her hips, and shakes her head. Her lips kink up at the corners.

"Catriona, my love, my darling," Alex says with enough sarcasm that nobody could miss it. He throws an arm around her waist and tugs her into his body. "I was only joking. You Scots are the most charming, intelligent people in the world, and the bravest too. I aspire to be as noble and righteous as you lot."

"Alex," Catriona says, shaking her head again, "you couldn't be righteous if your life depended on it."

"Did I say righteous? I meant *self*-righteous."

Catriona punches him in the side, though not with much force. "If ye donnae behave, *mo leannan,* I'll have to insist you wear a tiara during the wedding ceremony. A pink, sparkly one."

"I volunteer to wear a tiara. Anything for the love of my life."

He doesn't sound sarcastic when he says that. He really loves his fiancée. When he gives her a quick kiss, they gaze at each other with a kind of adoration I've never seen in the eyes of any man I've ever dated. Not even Domhnall, who I'd been ready to marry. Hadn't I? Not sure. I said yes when he proposed, but I'd avoided setting a date.

My gaze snaps to Grey, and I feel a strange pressure in my chest.

"I should go talk to Domhnall," I say. "Where is he?"

"Ask Ollie," Alex says, waving toward the big building. "He assigned everyone's rooms in the guest house. There's been some overflow, what with an army of MacTaggarts in residence. Some are staying in tents, and others found rooms in town. At any rate, Ollie is the one to talk to."

A blond man is standing near the guest house talking to a dark-haired woman. That must be Ollie. He kisses the woman's cheek, and she combs her fingers through his hair. They smile at each other the way Alex and Catriona had done a minute ago.

Jeez, does everyone have a significant other except for me?

Well, Grey doesn't have a girlfriend. Not yet. Considering how many beautiful women are coming to this wedding, he'll probably have a girlfriend by tomorrow.

That pressure in my chest comes back. It's stress related, I'm sure.

"We'll be on the lawn," Alex tells me. "You and Grey are the last to arrive, so it's time for the opening ceremony."

"I thought the wedding was Saturday. This is Monday."

"The opening ceremony for the nuptial week festivities, that's what I meant. It's like the Olympics, but with lots of angry Scots who want to murder me. I'm used to death threats."

"Oh. I get it."

But no, I don't really. Before I met Alex, I'd kind of assumed Grey was exaggerating when he told me his brother is "barmy." Nope. As usual, Grey speaks the truth.

"I'm off," I say. "See you guys later."

Grey's shoulders sag, and his expression wilts too.

He never liked Domhnall, but he has no reason to be depressed because I'm going to talk to my ex-fiancé. Maybe like me, he's a little bummed by the lovey-dovey displays that seem to be happening everywhere.

Maybe Grey is suddenly kind of bummed because he's wiped out from the long trip to get here. Every other wedding guest arrived yesterday, but a "work emergency" had kept him from flying over with Alex and the Scots in a private jet owned by one of the MacTaggarts. What kind of emergency a business intelligence analyst could have, I don't know. It's computer stuff, not nuclear weapons. A MacTaggart whose name I can't remember sent his jet all the way back to the UK to collect Grey, and Grey had picked me up in Des Moines. The time difference meant he'd left and arrived this morning, local time, though it must be late afternoon in the UK by now. Or maybe it's evening. Or it might be tomorrow or yesterday or...something. Since he slept on the plane, I don't know if he has jet lag or not.

I'll give him a hug later. That always makes him smile.

The blond man and his raven-haired companion smile when I approach them. They're both wearing uniforms—charcoal pants and forest-green polo shirts that have the resort's logo printed on them. They wear charcoal sneakers too.

"Welcome to Au Naturel Naturist Resort," the man says, offering me his hand. "You must be Jessica O'Connor. Alex Thorne sent us photos of everyone just in case there were any gate-crashers. I'm Oliver Jackson, but everybody calls me Ollie."

I shake his hand. "Nice to meet you, Ollie. This is a beautiful area. I've never been to Oregon before."

"You'll love it here. We have a hot spring and a lake, both on our private property." He drapes an arm around the woman's shoulders. "This is my wife, Mara."

I shake her hand too. Wow, she's a knockout, even in her work uniform.

"You'll love where you're staying," Mara says. "Alex Thorne was adamant that you and his brother should have the new two-room bungalow we built a few months ago. It's separate from the guest house, kind of hidden behind it. We'll show you."

"Um, I need to speak to Domhnall Sterling first."

"Oh, right," Ollie says with a grin. "The ex-fiancé. Sounds like we could have some drama on our hands, but it's not the first time."

Mara fake pouts. "I missed the first big smackdown that happened here."

"Yeah, but you made one of your own when you scissor-kicked your ex-husband in the balls."

"Not a scissor kick. You're making me sound like a ninja."

I raise my hand. "If you could just point me to Domhnall's room..."

"Sure," Ollie says. "Second floor, Room 210. Just go through the door behind us, down the hall to the stairs, and up to the first landing."

"Thanks."

I hurry into the guest house, following Ollie's instructions, and reach the door to Room 210. Though I raise my hand to knock, I freeze with my fist an inch from the wood. My ex-fiancé is inside this room. He followed me here. That must mean he wants me back, but it's too late. He wrecked our relationship months ago, and I will never forgive him for what he did.

But I should confront Domhnall, once and for all.

So I knock.

The door swings open, and Domhnall Sterling grins at me. "Jess, I've missed you."

He flings his brawny arms around me and hauls me into an embrace, squeezing hard enough to make me wince. My face is smashed against his chest.

I wriggle but can't get free. "Let go of me, Domhnall."

Though he steps back, he keeps his hands on my upper arms. "You look bonnie as ever, Jess."

He looks good too, of course. My ex couldn't have shown a little courtesy and gotten flabby or developed a strong body odor. Nope, he smells good and looks even better. Not that I'm still attracted to him. But I am a woman, and he is a muscular, sexy man, which means I can't help noticing all that. Still, I don't feel the teeniest inclination to admire his biceps or run my hands over that chest. I used to love doing that, but not anymore.

"You need to go home," I tell him. "This is a private wedding, and you are not going to ruin it for Alex and Catriona."

"Ahmno leaving, Jess. Not unless you're going with me."

"It's over, Domhnall. Finito. The end."

"No, it's not." He brackets my face with his hands. "I love you, Jessica. We both know why you broke off the engagement, and it had nothing to do with me."

"Yes, it did. You issued the ultimatum."

"What else could I do? You need to cut that wee scunner loose. He's keeping you from having what you really want, what you really need."

"Oh, let me guess. You think I want and need you." I push his hands away and lift my chin. "No way, Domhnall. If you really loved me, you would never have said those words to me."

"Ye make it sound like I made an unreasonable demand."

I huff. "Of course you did."

"Maybe I need to say it again." He leans in so close to my face that the stubble on his chin tickles me. "End your friendship with Grey Dixon. He's a lead weight dragging you down. Cut him loose, Jess, and we can have the life we both want—together."

"What you actually said was 'Grey Dixon is a *bod ceann* who's poisoning your mind against me.' Then you ordered me to end the friendship."

"Aye, and it's what you need to do. Now, Jess, before it's too late."

"How could you think calling my best friend a dickhead was acceptable?" I take two big steps backward and clench my teeth. "If I told you to dump your closest friend, how would you feel? You're nothing but a selfish prick who got jealous of my relationship with Grey. Who, by the way, is a better man than you'll ever be."

"That's him talking, not you."

"Ugh. I think for myself. And only an asshole would tell me I don't. How can you not realize how condescending that is?" I hold my hands up when he starts to move toward me. "No, Domhnall, we are never getting back together. It's over. Go home."

I stalk down the hall and out of the guest house.

No, I will never cut Grey loose just to make a jealous jerk happy. Don't care how amazing the sex was. Domhnall has no right to issue insulting ultimatums, and he absolutely has no right to follow me here as part of some asinine plot to win me back. Never going to happen.

Domhnall isn't a horrible person deep down. The real Domhnall Sterling, the one I knew and cared about for two years, is stubborn but also smart and charming. I can't understand why he's behaved like such an ass ever since the day we broke up. His determination to drive a wedge between me and Grey has started to verge on obsession.

I bump into Carly just outside the guest-house door.

When she sees me, she bites her bottom lip and hunches her shoulders. "Jess, I'm so sorry. Domhnall was very convincing when he told me he just wanted to see you again so he could apologize for everything. I didn't realize until we got here that he, um…"

"Lied to you? Yeah, Domhnall Sterling can be very persuasive. Why didn't you warn me he'd be here?"

"He wanted it to be a surprise." She grimaces. "Guess that should've been a clue, huh? I'm such an idiot."

"No, I don't blame you." I never told Carly the details of why Domhnall and I broke up. We're good friends, but not BFFs. That title belongs to Grey Dixon. "It's okay, Carly. I'm not mad at you."

"I hope you told him to leave."

"Yes, I did." But maybe I should ask Alex Thorne to kick him out. I mean, this is his and Catriona's wedding get-together.

Time to find Grey and give him that hug. I'm so glad I have him as my best friend.

Chapter Three

Grey

I HATE DOMHNALL STERLING. NEVER IN MY LIFE DID I hate anyone until I met him. The wanker thinks he owns Jess. What if he uses his smarmy charms, which some women inexplicably think are attractive, and wins her back? I lost count of how many times Jessica cried on my shoulder because of something the Scots lout did. Most of his loutish behavior involved his ex-wife. He kept her in his life despite the fact she'd married someone else and despite the fact it made Jess miserable.

Of course, Jessica also told me what a fantastic lover he is. Repeatedly. I'm glad she never shared the graphic details, but hearing how amazing he is... Well, I suppose it made me slightly jealous. Jessica took up with Domhnall three weeks after she and I had sex. Should I view that as a compliment? Jess cried after our one and only sexual encounter. She was terrified our friendship would be destroyed by it.

That disaster had almost done us in, but we recovered from it.

And Jess always gushed about Domhnall's prowess in bed.

"Fuck," I hiss, kicking a pebble. It flies several feet away, landing in the grass. I'm leaning against the back of the guest house so I can glare at the woods and try to figure out why I can't make Jess love me the way I love her. It's pathetic and humiliating, but I can't stop my mind from tormenting me with what-ifs.

"There you are, wee brother."

I glance at Alex and roll my eyes. "Thank you. I needed to be insulted again, and by my own flesh and blood."

"How have I insulted you?"

"By calling me your 'wee' brother."

"Would you rather I call you Greybee?"

"Can't you just use my name?"

Alex leans against the wall beside me. "I was experimenting with a Scottish word. Cat spouts them constantly, and I'm starting to feel left out what with all these kilt-wearers around."

Right, Alex the shameless show-off feels rejected. I'll believe that on the day the sun turns into a smiley face in the sky.

My brother sets a hand on my shoulder. "Cheer up, Grey. Jessica told Domhnall to leave. The news is making its way through the grapevine as we speak."

"But he hasn't left yet, has he? Can't you order him to go?"

"Yes, I could. And if that's what you really want, I will do it." He squeezes my shoulder. "But I think you'd be missing out on a great opportunity if we send him packing."

"What opportunity? More chances for him to sweet-talk Jess into going back to him? That arsehole is some kind of Svengali."

"Jessica had a private conversation with him, and it resulted in her telling him to leave. If Domhnall Sterling ever was a Svengali, Jessica has become immune to his powers of persuasion." Alex stuffs his hands in his trouser pockets and crosses his ankles. "I think you should invite Domhnall to stay, as a peace offering."

"What?" I jerk my head to stare at him. He must be joking. Ask the enemy to stay? It's insane.

Alex sighs. "Calm down, Grey. I'm not suggesting you and Domhnall become best mates. Letting him stay would be a strategic move. You'll have the chance to show Jessica how much better you are than Domhnall."

"He's better at sex. Can't do anything about that."

My brother regards me in silence for a moment, but I recognize the expression on his face. He's sizing me up and deciding what sort of bollocks to feed me. I like Alex, but we haven't known each other long. He was raised by our grifter mother until he was taken into care at age eight and then taken in by a nice couple who adopted him. I was raised by my father, a decent, hard-working man who never conned a soul—though our mother conned him and left me behind.

Alex can't help being a bit...dodgy, at times. It's his nature.

I can't help being strangled by the need to do the right thing all the time, even when that means I lose out to someone like Domhnall.

Maybe I should try to be more like Alex.

"All right," he says. "It's time to tell me the details about what happened when you and Jessica shagged."

"Details? No, absolutely not."

"Can't help if you don't share."

I frown, scratch behind my ear, and avoid looking at him. Am I actually going to tell him everything? The "details"? I can't. My brother doesn't need to know how I bollocksed up sex with Jess. Every girl I've ever slept with told me I'm rubbish in the bedroom. Well, almost every girl.

But Alex seems to know all about those things. Catriona always comes across as very happy and satisfied. I've stayed at their house several times, and I sort of inadvertently overheard them going at it. The things she said... Christ, if Jess shouted the things Catriona did, I'd be the happiest bloke on earth.

"Fine," I say with so much resignation in my voice that it's embarrassing. "I'll tell you. The whole thing lasted about five minutes, and it ended with Jessica sobbing."

Alex winces. "That's not good."

"It started out perfect. We were kissing and touching each other, then we took our clothes off. There was more kissing and touching, and things started to heat up. It was incredible." I rub my eyes with the heels of my hands and groan. "But as soon as we started to shag, everything went wrong. She said 'ouch' several times. Then I, um, sort of, ah...went off too soon."

Alex makes a pained face. "I'm guessing that's when Jessica started to sob."

"Yes. She wouldn't speak to me for days after, and she couldn't look me in the eye for at least a week after that." I let my head fall back against the wall. "Three weeks after we had sex, she met Domhnall Sterling."

"Hmm, I do believe I'm starting to see the whole picture." Alex gazes out at the woods for several seconds, seeming to consider the problem of me. "You mentioned that every girl you've ever slept with thinks you're rubbish. Have you really never had one good sexual experience?"

"Maybe one."

"Tell me about it."

How many embarrassing things am I meant to tell him? Humiliation has become my lot in life, so I guess it doesn't matter what I confess to my brother.

"The first time," I say. "That wasn't rubbish. The girl seemed to enjoy it, and so did I."

"No premature explosion?"

I shake my head.

Alex gives me his analytical look again. "You met Jessica at university, correct?"

"Yes. Our first year at Bournemouth. She wanted to see more of the world, and England had always fascinated her. So she decided to study there."

"Did you have sex only once before you met her?"

"Uh, yes." What is he getting at?

"Did Jessica start calling you Greybee before or after your ill-fated attempt to shag her?"

Once again, I have no ruddy clue what Alex is trying to get at. But I answer anyway. "Before. She's called me that since a few days after we met."

"Ah-ha," he says like that explains everything. "Did she have nicknames for the Scot?"

I rub the back of my neck, staring down at the ground. "She called him Domhnallicious, the Gaelic God, and King O. I think that refers to, you know..."

"Orgasms. Yes, I figured that one out." My brother smiles with smug satisfaction. "At last, the picture becomes clear."

"In what way? Doesn't seem any clearer to me."

"Firstly, Jessica's pet name for you is affectionate. Her names for Domhnall are all related to sex."

"Am I meant to be happy about that? I'm her fluffy little puppy, and he's her sex god."

"You're missing the point, but I think you need to realize that on your own." Alex pushes away from the wall and pats my shoulder. "There's another point you're missing too, but I'll give you more of a clue to this one. You did all right the first time you had sex, but after meeting Jessica, you suddenly became rubbish at it. Mystery solved."

"What on earth are you implying?"

He gives my shoulder a shake, slanting in so close that I can see the darker specks in his irises. "You're in love with Jessica. You can't get a proper leg over with anyone else because you want her and only her."

"I've already admitted to you, months ago, that I'm in love with her. And even if it's true that I can't do it properly with other women because I want her, that doesn't explain why I cocked it up *with* her."

"Honestly, it should be obvious. You were nervous. After years of fantasizing about her, you finally had Jessica naked, and you lost your nerve."

Even if that's true—and I'm pretty sure he's right about it—I don't see how recognizing that fact helps me at all. I'll be even more nervous if I try to seduce her again. Might as well give up and join a monastery.

"What am I meant to do?" I ask, and though it's a rhetorical question, my brother answers.

"Show Jessica you are the better man," Alex says. "Be yourself, but stop being so...twitchy. You need to prove to her that you are a mature man who knows what he wants and knows how to give a woman what she wants."

"But—"

"I wasn't finished." He smiles in that devious way, the one I know means he's plotting something. "You also need to talk to a neutral party about your sexual problems."

"A neutral party?" I get a sinking feeling in my gut that warns me I know which so-called neutral person he's going to suggest I talk to about the most embarrassing problem I've ever had. "No, Alex."

"Yes, Grey." He slaps my arm. "I'll let Jack know you need to have a chat to him."

"I said no."

Alex ignores me and starts to walk away, toward the crowd of Mac-Taggarts gathered on the lawn.

"Did you not hear me?" I call after him. "No way, Alex. I'm not talking to a psychologist, much less a Scottish one."

My brother flashes me another devious smile over his shoulder. Then he shouts to someone I can't see, "He's around the back. Give my brother a good firm hug, would you? He's too tense."

Alex, you sodding arsehole.

I want to run after my brother and throttle him before he finds Jack MacTaggart, but I see Jessica coming around the corner of the guest house, so I give up and slump against the wall. When Jess reaches me, she chews on her bottom lip the way she always does when she's worried. I'm too tense, Alex told her. Give him a good firm hug, my devious brother also said.

"Are you okay?" Jess asks. "You do look kind of weird."

Wonderful. Now she thinks I'm rubbish at sex and weird.

"I'm fine, really," I tell her. "Alex is a lying arsehole, so don't believe a word he says."

"Oh come on, you like your brother. He's very strange, but he cares about you."

"Yes, I know. In his bizarre way, he's trying to help."

"Well, he's right about one thing." She throws her arms around me, crushing her body to mine. With her mouth grazing my ears, she whispers, "My Greybee does need a hug."

She squeezes me tighter, mashing her breasts to my chest. Her warm, soft body feels so good, but the way her hair keeps tickling my cheek and her fingers tease my nape... That feels bloody wonderful. If I don't push her away soon, I'll develop a problem that won't help the situation.

Jess kisses my cheek and pulls away. "Better?"

"Uh, yeah, sure." At least she stopped hugging me before my brain decided to relocate all the blood in my body down to my dick. "How did it go with Domhnall?"

She shrugs. "I told him to leave, but I don't think he'll go voluntarily. Maybe Alex could toss Domhnall's ass off the property."

I just manage to suppress a grimace. She didn't even think to ask me to do that.

Alex is right. I need to show Jessica I am a man, the sort who tosses cabers and makes love to women so well that they never want anyone else. I need to be like Alex. Shameless. Bold. Unafraid.

How am I going to do that? Not a clue, but I'll figure it out. I'm cleverer than Domhnall, aren't I? So, all I need to do is outwit the Scots lout. No problem.

I'll start by taking Alex's advice.

"Let Domhnall stay," I tell Jessica. "The more the merrier, right? This is the wedding of the century after all, according to Alex. Maybe Domhnall will meet someone new here."

Jessica's eyes widen, but only for a second, then she smiles with a sort of appreciation I haven't seen from her before—not when her smile is aimed at me, at least. "Wow, Grey, that's so generous of you. I mean, I know you don't get along with Domhnall. He's not a total jerk, though he's doing a fantastic impression of one lately. But you're right. He could meet someone new here."

Maybe I can make sure that happens. Somehow. By channeling my grifter brother and learning how to be devious.

I will do anything for Jess. Anything.

She hooks her arm around mine and urges me to start walking. "Let's join the crowd, so you can introduce me to all those MacTaggarts."

Though I know I have to do that, since it would be rude not to, I'm also plotting all the ways I can prove to Jessica that I am the right man for her.

Chapter Four

Jessica

GREY KEEPS HIS HAND ON MY LOWER BACK WHILE HE SHEP-herds me through the crowd of Scots, heading for who-ever he thinks I should meet first. I hadn't met most of these people before today, except for Alex and Catriona. I'm excited to be introduced to so many new faces. I'd met Grey's brother several times when I visited Grey in England. Grey had taken me to meet his cousins too—Chance, Reese, and Dane—as well as their friends, the twins Richard and Nick Hunter. I'd also met everyone's wives who are, oddly, all Americans. Well, except for Catriona.

The Dixons and the Hunters are here today, but I haven't seen them yet. Grey's cousins aren't technically related to Alex, but they call Alex their cousin anyway. It's like an honorary title or something.

My best friend guides me to a group of MacTaggarts that's off to the side, distanced a bit from the rest of the throng. Grey approaches them, evincing a confidence I've never seen in him before. He's not shy, exactly, but he doesn't do well with strangers. Of course, he's probably met these people before since his brother is marrying a MacTaggart.

Domhnall never introduced me to his family or his friends, other than his business partner, and never suggested he might want to in the future. When I asked him about that, he grunted and shrugged.

Grey volunteered to introduce me to his friends and family.

His hand touches my back so lightly, but that faint pressure makes me feel... I don't know. I can't describe it. Whenever Grey touches me, even the tiniest bit, I get this indescribable feeling. It's not bad. In fact, I like it.

We reach the smaller group of MacTaggarts, and Grey stops us there.

A man with light-brown hair and pale-blue eyes, who seems older than the rest, smiles at us. "Grey, is this your girl? We've been looking forward to meeting her."

"She's not—" Grey scrunches up his face, but only for a split second. It's doubtful anyone else noticed that. "This is Jessica O'Connor, my best friend. Jess, this is Iain MacTaggart. He's an archaeologist, like Catriona."

Iain and I shake hands.

Back before I'd met any of the MacTaggarts, I'd kind of assumed Grey hated all Scots. Clearly, that's not the case. I guess he only hates my ex-fiancé. Does that mean... No, Grey could not be jealous of Domhnall.

My gaze wanders to him, and he's already looking at me. He smiles and gently rubs his hand over my back. A tiny shiver makes the hairs on my arms lift. Yeah, I *really* like it when Grey touches me. We tried sex, and it almost wrecked our friendship, so I won't ever go there again. I love Grey, but not in *that* way. Sometimes I wish I did. Well, maybe I feel...something.

But no, I will never risk losing him by giving in to whatever this is I'm feeling. So what if this unnamed thing I'm experiencing has been getting stronger lately? It means nothing. Well, it means one thing. I haven't had sex in months, not since the night before I broke up with Domhnall. I'm horny, that's all. Grey is attractive, and I don't meet many guys in my line of work. The ones I do meet can't speak because their entire mouths are numb, and they've got metal implements in there too. Yeah, being a dental assistant is not conducive to meeting eligible men. I don't love my job, but I don't hate it either. A career in dentistry had been a practical choice, not my passion, something I trained for when I couldn't get a job with my teaching degree.

After work, I'm usually too wiped out to do anything other than talk to Grey on the phone or do a video chat with him.

Does that mean something? Nah.

Grey introduces me to everyone in this little splinter group of Scots, including the Three Macs aka Catriona's three brothers—Lachlan, Rory, and Aidan. The Three Macs and their sisters Jamie and Cat married or will soon marry Americans. Alex Thorne might be British by birth and by accent, but he's also an American citizen. He has dual citizenship which Grey tried to explain to me once, but my head started to spin, so he gave up. Is there such a thing as triple citizenship? Don't think I want to know the answer.

I also meet some of the Three Macs' cousins. Iain is just one of them. There's also Evan the billionaire, Logan the ex-MI6 agent, and Jack the psychologist. Grey gets a funny look on his face when Jack approaches us and shakes my hand. Jack seems nice, but Grey acts uncomfortable around him. He flattens his lips and glances around like he needs to make sure no one can hear whatever he and Jack might say to each other.

Things get even weirder when Jack places a hand on Grey's arm and leans in to whisper to him. I can't hear what's being said since he's speaking too softly, but I do hear the last thing he tells Grey.

"I'm in Room 312. Come to me whenever you're ready."

What on earth? That almost sounds like Jack is propositioning Grey, but my best friend is not gay. I've heard that Jack's wife left him two years ago, but nobody said why they broke up. Maybe Jack is gay. I have no idea. When Grey and I had sex, it was awful, so maybe he's finally realized he prefers men. I have trouble believing that, but I will be totally supportive if that's what's going on. He's my best friend no matter what.

I feel a little queasy when I think about Grey being gay. My mind travels back in time to that night when he'd kissed me and done it so well that I still dream about that kiss sometimes. Often, actually. Okay, more than often. I've thought about it way too much ever since I dumped Domhnall. But if Grey is batting for the other team now, I'll never get to kiss him again.

Which doesn't matter. I'm not interested in more than friendship with him. So yeah, I'll support him all the way in whatever life changes he wants to make.

But that kiss...

"Jessica, are you all right?" Grey asks.

I jerk my thoughts back to reality, blinking several times to clear my mind. "Huh? Yeah, I'm fine."

That's when I realize Jack is gone. Grey and I stand here alone, several yards from the nearest congregation of MacTaggarts.

"What happened to Jack?" I ask.

"He left while you were semi-catatonic, staring at the trees or my shirt. Not sure which." Grey studies me for a couple of seconds. "Are you sure you're all right?"

"Positive. What were you and Jack talking about? Sounded serious."

Grey averts his gaze, hunching one shoulder. "It's a personal matter. Private."

"Oh." We used to tell each other everything. If he's keeping secrets from me, that must mean something big is up. I desperately want to grill him about that, but I can't make myself say the words. Unless and until he wants to share his secret with me, I have to live with not knowing.

Grey narrows his gaze on me and folds his arms over his chest. "Jessica, I know when you're upset, so tell me what's wrong."

Yeah, he always knows when I'm unhappy even when nobody else notices.

So I tell him the truth. "You and Jack have a secret. I used to be the only person who knew things about you that nobody else did. You and Jack must be getting really close."

"Close? I met him recently and haven't spent much time around him, so I wouldn't say we're good mates."

"But you, uh..." It's none of my business. I shouldn't ask him, but I'm dying to know the answer. "Never mind."

Grey moves closer, settling his hands on my arms, and bends his head so our gazes align. "That's rubbish, Jess. You're upset about something, and it seems to be about Jack. Tell me what's going on, please."

Sometimes I wish I were good at lying, but no, I suck at it.

"Your life choices are none of my business," I say. "Honestly, I don't care if you guys are involved. You'll always be my best friend, no matter who you choose to love."

His brows squish together over his nose, but it's not like that crinkly thing he does when he thinks about his dad. His mouth falls open a smidge. "What in the world are you talking about?"

Now that I've completely stepped in it, I might as well roll around in the shit pile I've made. "You and Jack. I don't blame you for falling for him. I mean, he is gorgeous and super nice."

"Falling for—" He jerks his head back, his eyes bulging so much I expect them to pop out. His mouth gapes open, but for several seconds, the only sound he makes is a tiny gasping noise. Then he covers his face with both hands and groans. When he raises his face to me again, his shoulders sag. "Jessica, I am not gay."

"But Jack invited you to his room. 'Whenever you're ready,' he said."

Grey shuts his eyes, his face pinched into a tight expression. Then he looks straight into my eyes. "He's a psychologist. Alex told Jack that I might want to talk to him about some, ah...personal issues. It's therapy, not a secret liaison."

"Therapy? What's happened that makes you need professional help? Are you okay?"

"Stop worrying, Jess. I'm fine. This is just…something I need to work out on my own."

"On your own but with Jack. Alex knows what's wrong too, doesn't he? I'm the only one who's in the dark." Oh God, now I sound like a harpy. Why does Grey's confession that he needs therapy make me feel like I've been rejected? It's dumb. "I'm sorry, Grey. Don't know what's wrong with me today. I'm glad Alex suggested you talk to Jack, and I hope he can help you figure things out."

"I want to tell you about this. I do, really. But it's complicated."

"You don't owe me any explanations. Please, let's just forget we ever had this conversation. I'm such an idiot." Jeez, could I have humiliated myself any worse? Since I don't want to find out, I latch on to the first lame excuse that pops into my mind, so I can escape from this conversation. "Gotta go. I'm hungry for, um, green beans. Think I'll go to the dining hall and get some."

Green beans? Really? Ugh.

Before he can say anything else, I hustle away from him, wending my way through the crowd to get to the guest house. I bump into several people, but they all smile and apologize like it's their fault. My freaked-out brain can't manage anything more comprehensible than "uh, sorry." I burst through the guest-house doors and stop. The hallway is empty, and the house seems silent. Everyone is outside, I guess.

What the hell is wrong with me? Grey's not gay, but I have no idea why the thought he might have been got me so upset. He still has a secret, one he doesn't feel comfortable telling me. That realization had hurt so much that, for a second, I thought I might throw up. Apparently, I've gone cuckoo today.

I shuffle down the hall but suddenly forget where I intended to go.

The door bursts open and bangs shut again.

"Jessica, wait."

I freeze when I hear Grey's voice. Inch by inch, I turn toward him, my face scrunched up.

"You're making your anxious face," he says, standing so close I can smell his aftershave.

Damn, I love that scent.

He shakes his head the tiniest bit. "Green beans? You don't even like those. What's gotten into you today? Is it because Domhnall's here?"

"No, it's not that." I can't explain it to him because I have no idea what's wrong with me. "I guess I assumed I was your number-one confidante. But that's selfish and stupid."

He moves even closer, cupping my cheek in one hand. "No, it's not stupid. You *are* my number-one confidante. You're my best mate, Jess, and that will never change. But there is one thing I'd be more comfortable discussing with another bloke, and Jack is a therapist. He counsels people for a living."

"Yeah, I know. You should talk to him."

"I want to tell you all about it, but not just yet. All right?"

"Mm-hm."

He lets out a long sigh. "I'm allowed to keep things to myself, you know. And I said I'll tell you later."

"Fine, whatever. It's none of my business, and I'm sorry I got bitchy about it."

"You're not bitchy." He pulls me closer, gripping my arms. "I want to tell you everything, Jess, I do. This is not a sign our friendship is falling apart. Do you believe me?"

"Of course I do."

He rests his forehead on mine and exhales another long breath. The warmth of it teases my skin, and the feel of his hands on my arms is affecting me in the strangest way. My skin starts to tingle where his palms touch me, the delicious sensation blossoming outward until my whole body comes alive with a sultry warmth. Why do I feel this way? Grey is my best friend, nothing more. I shouldn't care if he keeps a few things to himself, and I really shouldn't love having him so close with his hands and his forehead in contact with my skin. And God, the way he smells. I absolutely should not love that, but I do.

With his face millimeters from mine, his lips achingly close, I can't stop my lids from sliding shut and my body from relaxing. Words escape my lips before I stop to think about what I'm saying. "Kiss me, Grey."

His hands stiffen, and I bet his entire body does the same thing. He lifts his head away from mine, but I still can't manage to open my eyes. "What did you say?"

"Huh?" I finally pry my lids open and see the stunned look on his face. My thoughts are still hazy, which is my only excuse for what I say next. "Kiss me, Grey. Please."

"Why?"

Does he have to sound so shocked and baffled? I mean, he's kissed me before. Once. Two years ago. Right before our awful attempt to have sex. Okay, I can see why he might be hesitant to kiss me again, especially considering the way I pleaded for it.

He stumbles backward two steps. "I can't. Sorry."

Grey rushes past me, heading deeper into the guest house.

I can't make my feet move. Should I run after him? Call out to him?

He gallops up the stairs and out of sight.

What if I just ruined our friendship? I can't even explain why I begged him to kiss me, but obviously, he doesn't want to do that. I don't want it either. I suffered one moment of madness, brought on by the stress of this day. A wedding at a nudist resort? Sheesh. And then Domhnall showed up. Now Grey wants him to stick around. Confusion, that's the cause of my insane request that Grey kiss me. Confusion and stress.

I need a drink. Right now. Vodka and the unhealthiest food I can find.

But as I hurry into the dining hall where snacks await, one thought torments me. Why didn't Grey want to kiss me?

Chapter Five

Grey

JESSICA BEGGED ME TO KISS HER. SHE *BEGGED*. I DIDN'T mishear that, did I? Like an auditory hallucination or something? No, I'm one hundred percent certain she said that. *Kiss me, Grey.* Well, I'm at least ninety percent sure. Maybe I wanted her to say that, so I imagined she had. No, she definitely said, "Kiss me, Grey. Please."

And I ran away.

You bloody stupid arsehole.

Since I'd cocked it up again with Jess, I decided to take Jack up on his offer. He was in his room unpacking when I banged on the door. Now, I'm lying on the double bed in his room while he sits in a chair near the foot where I can see him if I open my eyes. I have them closed right now, and I'd rather not see the look on his face. He must think I'm a nutter and a moron. What sort of man runs away when the woman he's loved for years pleads for a kiss?

"Are you going to tell me about it?" Jack asks in a patient tone I assume all psychologists learn at school.

"What?" I'm pretending I didn't hear him the first time he asked that or the second time either. Anything to delay the inevitable shame. Why did I come here if I don't want to share everything with Jack? He'll keep it all confidential. Won't he?

"You heard me both times I asked," Jack says. "What happened when you and Jessica had sex? And when was that, anyway?"

"Two years ago." I rub my eyes and groan. "I mucked it up, that's what happened."

"Details, Grey. I can't help unless I know everything."

I groan again, then I tell Jack what I told Alex earlier. Verbatim, I think. Once I'm done, I say, "That's the kaleidoscope of my shame. Happy now?"

Jack chuckles softly. "You're more like your brother than you think. He resisted therapy too and used sarcasm as a shield. But you won't be as resistant as he was, I can tell."

Should I be flattered or insulted that he compared me to Alex? My brother can be confusing and irritating, but he's also clever and strangely entertaining, not to mention quite serious about helping me with my embarrassing problem. But he also lies, or at least evades answering questions. I don't do either of those.

Except when I told Jessica I couldn't kiss her.

I can, obviously. I'm physically capable of kissing her. But she must have assumed I meant I don't want to do it, and I let her believe that. I am a liar, aren't I? Just like Alex.

"Resistance is futile," Jack says. "I'll get my hands in your mind one way or another."

The strange hunger in his voice makes me open my eyes.

Jack is smiling. He points a finger at me and laughs. "See? I got you to look at me. That's how good I am."

"Aren't psychologists meant to be comforting?"

He laughs again, louder this time. "Alex asked me the same question, almost verbatim, during our first session. The answer is that I'm not your typical therapist. I tailor my technique to each client, and everything will be completely confidential. So, relax and enjoy it."

"I don't see how I'm going to enjoy this."

"You can tell me anything because I won't tell a soul." He props one ankle on the opposite knee, clasps his hands over his belly, and slouches a little like he's very relaxed. "Now, let's talk about why you cocked it up when you had a poke with Jessica."

"Not a clue. That's why I'm here. You're meant to explain it to me."

"That's not how therapy works, laddie. I ask annoying questions until you're fair certain I'm a dunderhead and an ersehole, then you suddenly realize the truth. And you thank me."

"Brilliant. Can we skip that, and you just tell me the answer?"

"Not how it works." He links his hands behind his head, eying me with no discernible expression. "What did Alex say about it?"

"Maybe he should be my therapist since all you care about is what Alex thinks."

"I may have been wrong. You might be even more resistant than he was. Bloody-mindedness runs in the family, eh? But you came to me, so I'm thinking you want my help. Cannae do that unless you participate in the session."

"Fine." I lay my hands on my belly, my fingers tapping, and stare at the ceiling. "Alex thinks I started having trouble with sex after I met Jessica because I've always wanted her and only her. The first time I slept with a girl, it was fine. But then I met Jess, and Alex has decided there's a connection. He also thinks sex with Jess was awful because I got nervous."

"Do you agree with him?"

I shrug. "Maybe. I don't know. Alex also implied there's some deeper meaning in the fact that Jessica calls me Greybee, which is a contraction of Grey baby, but her pet names for Domhnall Sterling are all sex-related."

"Really?" Jack says like that's the most fascinating fact he's ever heard. He leans forward, setting his elbows on his knees. "Tell me those pet names."

My humiliation knows no bounds, does it? "She called him Domhnallicious, the Gaelic God, and King O. The last one is a reference to, um..."

Just like when I'd told Alex about those pet names, I still can't speak the word orgasm. Why? I'm not a teenager. I'm a grown man who should have no problem talking about sex.

"Pretend I can't guess what the O stands for," Jack says, "and explain it to me."

I squeeze my eyes shut because I cannot look at him, or even look at the vicinity of him, when I say it. "King O means King Orgasm. Jessica used to tell me what an 'outrageous stud' Domhnall is. Honestly, I don't see how the other pet names relate to sex. They're just about how amazing that damn Scot is." I wince, suddenly realizing what I've said. "Sorry. I didn't mean to insult all Scots. It's only Domhnall I can't stand."

"No worries. I'm not easily offended. But I agree with Alex that Jessica's nicknames for her former lover probably are all references to sex. How does that make you feel?"

"Ruddy awful, that's how."

"Why do you think you feel that way?"

I push up on my elbows to glare at Jack, but I've never been good at expressing anger. Not that I am angry. Not at Jack, at any rate. My attempt to glare at him probably looks like I'm constipated. "If I knew why I feel this way, I wouldn't be here talking to you, would I?"

"Aye, but you need to root out the core feeling before you can deal with it." Jack still has his elbows braced on his knees, and he's gazing at me with a faintly amused slant to his lips. "Answer one question. No sidestepping, no 'I haven't got a sodding clue' responses, just an honest answer. Will you do that?"

"Yes." Am I going to regret agreeing to that?

Jack stares at me for a moment, then he asks, "What are you most afraid of?"

"That if I tell Jessica how I feel, she'll say she doesn't love me that way and it's because I'm so horrible at sex. Oh, and she'll announce she's marrying Domhnall. They're going to have arrogant little Scots children, and I'll never see her again."

"Didn't Jessica break up with him?"

"Yes, but he's here now. He wants her back."

Jack bows his head, steepling his fingers under his chin. "When exactly did she take up with Domhnall?"

"Three weeks after we had sex."

"I see." Jack gets up and walks to the window, leaning against the frame facing me. "Why do you think you dislike Domhnall so much?"

I huff and throw my hands up, flopping back down onto the bed. "Because he had Jess. For two years. Bad sex with me made her realize all she wants now is great sex, even if the man she's with is a wanker."

"Did she live with Domhnall?"

"No. Jessica said she needed to maintain her independence."

"Hmm." He eyes me with his narrowed gaze. "You think she was with him for the sex."

"Maybe, I don't know. If he's her true love, I'm doomed."

Jack's brows hike up. "So, you're afraid of abandonment. You were an only child until a few months ago. Never knew your mother, right? And your father died several years ago. Alex told me about that."

"And it's all spot on. Yes, I'm a bloody moron who's afraid to be alone, afraid no one will ever love me, et cetera." I sit up, swinging my legs off the bed, and frown at my shoes. "I really am pathetic, aren't I? No wonder Jess doesn't want me."

"She wanted you to kiss her. Why did you say no?"

"I didn't say no. 'I can't,' that's what I told her."

"Hmm."

Bugger me. If he makes that noise again, I might scream.

Despite that, my eyes decide now is a good time to look at Jack. I wish I hadn't done it when I see his expression. Smug is the best description. Smugly certain. He seems to think he knows what my problem is and how to fix it, but of course, he's not going to share the information. I'm meant to figure it out on my own.

"Here's my advice," Jack says. "Stop feeling sorry for yourself. Stand up straight, look everyone in the eye, and act like a mature adult."

Is he calling me a childish idiot? I think he might be.

Jack is right, though. Lately, I've complained about my life, but I've done sod all to change it.

"Point taken," I say. "I'll give it my best shot. No, I won't try. I'll do it."

"Excellent." Jack pushes away from the window and slaps my arm. "Now, here's your assignment for today. Kiss Jessica."

"What?"

"Kiss her. She wanted you to do it, you want to do it, so just do it." He walks to the door and swings it open. "Your first session is over. Congratulations, you did much better than Alex did on his first try."

I did better than my brother? I suppose shouting and pumping my fists in the air would be impolite. Childish too. So I won't do that. Not here in Jack's room.

"Thank you, Jack," I say as I hold out my hand to shake his. "I appreciate your help. And I can see why Alex calls you both a bloody annoying wanker and the best psychologist on earth."

Jack laughs. "That's Alex all right."

I turn to leave.

"Remember," Jack says. "You have homework to do."

"Yes, I know."

I shut the door behind me and head downstairs, hurrying through the main hallway and out the doors. Just outside the guest house, I stop to scan the crowd for Jessica. She sees me at the same instant I see her, then she smiles and waves.

And my brain still shuts down whenever she smiles. Christ, she's beautiful. And sweet. And clever. And just all-around wonderful.

Kiss Jessica, my so-called therapist had said. *You have homework to do.*

"Attention, all guests," a woman's voice says through what sounds like a megaphone.

I glance around until I spot the woman who spoke. It's Eve Silva, the strawberry blonde who had greeted us earlier. She's standing on a wooden box at the other end of the lawn. Her husband, Val, stands on the ground beside her.

"Welcome to Au Naturel Naturist Resort," Eve says, waving to the crowd with her free hand. "I know Val and I have already introduced ourselves to you guys individually, but this is your official group welcome. We're thrilled to be hosting our very first on-site wedding. Congratulations to Alex and Catriona."

Val says something to his wife that the megaphone doesn't pick up.

"I know, honey," she says. "I was just getting to that."

She pats his cheek, and Val grasps her wrist so he can kiss her palm.

"Listen up," Eve says. "This is a private party, for the next seven days, which means no one who's not on the guest list will be allowed on site. All guests will receive a code to open and close the gates. If you leave the property, the gates will close behind you automatically, so make sure you have the code with you when you come back. There will be someone in the office twenty-four seven—either me, Val, Damian Petrescu, or Ollie Jackson. If you forget your code, give us a call. Wave hello to the guests, guys."

Two men stand up and wave. They must be Damian and Ollie. The blond bloke wears glasses and a resort uniform while his dark-haired mate dresses all in black.

Everyone is watching Eve and, presumably, listening to her speech.

"Here are the resort rules," she says. "Nudity is optional, but if you choose to try the naturist way, you must obey the rules. Everything I'm about to tell you applies to nudists only. First, no staring at women's breasts or anyone's private parts. Maintain eye contact."

"So we can stare at your breasts as long as we're clothed?" someone shouts.

I glance around until I see Nick Hunter, who's a mate of my cousins. Yes, he's exactly the kind of man who shouts inappropriate things. His twin brother, Richard, is mature and level-headed. Nick...isn't. He's lots of fun, though.

"Be polite all the time," Eve says. "Moving on. When you're naked, we recommend footwear if you leave the lawn. The woods can be hard on your feet, and there are biting ants out there. Do not walk around in only your underwear. Total nudity or clothes on, those are the options."

My gaze wanders back to Jessica, who's watching Eve and listening to the woman's speech about the rules. Will Jess choose to try naturism? Not sure how I'd feel about other blokes seeing her naked. But if we're alone...

"Always shower before using the sauna or the hot spring," Eve continues. "Always put a towel on a chair or other surface before sitting down on it. No PDAs—public displays of affection—other than a quick hug to say hello or a quick peck on the cheek. Hand-holding is acceptable. No barn doors open when you're sitting or lying down in the presence of other guests. That means don't have your legs spread so everyone can see your privates."

Jess glances at me.

I wave for her to come over here, and she starts making her way through the crowd toward me.

"No reaching during meals," Eve tells us. "If you need anything, ask someone to pass it to you." She waves a finger toward Val's groin. "Make sure none of your bits intrude on anyone else's space. And if you absolutely must relieve yourself outdoors, whether it's number one or number two, please find a secluded spot where you can take care of things. No photography without express permission from the people involved. That goes for everyone, not just the naturists. If you have a cell phone, please come to us and we'll give you red dot stickers to put over the camera lenses. And guys, if you get an erection when you're outside of your room, please put a towel over your lap or roll over onto your side. If you're in the hot spring or the lake, you can just stay put until the problem subsides."

Did Eve just say the word erection in front of the entire crowd? Oh bloody hell. What if I get one of those around Jessica? No public nudity for me, that's my new rule. I can't risk more humiliation.

"You'll find welcome kits in your rooms," Eve says. "That's all. Now, go have a good time. Lunch is normally served at noon, but since most of you came from the UK and probably have screwed up internal clocks, we'll be offering a special twenty-four-hour buffet so you can eat breakfast, lunch, or dinner whenever you feel like it."

Alex must have paid Eve and Val an enormous amount of money if they're willing to host a round-the-clock buffet for us.

Jess finally reaches me, smiling in that sweet way I love, her lips sealed but curved up at the corners. "What's up, Greybee?"

Kiss her, Jack had told me.

"Could we talk privately?" I ask.

"Sure. Let's go to our bungalow. I haven't even seen it yet."

"Fine, let's do that."

I follow Jess behind the guest house, but suddenly, I can't wait one second longer to do what I've needed to do for two years. I grab her arm to stop her.

Jessica turns toward me. "Something wrong?"

"Not exactly." I cradle her face in my hands. "Need to do this now."

Chapter Six

Jessica

BEFORE I CAN PROCESS WHAT HE JUST SAID AND FIGURE OUT what it means, Grey presses his mouth to mine. His lips feel warm and faintly damp, like he licked them a minute ago. He keeps us like this for several seconds, his hands covering my cheeks and his mouth fused to mine, and my body reacts of its own volition, softening and warming, triggering a tingle that chases over my skin and raises every hair on my body. The sensation sweeps over me from head to toe, then dives deeper to awaken the most intimate parts of me.

He exhales the breath he must've been holding, and the heat of it blusters over my skin. He groans, the sound so hungry that it makes my nipples go hard.

I melt into him, fisting my hands in his shirt, and my mouth opens just enough that he can't possibly misinterpret what I want. God, I'd wanted this earlier. Wanted it so badly. *Kiss me, Grey,* I plead in my mind like he's psychic and will hear it, *kiss me all the way.*

He thrusts his tongue between my lips, curling it around mine, teasing the roof of my mouth before diving in deep.

A moan of intense pleasure vibrates in my throat. I plunge my tongue between his lips, loving the feel of his mouth, the heat of it, and the taste that drives me crazy in the best way even though I can't figure out what he tastes like. Doesn't matter. I need him to keep kissing me forever. I burn for him to slide his hands down to my shoulders, and lower still to my breasts. I want his hands on me, everywhere, exploring my body the way he's exploring my mouth.

He pushes his fingers into my hair and tips my head back, giving him deeper access.

I fling my arms around his neck and hold on tight.

This is even better than our first kiss two years ago. Way better. Like, alternate-universe better. If this is a doppelgänger of Grey Dixon, I want to keep this version of him. He's kissing me with so much passion and hunger that I can't help praying he'll drag me into our bungalow and tear my clothes off.

Grey rips his mouth away from mine but keeps our lips a hair's breadth apart. His chest heaves with every breath. "Jess, I want to—"

I shove a hand between our mouths to silence him with my fingers. "Wait. I need to, um, think."

We both sound breathless, and I'm breathing as hard as he is. Holy shit, that kiss. It was so far beyond amazing that I can't find a single word to describe it.

A chill shivers through me. I just made out with my best friend. I'm burning for him. Ravenous for him. Wet for him. The one and only time we had sex, it had been so bad I couldn't speak to Grey for days after that incident. I swore to myself I would never, ever again give in to my attraction to him. He's my rock, my go-to person for those moments when I need a shoulder to cry on or a wall to pound my fists on, metaphorically. I've never actually pummeled Grey, though I have cried while he held me.

Like the day after I broke up with Domhnall. Grey had flown to America just to be there for me.

As much as I loved our second kiss, I cannot risk our friendship over one lustful impulse.

I stumble backward a few steps, shaking my head. "No, no, we can't do this. It's wrong. I'm sorry, Grey, I'm so sorry."

And I run to the bungalow, fumbling to unlock the front door.

Grey comes up behind me.

I can't see him, since I'm focused on trying to open the door, but I know the shadow looming over me is him. I can feel it. That's dumb, but it's the truth.

"Jessica."

His voice makes my skin tingle again. I'm way too turned on to risk looking at him. Even the fear that has me in its grip can't overpower my lust. Why do I want him so much? It's crazy.

Grey plucks the keys out of my hand, then he unlocks the door and pushes it inward.

I stagger across the threshold and trip over something I didn't see because I'm lost in my own fearful thoughts.

He catches me, picks me up, and kicks the door shut. Carrying me to a sofa, he sets me down. Then he sits beside me but leaves a discreet distance between us.

That's my Greybee, always polite and considerate.

I start tingling again, but now the sensation is only in my breasts and between my thighs. The way he'd swept me up in his arms... Wow, I hadn't realized until that exact moment how big and strong his biceps are.

Grey turns slightly to face me. "What's wrong, Jess?"

"Told you. I won't risk losing you just so I can give in to one moment of lust." I glance at his biceps, and that heat shimmers through me again, making my nipples go stiff. I wrap my arms around myself to hide those two little signposts that advertise the fact I'm still turned on despite my freak-out. "We tried this once before, and it almost destroyed our friendship."

"I was anxious the first time. I'd wanted you for so long that when you said yes, I wasn't prepared for it."

"Even if the sex is good this time"—or totally amazing, which I can now imagine happening thanks to that kiss and his biceps—"we might still wreck things. I might wreck it, or you might, or we both could. It's not worth the risk."

"Please stop saying the word risk. You make it sound like I'm the embodiment of a statistical certainty."

I can't prevent my lips from curving into a smile. Really, he's adorable when gets all geeky on me. It's kind of hot too, and my gaze gravitates back to his biceps. The shirt he's wearing hides them somewhat, but my mind can fill in the blanks. I saw him naked once, two years ago, but I swear he's gotten more muscular since then. When we had sex, the lighting had been too dim to give me much of a look at his body. He's not as overdeveloped as some of the MacTaggart men, or Domhnall, but bulk matters less than what a man does with those muscles.

"Jessica?"

Blinking swiftly, I veer my gaze to his face. *Focus on his eyes, not his biceps.* "What? No, you're not a statistical whatsit."

He studies me for a moment, his lips tight and his brows lowered. "Did you calculate the probability of success when you leaped into a relationship with Domhnall Sterling?"

No, I hadn't. Domhnall is smokin' hot, smarter than he lets on, and nothing like Grey. Was that why I picked Domhnall? Jeez, I hope not. Domhnall and I had fantastic sex, but we argued about a lot of things—most notably,

Grey Dixon. Domhnall always had a weird fixation with my best friend and hated him from the second they met. I think Grey might've been cool with Domhnall if my fiancé hadn't blared the first note of discord. Grey liked all my other boyfriends. Well, at least he seemed to like them. And he dated too, so it wasn't like he'd been secretly pining for me for years.

Unless I've been oblivious to the truth. No, I understand Grey. I would know if he... Would I? We had sex, and I still thought he didn't have feelings for me beyond friendship.

Maybe I am oblivious. Totally blind. A complete freaking idiot.

That does not change the facts. I cannot, will not, lose my best friend.

Does the fact I'm not using contractions mean I'm desperately denying the obvious?

Grey moves closer, laying an arm on the sofa's back behind me. "We know each other, Jess, very well. Most couples have to work at developing the kind of emotional intimacy we already have. Doesn't that make us ahead of the game?"

Sure, maybe. But friendship is different from love. I can't make those words come out of my mouth, though. Different ones spill from my lips instead. "I need time to think about this, Grey. Preserving our friendship is the most important thing to me."

"Take whatever time you need." He brushes a fingertip down my cheek. "I'll wait for you, Jess, as long as it takes."

Domhnall had been more about ultimatums than patience. Grey is the sweetest man on earth.

"I need to think," I say again. "Honestly, I'm terrified that if we have sex again, it'll be worse than before. Then I will lose you, for sure."

"Sex isn't everything."

"True, but it's important in a relationship. It's kind of required for having kids. Unless you're planning on us doing in vitro."

"In vitro?" He jerks his head back, his mouth open, and then scrunches up his entire face. "You're being ridiculous. It wasn't that bad the first time."

"How did my crying convince you that it wasn't so bad? Or maybe you just don't care if I enjoy it as long as you get your seed in my womb or whatever." Why am I getting angry? I should end this conversation now, but I can't help feeling wounded by his claim that I'm being ridiculous. It's not my fault we aren't sexually compatible.

But the way he kisses me...

"My seed in your what?" Grey almost shouts. He clenches his jaw so tightly that a muscle ticks in it. "Stop making me into the villain. Maybe the real issue is that you care more about sex than having a real adult relationship. How many times did I wipe away your tears while you were crying over something Domhnall did? You went back to him over and over. But being with me is still impossible." He covers his face with one hand, his head down. "Maybe we both need time to think."

"I'm sorry, Grey. This isn't easy for me."

"Not for me either." He jumps up. "I'm going out to…see what everyone else is doing."

He hurries out of the bungalow, slamming the door.

Jeez, did he have to flee at cheetah speed?

Since I have nothing else to do, I explore our new digs. Someone brought our bags in earlier and left mine in one room and Grey's in the other. My room lies on the right side of the bungalow while Grey's is on the left side, and the living room, bathroom, and kitchenette are between them. I start unpacking my stuff, doing it by rote because I can't stop thinking about my argument with Grey. We've never argued before. Grey never gets upset about anything. Well, except for when his dad died. He had cried then, but only once and only for a minute. I wrapped my arms around him until he was done, and neither of us ever mentioned that incident again. He'd been shattered by the loss of his father, and I couldn't leave him alone in that state, so I stayed with him twenty-four seven. Grey means more to me than anyone in the world.

But he's never been good at relationships—with women or with friends. I know he's still struggling to get comfortable with the idea he has a half-brother, especially one as strange as Alex Thorne. Grey gets along great with his cousins and their friends. He's bonding with the MacTaggarts too. Maybe he is ready for a real adult relationship. Maybe I'm the problem here.

Why did I hook up with Domhnall right after Grey and I had our bad-sex experience? I know why I stayed with him for so long. I'm a coward. And yeah, the sex was incredible. But mostly, I'm a coward who couldn't face another failure.

If Grey and I tried being a couple, and things went sideways, I couldn't handle that.

While I'm unpacking, Carly calls to tell me she's on her way to the airport. Her boyfriend has appendicitis and is going into surgery right away. She wants to be there, which I completely understand. I tell her to call if she needs anything, and we say goodbye.

Domhnall won't have a date for the wedding, but that's his problem.

Once I've finished unpacking, I head out to the lawn to see what's up. Maybe I can join a badminton game or something. I'll take any excuse to distract myself from the Grey problem. I'm staring down at my feet while I walk, and though I try not to, I keep thinking about Grey. When I reach the lawn's periphery, I lift my head—and freeze.

Naked people. On the lawn. Lots of them. Four people are playing a strange game that involves tennis balls, and they each wear a weird, wedge-shaped box over one hand. They bat the ball around with those boxes. The four people enjoying the strange game are Alex Thorne, Catriona Mac-Taggart, Cat's cousin Logan, and Logan's wife, Serena. Cat is pregnant, but the only sign of that fact is a slight rounding of her belly.

They've all become nudists. Or naturists, or whatever.

And they're not alone. I see various other MacTaggarts and even a few Dixons lounging on lawn chairs in the nude while they watch the game. Grey is not among the nude Dixons. His cousins Reese and Chance are, but I don't see Dane anywhere. Maybe he ran away when his brothers stripped. Elena and Arden, the wives of Chance and Reese, lie on lawn chaises alongside their husbands who occupy separate chairs. Arden is naked, but the very pregnant Elena wears a loose-fitting dress. Richard Hunter and his fiancée, Maddie Solberg, have ditched their clothes. So has Nick Hunter.

I try not to gawk at the naked wedding guests, but honestly, I can't help it. I've never seen them in the buff before. Logan MacTaggart has the most impressive bod currently on display, but the others are damn hot too. I don't feel lust for them, though, not even a twinge. Detached appreciation is more like it.

Eve Silva walks up beside me, and thankfully, she's wearing clothes. It's her work uniform that has the resort logo on the shirt.

"Is this your first time at a naturist resort?" she asks.

"Yeah. I wasn't mentally prepared for this." I watch Alex bat the tennis ball over the net with his box-covered hand. Naturally, he has an impressive bod too. "What is that game they're playing?"

"Miniten. It was invented by naturists a long time ago. Most nudist retreats don't have a lot of space and can't accommodate a full tennis court, so somebody got the idea to create a special version of tennis. Miniten is short for mini tennis." She points toward the wedge-shaped box on Alex's hand. "Those are called thugs. There's a kind of handlebar inside it so the box won't slide off the player's hand. You grip the bar to keep the thug in place."

"I didn't realize nudists had their own game, but that's cool." I glance around, suddenly realizing something. "Where are the kids? I know a lot of the wedding guests have children, but I haven't seen them."

"Oh, they're in our new daycare center. We just built it a few months ago." Eve points toward a building adjacent to the guest house. "There it is. Children are welcome outside, but some parents prefer to keep them away from the nudists, and we're happy to oblige. We do have two teenagers here, but they're both hiding indoors right now. Serena's son, Chase, seems embarrassed by nudity. Malina, Iain and Rae's daughter, is staying inside but keeps peeking out the window."

Eve points toward a window on the second floor of the guest house.

I spot a face in that window, framed by the curtains.

"As for the older relatives of the guests here," Eve says, "they're staying at a hotel in town. We didn't have room at the resort."

Finally, I see Grey. He's just walked up to the Dixons, but he's wearing clothes.

Am I disappointed by that fact? No, of course not. Well, maybe just a teeny smidge of an eensy bit.

I see Domhnall too. He's fully clothed, thank goodness. Not that I would feel the eensiest bit tempted by his naked body. But if Domhnall did chuck his clothes, I'm sure he would be doing that strictly to intimidate Grey or make him feel unworthy or whatever. Grey has nothing to worry about. He's sexy enough for me.

No, not for me. Friends only, that's what we are. His hot bod makes no nevermind to me. Yeah, I'm determined to pretend I'm not attracted to him, which is pathetic.

Luckily, Domhnall leaves the vicinity and disappears behind the guest house. I don't want to talk to him. Grey might've invited my ex to stay for the festivities, but that doesn't mean I have to speak to Domhnall.

Damn, I need a break from the ex-lover versus best friend drama.

Eve is still standing beside me, so I ask her, "Somebody mentioned nature trails. Where are those?"

"Right there." Eve points toward a path I can just make out, though the darkness of the woods obscures it somewhat. "That's the main trail. Signs tell you where each offshoot trail goes. We have a hot spring and a private lake, not to mention lots of great spots for birdwatching and observing wildlife."

"Awesome. Think I'll go for a walk."

"Let me get you a map."

Eve dashes into the caretaker's house, returning a moment later with a folded map. "Take this. Cell phones do work out here since there's a tower on the state land that's right next to the resort property."

"Thanks, Eve."

I take the map and make a beeline for the nature trail.

Time alone. Time to think. That's what I need.

Chapter Seven

Domhnall

AFTER WATCHING THE NUDISTS KNOCKING A TENNIS ball back and forth for a few minutes, using odd boxes that cover their hands, I retreat behind the guest house to think. To plot might be more accurate. How can Jessica not see what Grey Dixon is doing to her? She'll never have a full and happy life as long as he's dragging her down. After a few minutes of focusing on that, my jaw starts to ache, so I must be grinding my teeth. *Bod an Donais.* I need to talk to Jessica. Now.

And do what, I have no bloody clue. But I set off to find her anyway. I need to convince Jess that Grey is toxic. Aye, I've had dead brilliant luck with that so far.

I see Jess walking away from the lawn, headed for the nature trail that starts just past the caretaker's house.

So I follow her.

I run after her, actually.

"Jess!" I call out as I catch up to her. "Wait, please."

She stops, turning toward me. "Are you stalking me now?"

"No, of course not. But we need to talk."

"About what?" She folds her arms over her chest, puckering her mouth in the way I know means she's irritated. "Let me guess. You want to trash-talk my best friend some more. Not interested, Domhnall."

"Donnae want to trash anyone. But somebody needs to show you the truth about that scunner."

She rolls her eyes. "Oh yes, every time you insult Grey, it makes me want you back even more."

The sarcasm in her voice makes me want to fist my hands and grind my teeth again, but I don't do it. "Why cannae ye see how that sc—Grey is manipulating you?"

"*He's* manipulating me?" She shakes her head. "You're the one who issued an ultimatum. It was either you or my best friend. So guess what? I chose Grey, and I will keep choosing him over and over and over."

"He's brainwashed you. Why cannae ye see how manipulative he is?"

"Brainwashed? If anyone's trying to mess with my head, it's you."

"The *sassenach* will ruin every chance you have at real happiness." I move closer, grasping her upper arms, and look straight into her eyes. "Jess, I love you. Don't throw away everything we had. Remember that weekend in Cancun?" I rub her arms, leaning in closer, wanting to kiss her so badly it takes all my willpower to stop myself from doing that. "We didn't leave the hotel room all weekend. We were naked the entire time, except when we ordered room service. I only put on trousers then so I wouldn't scare the lass who brought our food. We spent hours making each other come so many times that we couldn't move anymore and we both fell asleep, then we woke up and did it all over again."

"What I remember is how you kept taking calls from your ex-wife, and meanwhile, you secretly muted my phone so I wouldn't know when Grey called me." She pushes my hands away and steps back. "That weekend was the second-to-last straw."

"Come on, Jess. That *sassenach's* dragging you down, but you're too soft-headed to see—"

"Soft-headed?" Her gaze narrows, and her lips tighten.

"I meant soft-hearted. You're kind to every person you meet, even the ones who donnae deserve it. Grey is—"

Jessica slaps me. Hard.

My cheek stings, and I rub my jaw while I try to figure out what to say to her.

"Are you all right, Jessica?"

The man who spoke those words is standing behind her. Grey Dixon must have sneaked up on us while we were arguing. That scunner is smirking like he heard our entire argument and thinks it's entertaining.

Jessica glances at him. "Everything's fine, Grey. Domhnall had a mosquito on his cheek."

Now *she* smirks.

Grey approaches us, pulls a tissue out of his pocket, and hands it to me. "Might want to wipe the mozzie guts off your face."

I glare at the tissue, contemplating whether I should wad it up, shove it in his mouth, and tell him to eat the fictional mosquito. But he probably wouldn't be intimidated by a threat to make him swallow a wee insect, even if one did exist.

Grey stuffs the tissue back into his pocket. "By the way, you have my permission to stay for the entire wedding week. My brother and his fiancée don't mind, so you're now officially a guest."

What the bloody hell? Grey Dixon despises me as much as I despise him, so I can't fathom why he's inviting me to stay. This must be a trick. Some sort of con he learned from his brother. Aye, Alex Thorne is a con artist—a fact I learned from the conversations I've overheard since I arrived here.

Now I'm an eavesdropper. Christ, what's wrong with me?

Grey Dixon offers me his hand, like he wants to shake mine. "Let's call it bygones and enjoy the wedding celebrations. What do you say?"

I don't believe for one second that he wants to be my mate, but I can play whatever game he's got in mind. This wee scunner will not fool me.

So I shake his hand. "Aye, bygones."

Grey and Jessica leave.

And I start plotting how to murder Grey Dixon while I stalk down the nature trail away from the resort and the nude people on the lawn. Nudity doesn't bother me, but the only person whose body I want to see without clothes on is Jessica. That won't happen ever again unless I can prove to her what a bastard Grey Dixon is.

I turn down offshoot trails without reading the signs that say where the paths lead, and I wind up at a natural hot spring. Two people are in the pool, surrounded by blue water with steam curling up from the surface. They're kissing, passionately. The man has the woman pinned to the rocky edge of the pool while she has her legs wrapped around him. Her blonde hair is damp and plastered to her face and chest. They're both naked.

And they're shagging.

I clear my throat.

The man pauses in fucking the woman and glances up at me. He lifts one brow. "Who the bloody hell are you?"

"Domhnall Sterling. Who the bloody hell are you?"

"Rory MacTaggart." He squints at me, his lips flattening. "I've heard about you. Alex Thorne says you're the man who wants to steal Jessica away from Grey Dixon. I donnae look kindly on men who poach lasses."

Poach? That sounds like I want to mount Jessica on my mantle as a trophy.

The blonde woman who's still attached to Rory MacTaggart wriggles out from under him and turns around to brace her arms on the rocky ledge. "Since my hubby doesn't want to introduce me, I'm Emery MacTaggart, Rory's wife. I'm American, by the way, not Canadian. Scots and Brits can sometimes confuse the two."

Should I say it's a pleasure to meet them? Rory doesn't seem inclined to friendliness, and these two are wedding guests which means they're on Grey's side. They're enemies. Maybe I should think about why I see everyone who doesn't batter Grey Dixon as an enemy. But I can't think about anything except Jessica O'Connor.

Am I obsessed with her? No, I love her and need to save her from that British *bod ceann.*

Despite the itch that's growing inside my chest, I know I'm in the right.

Rory MacTaggart grasps the ledge and levers his body out of the water, springing to his feet to approach me. He's naked, but I'm not shocked by that. This is a nudist resort, after all. I've been to nude beaches, so if Rory is trying to intimidate me by not wearing clothes, he'll need to try much harder.

"You weren't invited," he says. "The only reason I'm not skelping you bloody and dumping your body in the nearest rubbish heap is because Grey Dixon wants you to stay. But if you ruin my sister's wedding, I will give you your head in your hands to play with—literally."

His wife laughs. "Rory baby, it's so cute when you get all bloodthirsty. But I thought getting your head in your hands to play with meant to punish someone, not commit murder."

Rory glances back at Emery. "That's why I said 'literally.' And I think this scunner knows what I mean."

"Yeah, he's a Scot, so he probably knows the secret language."

"I know what your husband means," I say. "And I have no plans to ruin the wedding. I'm here for Jessica, that's all."

Emery plants her hands on the ledge like she's about to push up out of the water.

Rory raises a hand. "Stay in the pool, Em. Being naked around the family is one thing, but I will not have my wife flouncing around in the nude in front of a stranger."

"You will not have it?" she says with a smirk. "Oh honey, you know better than to try commanding me to do anything."

He huffs. "Aye, I do."

She folds her arms on the ledge again, relaxing into the water. "Maybe we should welcome Domhnall instead of threatening him. He is a guest now."

Rory rolls his eyes and twists his lips into a strange expression that's halfway between a smile and a scowl. Then he looks at me. "If you're staying, you should talk to my sister Fiona. She's in charge of organizing the wedding nonsense."

"I thought your sister's name was Catriona."

"Aye, she's the one getting married. I have three sisters, though, and Fiona is the one you need to speak to. She might need to rearrange the seating chart or whatever bollocks she's been handling."

His wife laughs again. "Honestly, Rory, a wedding is not bollocks. Don't mind him, Domhnall. My hubby likes to pretend he's a confirmed cynic when other people are around, but he's really a big old teddy bear."

Since I have no idea what to say in response to that, I tell Rory, "Thank you. I'll speak to your sister Fiona."

"You'll find her in the guest house, in the dining hall."

I march back down the trail and manage to find my way to the main resort area, emerging from the woods near the lawn where guests had been playing that strange game earlier. Now, I see a smattering of people relaxing on chaises or Adirondack chairs and a few more gathered on the green where the net had been set up, though now it's gone. I jog past the other guests, who are laughing and talking, and go inside the guest house, slowing to a walk while I make my way down the corridor to the dining hall. When I cross the threshold, I see one person in the large space.

The woman has light-brown hair like her brother Rory and a slim figure. Her face, bonnie and sweet, reminds me of a statue of the goddess Aphrodite that I'd seen in a museum once. She's standing at a table where she has papers spread out on the surface, and she bites her lip every time she picks up a paper to examine it.

I stop on the opposite side of the table. "Are you Fiona?"

Her head pops up. "That's right. And you must be Domhnall Sterling, the ersehole who wants to steal Jessica away from Grey. I'm quoting Alex Thorne, not stating my own opinion."

"Aye, I'm Domhnall Sterling. What *is* your opinion of me?" Why do I ask? I shouldn't care what a stranger thinks, but for reasons I can't explain, I want to know if this bonnie lass thinks I'm an ersehole.

She shrugs. "I don't know you, so I can't have an opinion."

"Your brother Rory threatened to give me my head in my hands to play with, literally."

Fiona laughs softly. "That sounds like Rory."

She has the loveliest laugh I've ever heard.

I clear my throat. "Rory said I need to check in with you since you're the one organizing the wedding events. Grey Dixon invited me to stay for the week, so I'm staying."

Fiona sweeps her gaze down the length of me, and as her focus travels back up my body, her tongue darts out to moisten her lips. "Aye, you should stay. We have lots of events planned. I'm handling the dinner arrangements and organizing the Highland games, but Eve Silva and Mara Jackson are taking care of the logistics. If you need a room..."

"No, I have one. Rory thought you might need to rework the place settings or some such bollocks."

She smiles. "Bollocks? Aye, you definitely talked to my brother."

Her smile gives me an odd warmth in my chest. That doesn't mean anything. I love Jessica, and no one else on earth can compare to her.

"Why do you want to stay?" Fiona asks. "You don't know anyone here except for Jessica and Grey, and you don't like him."

"I'm here for Jessica. To stop her from making a terrible mistake, and to stop him from taking advantage of her."

"Does Jessica want your help? If not, maybe you're the villain, not Grey."

My jaw aches—because I've started to grind my teeth again. "I came here to tell you I'm staying, so you can rearrange whatever it is. Thank you for your opinion, but I know Jessica better than Grey Dixon does."

"Time will tell, eh?"

I want to bark at her to sod off, but I never say things like that to women. Besides, I suddenly have a much better idea. "Did you say there will be Highland games?"

"Aye. My brothers and cousins love to show off for their lasses."

"I want to compete in the games. If that's all right with you and your family."

Fiona studies me for several seconds, tilting her head to the side. "You're a guest, which means you have the right to compete. If anyone complains about that, I'll remind them they put me in charge of the Highland games. That ought to shut them up."

"Even your brothers?"

Her lips slide into a sly grin. "Especially my brothers."

The look on her face convinces me that Fiona MacTaggart can handle her brothers under any circumstances, and she won't even flinch if they get angry. She's quite a woman.

But I'm not here for her. Jessica is my only concern. I know her best, I love her the most, and I will do anything to keep Grey Dixon from worming his way into her heart.

And the Highland games gives me the perfect opportunity.

Chapter Eight

Grey

WHEN ALEX MENTIONED AN "OPENING CEREMONY" for the wedding week, I'd assumed he was referring to Eve's speech about the resort rules. But no, my brother would never accept that as a proper start to what he has labeled "the wedding of the century." I should've expected he would come up with something outrageous, embarrassing, and slightly dirty. The man wrote a book about sex in the ancient world, one that includes explicit illustrations and a glossary of sex terms in English and various dead languages. Yes, I've read his book. It won't be published for a while yet, but Alex wanted me to read the manuscript. He showed me the illustrations too, and I think I blushed when I saw them.

Isn't that so manly of me? At least Jessica wasn't there to see it.

When I'd seen Jessica heading down the nature trail this afternoon, and Domhnall hurrying after her, I had suffered from an intense urge to follow them. To make sure he didn't harass her, that's all. Honestly, I swear that was the only reason. Well, maybe I also wanted to ensure the Scots lout didn't do his sweet-talking Svengali thing again.

By the time I'd caught up to them, they were arguing. I heard only the end of their conversation, but it was enough to convince me Domhnall is indeed a sodding wanker. And yes, I'd been smugly pleased when she slapped him. I don't like feeling smug about anything—it's not in my nature—but Domhnall Sterling turns me into the sort of bloke I'd never imagined I could be. Am I jealous of him? No, it's more like I feel vengeful. He hurt Jess, so I want to hurt him. Not that I would ever assault him. That's also not in my nature, and maybe that's why Jessica wants me as a friend and nothing else. She can't see me as a man, but only as her asexual mate.

Then again, she did ask me to kiss her. But immediately after that, she declared it was wrong and she couldn't do "this." Whatever that meant.

So, I'm back to being the asexual best mate. Bloody hell.

But if she's afraid to get into a real relationship with me, that must mean she does think of me as more than a mate. Doesn't it? Since she mentioned how I bollocksed up sex with her, I don't think it matters. She will never love me the way I love her unless I can prove I have the maturity and the sexual skills to become the kind of man she needs.

Though we had walked out of the nature trail together, once we reached the lawn, she announced she wanted to get lunch to go and eat alone in the bungalow because she needed time to think about everything. I knew that already since she'd said the same thing earlier. But now she's made it painfully clear that "thinking" means being away from me. For how long? I wanted to ask but couldn't summon the nerve to do that.

My only option at this point is to work on my problems while she thinks about hers and to do whatever it takes to keep Domhnall away from Jess.

I spend the rest of the afternoon avoiding Jack and Alex so I can think about everything without their well-meaning interference. I did what Jack ordered me to do. I kissed Jessica, and it didn't help. So I don't think I want advice from anyone anymore. I need to sort this on my own. I avoid the bungalow too because Jessica might be there. I'm not being childish. I'm giving her what she asked for—time alone. That means I hide out in the entertainment room in the guest house until dinner, then I grab some food and retreat into my room in the bungalow to eat alone and distract myself with work.

Jessica stays in her room, which I know because of the light leaking out under the door.

We now have food in our refrigerator, so I assume Jess gathered that stuff and ate here, alone.

Once the sun sets, and the children are asleep, the adults gather on the lawn to sit in various chairs or to relax on blankets. I'm alone on my little blanket, the plaid one Alex gave me. When I made a snarky comment about the Scottish overtones of this fabric, he shook his head and told me to "try taking the offensive instead of playing defense." Since when does Alex use sports metaphors? For all the time I've known him, he's been more likely to spout archaeology jargon. But I do appreciate his effort to boost my spirits with strange advice.

A makeshift stage has been set up at one end of the lawn, so every chair and blanket faces in that direction. The stage consists of a flatbed trailer outfitted with a loudspeaker as well as a microphone attached to a stand. A portable spotlight has been positioned on the trailer too. No one is on the makeshift stage yet. Alex will, naturally, want to make a grand entrance.

"Mind if I sit with you?"

Jessica's voice startles me out of my thoughts. I glance up at her, and the familiar lump forms in my throat, the one I always get when I see her. This far from the stage, the spotlight casts her in a moon-like glow, as if she's an angel come down from heaven. Angels, at least the male ones, did often shag humans, so maybe...

Oh bugger. I'm a complete idiot, aren't I? Yes, Jessica is going to let me shag her again because she looks like an angel tonight.

"Well?" she asks.

"Uh, yes, please sit down." I pat the blanket. "I'd love the company. Alex is about to do God-knows-what to kick off the official wedding rubbish."

She settles onto the blanket, tucking her feet under her cross-legged. With a sly smile, she says, "You know, the more time I spend with your brother, the more I realize how alike you two are."

"Jack MacTaggart said the same thing. I'm not sure if it's a compliment or an insult."

"Compliment for sure, Greybee. Alex might be weird, but he's a good person." She pokes her finger into my chest. "Just like you."

Her smile, her voice, her words, it all makes me want to kiss her again. Right now. In front of all these people. But I can't do that because I promised to give her time. She's here now, with me, so does that mean she's done with the time she needed?

"I'm glad you're here," I say, "but I didn't expect to see you again today."

"Just because I want time to think things over doesn't mean I won't see or speak to you in the meantime."

That's what I thought it meant. Do women have a different definition of "I need time to think"? I can't be the only man in the world who assumes that means "stay away from me, you arse."

But I'm so bloody relieved it doesn't mean that.

"I'm sorry about earlier," she says. "I didn't mean to imply it's a statistical certainty that we won't make it as a couple. You know how bad I am with numbers, anyway."

She hits me with her teasing smile, the one I've seen a lot more of lately. I love that smile. I love her, full stop. As much as I want to tell her that, though, I shouldn't do it yet.

"Have you seen Domhnall again?" I ask, trying to sound casual, like I don't give a toss about the answer.

"Nope. Not sure where he got to, and it doesn't matter."

And I'm even more relieved to hear that.

"I hope things won't be awkward between us," I say. "Because of the kiss, I mean."

"You are such a worrier. Chill, Greybee, or you'll get an ulcer."

Before I can speak, the spotlight goes out, plunging the entire lawn into darkness. Only the faintest lights inside the guest house pierce the shadows. Well, that and the moon. And the stars. So not total darkness after all.

Everyone falls silent. The only sound is a soft creaking which I take to be the sound the trailer makes when Alex steps onto it in the dark.

Music blares. It's that music from the movie *2001*, though I know it's really a classical song. Bahhh, *bahhh*, BAHHH, *BAH-BAHHH*. Boom-boom, boom-boom, boom-boom.

Oh for pity's sake, Alex. Did you have to go for the overkill?

The spotlight flares on, blinding me for a second or two. Then I see Alex standing there on the makeshift stage in front of the microphone. Naturally, he's smirking. And naturally, he speaks in an overly dramatic, almost sensual tone when he announces, "Welcome to the wedding of the century, ladies and gentlemen and Scots. Those kilt-wearers are a category unto themselves."

He winks.

Someone—Logan MacTaggart, I think—shouts, "Donnae insult the folk who are allowing you to corrupt our Catriona with your heathen wedding. Unless you're wanting a skelping, the likes of which no one has ever witnessed before."

"Come on, Logan," Alex says, still smirking. "We all know you've corrupted Serena thoroughly, not to mention all those lasses you shagged before her."

"Got me confused with Iain. He's the one who shagged all the unattached women in Loch Fairbairn and half the lasses in the whole of the Highlands."

"Yes, yes, you are hilarious," Alex says, rolling his eyes. "But we're digressing. Catriona and I have devised a week of activities designed to keep everyone entertained—Scots, Brits, and Americans alike. I fall into two of those categories, and Cat seems determined to make me a Scot too, though not officially. Now, about the entertainment..."

He pauses for dramatic effect. Alex loves to do that.

Maybe I should try adding some drama to everything I say. But I don't want to veer too far into Alex territory. I need to be myself, only better—and with a few of Alex's tricks for extra impact.

"In the daytime," Alex tells us, "we'll have family-friendly events. But after dark, the bacchanalia begins."

And of course, he speaks the last bit in a deeper voice, like he's the devil tempting all of us to sin like mad. I know he's only joking, though. Even Alex wouldn't host an orgy.

"I mean drinking and carousing," Alex says. "Whatever else you lot get up to is entirely your own decision. Everyone will receive a list of up-coming events. It should be waiting for you in your room by now. Thank you, Fiona, for handling that task. And now, the show."

Jessica leans in to whisper in my ear, "Does he do this kind of thing all the time?"

"Haven't you seen the video of his sex lecture?"

"No." Her voice takes on an almost excited tone when she adds, "Is it online? You should send me the link if it is."

"Fine, I'll text it to you."

Not sure I want Jess watching that video, but I can't stop her. She'll find it eventually on her own.

"Catriona, my darling, my love," Alex says in that phony saccharine voice he'd used earlier today. "Get your bonnie little arse up here."

She hops onto the stage and into the glare of the spotlight, coming up beside Alex. "Are we starting the lecture now?"

"Of course, love." He surveys the crowd. "Cat and I are going to teach you naughty Gaelic. She will say the Gaelic word, and I'll translate—in my own way. Ready, Cat? Let's start."

"*Bod an Donais,*" she says.

Alex keeps his gaze on the rest of us. "Can't tell if she's swearing at me or starting the lecture. I'll assume the latter. That one means the devil's penis. I'll take it as a compliment since I'm sure Satan has the biggest equipment in the universe."

"It's a swear word, Alex," Cat says. "It's similar to 'dammit,' but for you, it also means 'Alex wishes he had a giant, forked penis.' Aye?"

"Let's move on, darling, shall we?"

"All right. *Mhac na galla.*"

"Can't argue with that. I am a son of a bitch, quite literally. But every-one knows about my dear incarcerated Mummy."

"This will cheer you up," Cat says with a teasing smile. "*An toir thu dhomh pòg?*"

"I love that one." Alex slings an arm around Cat's waist and pulls her close. "It means 'please, Alex, give me a kiss that will make me beg you to have a poke at me.' I never like to disappoint a desperate woman."

Alex kisses Catriona—and the kiss turns passionate.

How can they do that in front of other people?

My gaze flicks to Jessica, who's smiling at the spectacle my brother is making of himself. Jess looks so beautiful when she smiles. Or when she doesn't smile. Or when she rolls her eyes at me. Or basically anytime she does anything, except when she cries. That makes me want to pull her into my arms and erase all her pain.

We sit through the rest of Alex's burlesque show, which I can't deny is entertaining, then Jess and I walk back to our bungalow. Why does the word bungalow suddenly sound filthy to me? Once we get inside the little house, I turn left toward my bedroom while she turns right heading for hers. I change into a T-shirt and boxer shorts, the clothes I always sleep in, then I go to the kitchen for a snack. A piece, the Scots call it. I've learned a lot of Scottish words from the MacTaggarts, but I learned even more tonight. Alex and Cat made sure I'll never forget how to curse in Gaelic.

By the time I've finished my sandwich, the light is off in her bedroom, so I assume she's asleep. I left the light on in my assigned quarters, so I get up and stretch and walk over to Jess's side of the house to flick the switch that shuts off the overhead light. As the shadows envelop me, I hear an odd noise. It sounds like a grunt followed by a gasp, or maybe a gasping grunt.

Is Jessica all right in there? I'd better check.

At her door, I hesitate with my fist raised to knock. Those noises... She's definitely gasping. And moaning. I hear the bed creaking too in a steady rhythm, but the pace accelerates little by little along with the frequency of her gasps.

"Oh Grey," she moans. "Yes, Grey, yes."

What the bloody fucking hell? She can't be—No, I must've misheard. She said "yes, hey, yes." Sure, she said that. It makes perfect sense.

To a ruddy moron like me.

She's getting off while thinking of me? I feel strangely smug about that. Jess is not wanking off while picturing Domhnall Sterling. She wants me.

I need to go in there and finish her off with my mouth, but I shouldn't.

My fist has a mind of its own and knocks on the door. My voice also seems to have become autonomous, since I hear myself saying, "Jess? May I come in?"

The creaking, gasping, and moaning stops.

"What?" she says, sounding breathless and slightly panicked. "Grey? What are you doing out there?"

Eavesdropping while you give yourself an orgasm. Is this really the level I've sunk to? But it's too late to take it back, so I might as well keep going. "I heard noises and worried you were, ah...having a seizure? Since we're both awake, maybe we could talk."

"Now?"

"Why not?"

"Gimme a sec." After a brief silence, there's a thump. "Ow! Shit."

"Jessica, are you all right?"

I throw the door open and take two steps into the room. Then all the blood in my body simultaneously floods down to my groin and freezes. My entire body freezes up too.

Jess is naked, on the floor, sprawled there in a way that lets me see every inch of her, including the glistening, rosy flesh between her thighs.

"Oh bollocks!" I essentially shout while I spin around and cover my eyes with my hands. "Sorry. I thought—oh God, so sorry. Are you okay? I heard a thump and then you shouted."

"I tripped and stubbed my toe. I'm fine."

Rustling suggests she's putting on clothes or at least a robe. I can't look, though. I won't look. Bursting in on her while she's naked and in the middle of doing what she'd been doing, that's not the way to convince Jess we can work as a couple.

Her body is even more beautiful and sexy than I remember.

I sense her coming closer. It's rot, but I can't help feeling that way. I sense her and smell her. Not just the scent of her lust, but also the scent of her, the way she always smells.

She peels my hands away from my face. "Relax, Grey, it's all right. I'm not mad."

"Why not? I was hovering outside your door listening while you—Well, I was acting like a sleazy...something or other."

She laughs. "You're so cute when you can't figure out what to say."

"I should go to my room. Sorry again. I swear I've never—"

Jessica seals my lips with two fingers. "Hush. I'm not upset."

"Were you, um, actually saying my name while you...did that?"

She bites her upper lip, glancing away briefly, then she meets my gaze. "Yes, I was. That kiss made me feel things that I need to think hard about."

I'm getting sick of hearing how much she needs to think, but I suddenly have an idea that might help us both. I grasp her shoulders. "I'll do better next time we have sex, I promise. But you could help me with that."

"Help you? How?"

Taking a deep breath, I bend my head until our faces are a hair's breadth apart. "Teach me how to make love to you, Jess."

She stares at me, not blinking, her lips parted.

"Just think about it," I say.

"Okay. That's one more thing I need to consider." She clears her throat. "Now, let's both get a good night's sleep. Separately. Not in the same bed or room."

"Will you think about what I said?"

"Uh-huh." She shoos me out the door, shutting it as she says, "Good night, Greybee."

And I go back to my room, alone, and fantasize about Jessica O'Connor while I have a wank of my own. Twice.

Chapter Nine

Jessica

LAST NIGHT I GOT OFF WHILE FANTASIZING ABOUT GREY, and he caught me in the act. That was the single most embarrassing moment of my life. But strangely, it was also the hottest moment ever. Since he wore a pair of boxers and a T-shirt, I didn't get a good look at his body. Still, I could tell he's definitely grown more muscles. I wanted to crawl up to him on my hands and knees, lick my way up his thighs, lift his shirt and trace the line of every one of his ab muscles with my tongue, then yank his boxers down so I could eat him up.

I've never done anything like that. Sure, I've given guys blow jobs, but never have I needed to do it as badly as I needed to devour my best friend.

And then he asked me to teach him how to make love to me. Oh yeah, that moment instantly took over the number-one position on the hotness chart. No man has ever asked me to show him how to have sex with me. He cares about what I want, cares about making sure I like it this time because he's just that sweet and considerate.

I'm still lying in the bed where I gave myself three climaxes last night after Grey left. Those orgasms were amazing, but I want him to make me feel that way. My hand cramped up after the third time, so I had to give up despite needing more. I wriggle under the covers, loving the silky texture of the sheets. Since I'm naked, I feel it all over me. God, I want Grey's hands on me, caressing my skin this way.

Can we work as a couple? I don't know. Can I survive not at least trying to have sex with him again? Probably not. If last night taught me anything, it's that I can't think of Grey as only my friend anymore.

He wants me to teach him. Maybe I can do that. I've never needed to try before since all the guys I've dated were not virgins, not even the first time I got naked with a guy, and they were all at least decent in bed. Grey says he was anxious the first time we tried it, and that's why he messed it up. How can I help him with that anxiety? I know how to make him feel better about everyday problems, like work stress and getting used to his brother. Sex is a different planet from that stuff.

But God, I want him to rock my world.

I get an idea and pull on some clothes, then grab my phone and place an order from my favorite online bookstore. Overnight shipping costs a lot, but this will be worth it if I can find a way to make sex with Grey as incredible as kissing him is. I still don't know if I can get past my fear of screwing up our relationship and losing him for good, but I'll go crazy if I don't at least try. Maybe one time with Grey will get rid of this lust.

Sure, then we can go back to being besties. *You're so full of it, girl.*

I've never done meaningless sex, but I need to do the nasty with Grey with no strings attached. Does that make me a hypocritical slut?

Screw that. The time to nip this thing in the bud has come and gone—last night, when I came three times while thinking about Grey.

After doing my morning bathroom routine, I head into the living room that also doubles as an open kitchenette. Though I love cooking, and Eve had helped me stock our fridge yesterday, I decide Grey and I should eat in the guest house, in the dining hall with all the other wedding guests. We could both use a bit of not-alone time to recover from our surprise encounter last night.

Since my best friend seems to still be sleeping, I decide to explore the contents of my welcome basket. Grey has his own basket, but it doesn't look like he's checked it out yet. I sit cross-legged on the sofa while I sort through everything the resort has given me. Sunscreen makes sense, but bug spray? Are insects that big a problem here? There's also aloe. I guess nudists have a problem with chafing.

Do I want to try naturism? Stripping naked in front of strangers doesn't sound like fun to me, but maybe I need to push myself further outside my comfort zone and try something daring. Some of Grey's cousins went nude yesterday, along with several of the MacTaggarts. But I'll need a little more time to drum up the courage to do that.

Would Grey ever try naturism?

My skin tingles when I picture that.

The welcome basket also contains a brochure outlining all the wedding events as well as a sign-up sheet for any activities I want to participate in. A guided nature hike sounds like fun. I can learn about the wildlife and the plant life. Grey likes that kind of stuff too. Then there are horseback tours and riding lessons.

My gaze lands on the big even—Highland games.

Grey and I saw those once in Washington State. It might be fun to watch the MacTaggarts and the Dixons toss cabers and hurl stones. Domhnall would probably love that, but I doubt Grey has any interest in it. That's a good thing. If my ex-fiancé competes, it's way safer for Grey to keep his distance. Domhnall has developed a strange obsession with getting me back, and he blames Grey for breaking us up. That's bull, but I can't seem to convince Domhnall of that.

"Good morning, Jessica."

My head pops up, and I smile when I see Grey standing at the other end of the sofa. He's wearing his usual jeans and a T-shirt and looks extra yummy this morning. Did he get hotter overnight, or am I just obsessed with sex?

Obsessed with his abs and his biceps is more like it.

"Morning," I say. "Ready for breakfast in the dining hall?"

"Yes."

I hold up the brochure. "Have you read this? It lists all the stuff that Alex and Catriona have planned for the wedding week. Events for their guests. I'd love to do the nature hike."

He sits down on the sofa near me, but not too near. "I'll do anything you want."

Anything I want? That would involve him naked.

Get a grip, girl.

"We need to sign up for the things we want to do," I say, pretending I'm reading the brochure again. It's strictly a tactic to avoid looking at him. At his body. At his face. At those gorgeous eyes.

He scoots closer and leans in to peek at the brochure. "Highland games?"

Why does he have to smell so good? Is that different aftershave? It must be because I don't remember him ever smelling this...delicious. I clear my throat and try to breathe through my mouth so I don't have to smell him. "Yeah, they're doing Highland games. That would be fun to watch, huh?"

Grey stares at the brochure with his eyes narrowed, and his lips tick upward the tiniest bit. "It says the games are a test of skill, strength, and strategy for men and women alike." He throws me a sideways glance, his brows lifting ever so slightly. "Will you compete?"

"No, of course not. I'm a lover, not a fighter." Oh crap. Why did I say the word lover? He might think I meant it as a come-on or something.

"I know that. But aren't we meant to leave our comfort zones? Alex told me that's the point of having the wedding here, at a naturist resort."

Oh good. He didn't think I was hitting on him.

Maybe I kind of sort of was. Unintentionally.

I imagine Grey tossing cabers, his shirt sweaty, his skin sweaty, and then he dumps a bucket of water over himself. Drenched Grey. Wet T-shirt Grey. Maybe he'd strip off his shirt...

"Jess, are you listening?"

"Yeah, sure." I wince. "What did you say?"

"I'm going to compete in the Highland games."

"What? No, Grey, you can't. Domhnall will trounce you."

His eyes narrow again, but he's not almost smiling this time. His lips are compressed, and he hisses a breath out through his nostrils. "You think I can't beat him."

Why did I say Domhnall would trounce him? I panicked, that's why. My sweet Greybee going head-to-head with my ex-fiancé? That's sure to end in an apocalypse.

"I didn't mean it like that," I say. "Domhnall used to be a wrestler. He was an alternate on the Olympic team during his second year of college. Now he teaches self-defense classes and owns a gym—where, by the way, he works out religiously. Domhnall is strong, believe me."

"You mean he's stronger than I am and better at sex than I am."

"Who mentioned sex? Not me. I was talking about physical fitness."

"No, you were explaining to me why I can't possibly beat the Gaelic God in the Highland games. The thing about sex was hidden between the lines."

I'm not touching that claim, not right now, not until he cools down. "You've been saying for months, ever since Alex first mentioned the idea, that you will never, never, never compete in the games." I hold up two fingers. "Twice I've heard you mutter under your breath that you'll murder Alex if he tries to talk you into it."

"Changed my mind." He snatches the sign-up sheet from me. "I will compete. Full stop."

How does a person prepare for the apocalypse of machismo? Maybe I should start hoarding peanut butter and toilet paper.

"Okay, fine," I say, raising my hands in surrender. "Do what you want."

"Thank you. I will." He sinks back into the sofa and drops his head onto it. "I'm sorry, Jess. I hate arguing with you."

"Me too."

"But I'm serious. I want to compete in the games. My brother will be competing, I'm sure, and he would want me to do it too. It's brotherly bonding rubbish."

"Yeah, I get that." I kiss his cheek. "I'm sorry too. I never meant to imply you're weaker than Domhnall. But I know how ultra-competitive he can be and how ruthless he is when he wants to win."

"I can handle it."

"Okay." Can he? Domhnall is laser-focused on getting me back and hyper-determined to convince me Grey is toxic. Which is ridiculous. Grey Dixon is the exact opposite of toxic.

"May I ask you a personal question?" Grey asks.

I can't help laughing, just a little. "Since when do you need permission for that? We talk about personal stuff twenty-four seven."

"This is a question about Domhnall."

Oh, *that* kind of personal. I'd rather not hear his question since we just had an argument about my ex and the Highland games. But I act like a good friend and say, "Sure, ask me anything."

"Why did you end things with Domhnall?"

"I told you. It wasn't working anymore."

"There's more to it. I know there is because I know you." He straightens, laying an arm across the sofa's back behind me. "And you were very upset afterward. But all you would say was that he was jealous and made an outrageous demand."

"It was an ultimatum."

"About what?"

"Um..." I squirm, which makes my back brush against his arm. Though I don't want to tell him, I've never been able to lie successfully to anyone, but especially not to Grey. "Domhnall ordered me to cut you out of my life."

"He's always despised me. Why did he suddenly tell you to do that?"

"Domhnall said, um, that you are..." I wince again, harder this time. "He said you're toxic and I need to scrub your poison from my life. It wasn't the first time he suggested you're a bad influence, but it was the first and only time he issued an ultimatum and called you toxic."

Grey's expression goes blank, his eyes wide and unblinking. He stares at me that way for a moment that feels like an eternity. "You broke up with him because of me?"

"Well, I, uh, guess so. I don't like ultimatums, and I won't stand for anyone saying nasty things about my best friend."

He tucks a lock of hair behind my ear. "I won't stand for that either. You are the most important person in my life."

I get a pang in my chest when he says that. Grey is the most important person to me too, and I never want to lose our friendship. Does it mean something that I dumped Domhnall when he commanded me to get rid of Grey? I have no idea, but I'd better figure that out.

Ugh. Maybe Jack MacTaggart can help me with that.

Grey gets up and offers me his hand. "Let's go, Jess. It's time to forget everything else and have fun. A nature hike, right?"

"Yep." I clasp his hand, letting him help me up. "Let's get to know the local wildlife. But first, I need breakfast. My tummy is grumbling."

He smiles and gently pokes my tummy. "I know, I can hear it. Though not as loudly as your snoring on the plane yesterday."

"I do not snore. That's a rumor you started."

"Don't be shy about it. Own your chainsaw snores."

This time I poke him in the belly. "You know what I'll have to do if you keep saying that."

He grins and shouts, "Jessica O'Connor snores like a rusty chainsaw."

And I tickle his tummy until his eyes are watering and his face is red from laughing so hard.

Then we head to the dining hall for breakfast.

Chapter Ten

Grey

WE EAT BREAKFAST WITH ALL THE OTHER GUESTS INSIDE the packed dining hall. The room is large and holds so many tables that I can't count them all, and every table is at full occupancy. That's what happens when you invite the entire MacTaggart clan to a wedding. They've got more relatives than anyone I've ever met—brothers, sisters, cousins, spouses, in-laws. Then I have to add in my cousins, their wives, and their friends. Blimey. No wonder the dining hall is packed.

Jessica and I sit at the table with Alex, Catriona, and their respective parents. Imogen and Henry Bennett sit across from my brother while Niall and Sorcha MacTaggart have taken chairs across the table from each other, and Jess and I have done the same. We're facing each other, but I can't really talk to Jessica. She's wound up next to Imogen, who keeps asking her questions that I can't quite hear. The number of conversations going on around us makes it difficult to hear anything.

Alex is beside me, so I wind up talking to him and only him. Luckily, he doesn't ask me anything about Jess or if I've shagged her or any other embarrassing things my brother loves to talk about. He chats to me about the wedding, but when I ask who his best man will be, he gets cagey. Alex hasn't wanted to discuss that topic, but the ceremony will be on Saturday.

"Don't you need to pick your best man?" I ask. "Or do you plan to forgo that and just have groomsmen?"

"Maybe I'll do that, maybe I won't."

"Which will or won't you do?"

He shrugs one shoulder. "What if I go a different way altogether? Or maybe I simply enjoy sidestepping questions."

Oh yes, he does love doing that.

"Logan will be your best man," I say. "He's the obvious choice since he's your best mate."

"Is he?" My brother eyes me sideways. "What if I think he's not?"

"Come off it, Alex. Logan is your best friend. Everybody knows it."

"Maybe you're right." He winks. "But I'd rather have a sexy little best mate like yours. She comes with all the benefits, doesn't she?"

No, she doesn't. Not yet. Not unless I can convince her to give us a go.

But I tell Alex, in a calm voice, "It's none of your ruddy business, you bleeding arsehole."

He chuckles. "I know I've hit a sore spot when you start swearing at me. And I'm always amazed at how you can make a nasty curse sound pleasant."

For the rest of our meal, we don't talk about Jessica—or Domhnall, though I see him sitting at a table with several MacTaggarts, including Fiona, Cat's older sister, who sits beside him. They're having a conversation and keep smiling and laughing. Part of me wishes Domhnall would fall for Fiona and give up on winning Jess back. Another part of me wouldn't wish that on Fiona, not even if it made Jess want me. Domhnall is the worst arse I've ever met.

Maybe my opinion of him has more to do with Jess than with his personality.

No, it's definitely him. He's an arrogant, self-important tosser. Who needs muscles that enormous? And of course, he has the kind of stubble-beard that women seem to love. I shave. Facial hair makes my skin itch, and it's such a bloody nuisance to keep trimmed. But maybe I should try not shaving for a few days and see how Jessica feels about that.

Yes, making myself look like Domhnall is sure to win her over.

After breakfast, everyone wanders out to the lawn where the first group event will take place. I didn't sign up for miniten, mostly because it requires nudity. Val Silva explained to me yesterday that miniten was invented by naturists, so that's why it's nudists only for this event. Jessica and I relax on chaises while Rory MacTaggart and his wife, Emery, face off against Richard Hunter and Maddie Solberg in the first match.

"Didn't sign up for this event, did you?" Jessica says with a teasing smile.

"No. Did you?" Christ, I hope not. Seeing her naked again will give me an embarrassing problem, and I don't have a towel to hold over my lap. Yes, I was listening to Eve's recitation of the rules and etiquette of a naturist resort yesterday. I always listen to and follow rules. Maybe that's my problem. I'm *too* good.

My plan to channel Alex sounds better every minute.

"No, I didn't sign up for miniten," Jess says. "Those weird boxes they wear on their hands look uncomfortable. Besides, I forgot to bring a sports bra, and it's painful to have my boobs flopping around."

Though I try not to picture that, my mind has other ideas. Vivid ones.

I bend one knee, pretending I just want to rest my hand on it when I'm actually hoping my leg will hide my growing erection.

After Richard and Maddie beat Alex and Cat, they take on Gavin and Jamie Douglas. Jamie is the youngest sister of the Three Macs, and she married an American just like her siblings did. It's odd to watch these people playing a strange version of tennis while naked. Eve Silva claims miniten is a laid-back game, and that's why naturists like it. But none of the people playing the game today got the memo about it being laid-back. They're leaping in the air to slam their thugs into the ball. Doesn't it hurt to have your dick flapping around like that? Makes mine hurt just watching Gavin and Richard.

"Think you'll ever try naturism?" Jess asks.

"Me?" I tear my focus away from the bizarre miniten match to look at her. "No, I don't think so. What about you?"

She shrugs. "Maybe. I mean, it would be nice to ditch the bras and undies. Besides, you know what they say. When in Rome…"

"We're in Oregon."

"Ha-ha." She folds her arms under her breasts, studying me with her head tipped to the side. "You know, I don't think I've ever seen you without a shirt on or in a swimming suit. I've seen you naked, once, but that doesn't count since the lighting wasn't great."

"What are you trying to say? That I'm a prude?"

"No, but you're kind of shy about showing off what you've got." She looks at my upper arms and licks her lips. "I only know you've got serious biceps because you picked me up yesterday when I stumbled, and I felt those bulging muscles. Why work out if you're not going to let anyone see the fruits of your labor?"

"I wanted to be fitter, not become a male model."

Jack MacTaggart walks up to our chaises, glancing at Jess before his attention settles on me. "A group of us are going to the lake. You and Jessica should come along. It's a bonnie day for a swim, and there will be a piece to be had too."

"Ooh, snacks," Jessica says, rubbing her palms together. "I'm in. What about you, Greybee?"

I lean toward her so I can whisper, "What have I told you about calling me that when other people are around?"

"Donnae worry," Jack says. "Everyone already knows about Jessica's pet name for you. Alex told Cat, who told Fiona, who told Aidan, and you know how Aidan is with secrets."

No, I don't. But I can guess.

To make sure I feel completely emasculated, Jack adds, "The news spread through the MacTaggart grapevine like wildfire. Cannae douse gossip once it catches a spark."

Perfect. Everyone knows Jess calls me Greybee. I'm sure Domhnall knows by now too. Even more perfect.

"Come on, Grey," Jessica says, touching my arm. "A swim would be fun."

She just told me that she's never seen me without a shirt on, much less in a swimsuit. I don't like swimming, but maybe I can use this outing to my advantage. She seems to like my biceps, though she hasn't seen them yet. She licked her lips when she glanced at my upper arms. If I show her the "fruits" of my labor, as she put it, maybe she'll like what she sees.

"Yes, I'd love a swim," I say.

Jessica claps her hands, though her palms barely touch, so it's more like the way people clap at golf games. "Yay! I haven't been swimming in ages. Or been to a beach. This will be sooo much fun."

Jack wags his eyebrows.

Whatever that means.

Because I have rubbish luck, Domhnall attends the beach outing and wears a scrap of skintight cloth that somehow passes for a swimsuit. I'm wearing swim trunks that Alex lent me. They're not baggy, but they aren't skintight either. Once we get to the beach, I take off my shirt.

Jessica is looking at Domhnall.

Is that appreciation on her face?

"Ready for that swim?" I ask.

"Uh-huh." She swerves her attention to me, and her eyelids flutter. Either she has something in her eyes or... Jess clears her throat. "Holy cow, Grey, I had no idea you'd been working out *that* much."

Domhnall saunters past us, which I'm sure he does on purpose to make sure Jess notices what he's wearing.

She keeps looking at me. Her gaze travels over my entire body, and she slides her tongue over her bottom lip several times. She sounds breathless when she says, "Wow, I really had no idea."

Maybe I'm not as ridiculously muscular as Domhnall and some of the other men here, but I've spent the last eight months trying to get in better shape. Working at a desk all day, for years, left me a bit out of shape. I swear I didn't start exercising to impress my best friend. That's an ancillary benefit.

And she still doesn't look at Domhnall, even though he's lying on the sand nearby, stretched out on his back. He's trying to gain her attention, I'm sure.

But she ignores him.

I feel a glimmer of triumph over that. Score one for the Brit.

"Let's go for a walk," I say, "down the beach."

Jessica smiles. "Sure. Then we can swim after."

"Yes, after." I get a twinge of something not pleasant when I think about swimming. I'm not skilled at that. But for Jess, I'll try.

We walk down the beach, talking about nothing much, but it's the longest conversation we've had in months. Since she ended her engagement to Domhnall, Jess hasn't wanted to chat to me as much as she used to do. The fact that she does now gives me hope for us, as a couple.

Luckily, Jessica decides she doesn't want a swim after all, so I'm spared from floundering in the water. I want to get her alone again, but my brother announces we're having a group picnic on the lawn for lunch. It's his wedding extravaganza, so I can't say no. The picnic is nice, and I get to talk to my cousins while we eat. They've always loved Jess, and she's always loved them, so it's nice to have all of them with me. My cousins do more talking than I do, but I don't care. Jess is smiling and laughing at Reese's jokes. Watching her is all the fun I need.

Alex spends the entire picnic with Catriona, Logan, and Serena.

Everyone keeps their kit on during lunch, thankfully.

In the afternoon, Jess and I watch the children playing silly games on the lawn, things like three-legged races and bobbing for apples. Even the two teenagers in residence, Malina and Chase, get in on the silliness. When Malina stumbles and falls down, Chase helps her up, and the looks on their faces make me think those two might be sweet on each other.

I spend most of the time gazing at Jessica.

Once the games are over, everyone separates into smaller groups to do whatever they want. Alex had announced, via megaphone, that we have the rest of the day to "play silly buggers." Free at last. I want to spend time with Jessica, but the American Wives Club, the women who married MacTaggart men, sweep Jess away for a "girls' outing," whatever that means. I spend the rest of the day in my room working on my computer. I'd promised Alex I wouldn't work during the wedding week, but a self-employed person doesn't really get days off. Besides, I like my job. And I need a break from the crowds and my brother's outlandish behavior.

Jack stops by to ask if I need another session.

"Therapy is good for the soul," he says, "and it's like riding a bicycle. You need to keep practicing to get better, but once you've mastered it, you never forget."

"I thought psychologists never cured anyone. It's an ongoing process, that's what I heard."

"Not the way I do it."

What does that mean? I don't know, and I'm pretty sure I don't want to know.

Jess comes back to our bungalow at eight o'clock in the evening, but she's too tired from her "girls' outing" to talk to me. The next day is what Alex calls "a day of freedom before the battle commences." Yes, he makes all this event rubbish sound so bloody wonderful.

Just after ten o'clock, a FedEx vehicle pulls up near the guest house. Jessica rushes over to accept a package.

Why would she order something to have it delivered here? I decide it's none of my business.

At lunch, Alex brings out the megaphone to address the crowd that's gathered for another picnic on the lawn.

"Attention, everyone," he says. "We have a surprise event for you this evening. It's a fancy dress ball, or as my American friends would say, a costume party. Don't worry if you have nothing appropriate to wear. Cat and I hired a selection of costumes that you can choose from. You'll find those in the exercise room, which we have commandeered for tonight."

Costumes? He must be joking. I *pray* he's joking.

"The ball begins at nine this evening," he announces. "No kiddies allowed, I'm afraid. This is for the grown-ups."

Why do I get faintly nauseous when Alex says that? Probably because he has bizarre and sometimes illegal ideas about what grown-up fun means. Well, maybe not actually illegal. But inappropriate, for sure.

Everyone starts to leave the lawn.

Alex comes over to me and Jess while I'm folding up the blanket we'd used for our picnic.

He claps me on the shoulder. "As my brother, it's your responsibility to attend the ball tonight. No wriggling out of it because you think fancy dress is embarrassing."

"Whether I try to wriggle out of it depends on what you think 'fancy dress' means. I remember your story about Aidan's birthday when Logan made you dress like a Scottish stripper."

"I was a medieval Highland warrior, not a stripper."

"But you told me you felt like a bloke in a male revue."

He squeezes my shoulder. "You should take Cat's approach and ignore three-fourths of what comes out of my mouth."

"Does that mean I should ignore everything you just said?"

Alex smiles in the enigmatic way he loves to do, then he leans in to whisper in my ear, "I've picked out a particular costume for you, Grey. It'll show your girl what a sexy, mysterious man you are. Women love that."

"Are we wearing masks at this ball?"

"Of course."

I roll my eyes. "Then how is she going to be impressed with my sexy costume if she can't tell it's me?"

"That's the mysterious part. Let her discover the truth for herself."

"Right. That worked out smashingly for you, didn't it? Catriona slugged you when you were wearing a mask."

"No, she slugged me on the green during the Highland games. At Aidan's birthday masquerade party, she threatened to slap me but didn't."

"Well, that's all right, then," I say, my voice dripping with sarcasm. I sound a bit like Alex when I do that, and I'm not sure that's a bad thing.

My brother gives me his enigmatic smile again and walks away.

Jessica is staring at me with a confused look on her face. "What was that secret confab about?"

"Nothing. Alex thinks he's giving me advice, but it's complete rot."

"Yeah, I think that's part of his charm. Being full of shit, I mean." She slips her hand into mine. "Let's go check out the costumes, hey?"

"Sure, let's do that."

While we head for the guest house, I send out a probably futile prayer that Alex hasn't arranged for me to dress like a male stripper. It turns out Alex has issued orders that all guests must keep their costumes a secret until the party tonight, so I have no idea what Jess will wear.

While she finds her costume, I return to the bungalow, intending to work again. But when I go into my room to retrieve my laptop, I notice something on the bedside table. It's a book. Someone has put a sticky note on the front cover so I can't see the picture on it. I pick up the book and read the note: "Your homework. J." Jessica likes to sign little notes that way. But homework? What does that mean?

Peeling the sticky note off the book, I stare at the cover. And I swear all the blood in my body relocates to my groin. Something like a tingle rushes over my skin, and my pulse accelerates.

The cover image shows a flower in mid bloom, halfway open. The words on the cover say, "Pleasure Practice: How to Make Sure Your Partner Gets Everything She Needs."

I swallow, hard. Jessica O'Connor has given me a sex manual.

Chapter Eleven

Jessica

'VE NEVER HEARD OF A COSTUME PARTY AS AN EVENT IN a week-long wedding celebration, but hey, this is Alex Thorne's big week. Of course he would want naughty, adults-only events as part of the whole shebang. Grey seemed kind of embarrassed by the idea, but I bet he'll warm up to it. He always thinks Alex's ideas are "barmy," but eventually, he gets into it.

Tonight, I'm leaning against the wall inside the dining hall, which has been transformed into a night club. A disco ball rotates over the center of the room, throwing off shards of brilliance. What looks like Christmas tree lights festoon the walls and the three long tables set up along one side of the dining hall to form a buffet. The rest of the tables are gone, leaving plenty of room for dancing. The DJ who has his stuff set up at the opposite end plays typical night club music, though at a lower volume than an actual club would play it.

Everyone here is wearing a mask, but I can recognize most of them by their smiles or the way they walk. Quite a few MacTaggarts are already dancing. The Dixons have just arrived, but I'm betting they won't wait long to join in the cheesy dance moves. They lift their masks when they smile at me. Aidan MacTaggart seems to be having the best time, doing something that looks like a cross between a meringue and a stripper dance. He's dressed like a vampire, which makes his dancing even stranger.

I spot Alex and Cat near the buffet, but they're too busy kissing to notice me. Seeing them like that makes my thoughts rewind to when Grey kissed me. It had felt so good. Today, I'd gotten the chance to see his body, and wow, he looks as good as he kisses.

Has he found my gift yet? Did he read any of it?

Can't believe I gave my best friend a sex book. I mean, that was basically me telling him I want to screw his brains out. If we go all the way, again, I want it to be good. Really good. Epic, actually. But I don't want to put too much pressure on him to, um, perform. Maybe we shouldn't have sex again. Maybe I should get out my vibrator this time and relieve my lust alone in my room. That would be the safest approach.

No, I will *not* be a spineless moron anymore.

More people enter the dining hall, and more couples take to the dance floor. Jack MacTaggart heads straight for the buffet. Another man follows him over there. They both remove their masks while they snack on the offerings on the tables, and I notice the other man resembles Jack. Maybe that's his brother, Callum. I've heard Jack has a younger brother, but I've never seen him. The new guy is as attractive as Jack, who's as attractive as every other MacTaggart here. That clan has the best genes on earth.

A man enters the dining hall alone, his head slowly swiveling left and right as he scans the crowd. He's dressed like a pirate, with leather pants that hug his thighs and a billowy white shirt that hangs half unbuttoned, revealing his muscular chest. His long black hair must be a wig since I haven't seen anyone here who has hair like that. A silver mask covers half his face, but I can see his mouth, and if he came closer, I'd be able to see his eyes.

I know that man. I saw that chest during the beach outing, and I recognize the way he carries himself with his shoulders back, but his overall posture relaxed. And that mouth. I've kissed those lips and felt them pressing into mine.

Holy shit. Grey Dixon is the hottest pirate I've ever seen.

My best friend saunters toward me with a phony cutlass swinging from his hip. At least, I hope it's phony. Though a sword fight between Grey and Domhnall might be hot, it could also be a huge disaster.

Grey stops an arm's length away, and the coruscating light from the disco ball flashes on his eyes, making them sparkle.

"Good evening, Jessica," he says, his voice seeming deeper and sexier. "You look incredible."

His compliment makes me feel warm all over. I'm wearing what Alex called a "pirate wench" costume. He suggested I should wear it, and now I see why. My outfit goes with Grey's. I have a bodice that hoists my breasts so they mound up. My shoulders are bare, but sleeves cover most of my arms, while the skirt is cut high on both sides so that if I bend either knee my thigh will be exposed. Thigh-high boots and a scarf tied on as a headband complete my outfit. The gold mask I'm wearing covers my eyes only.

I felt silly dressed like this—until Grey looked at me.

"How did you know it's me?" I ask.

Grey pushes his mask up onto his forehead. "I'd know you anywhere, even if I were blind and deaf."

With his attention trained on me, and his mask pulled up so it doesn't obscure his face, I swear his gaze sizzles over my skin like he's dragged his tongue up my throat. An impulse seizes control of me, one I can't and don't want to deny, so I bend one knee and brace the stiletto heel of my boot on the wall. My skirt falls away from my leg.

Grey rubs a hand over his mouth, his gaze riveted to my thigh.

"I love your costume," I say. "It's so hot."

His focus veers to my face. "*You* are hot, Jess. So fucking sexy."

Maybe I've gone crazy tonight, but I no longer care about propriety or any of that shit. I want Grey. Now.

I seize his shirt with both hands and haul him into me. "Did you read the book?"

"Yes." He lifts my mask, resting it on my forehead, then settles his hands on my hips. "I read it from cover to cover. Twice. And I studied the pictures in depth. Did you know there's a website too, with animated illustrations?"

"No." But I wish I had known because that's super hot. What gets me even more aroused is knowing he couldn't wait to read about sex because he wants me that much. "I only gave you that book this afternoon. How did you get through it so quickly? I know you're a fast reader, but that's...really fast."

"I can speed read when the content excites me." He dips his head until his lips graze mine. "You excite me, Jess. Maybe it's the costumes or the night-club atmosphere, but I don't care. All I know is that I want to show you I can be a good lover, I can give you the kind of pleasure you deserve."

Oh God, I want that too. All my worries about ruining our friendship vanish from my thoughts. All I can think about is Grey Dixon, the sensual pirate who wants to ravish me.

And I have a fabulous idea. I'd gotten wet the moment I saw him walk into the room, but this idea I have makes me even wetter, even hotter, so much that I can't stop myself from doing the most insane and outrageous thing I've ever done.

Where we're standing, there are no lights hanging on the wall. Only the oscillating glow from the disco ball reaches this spot, leaving us mostly in shadow. Someone might still see us, but I don't care.

I grasp Grey's shirt again.

Part of me wants to rip his pants open and eat him up. But he's been anxious about ensuring things are better this time, so I don't want to rush it and make him even more anxious. There's plenty I can do to him without even unzipping his pants. Domhnall had never like a slow build to the main event. I wanted to play, not just go for the wham-bang. But I have a feeling Grey will love the build-up, and once he's comfortable with the preamble, I bet he'll want to play too. He's the most patient man I've ever known and the most considerate.

I tug him closer until our bodies meet. The bulge in his pants is pressed into my belly.

He coughs, then swallows hard enough I can hear it. "Would you, ah, like to dance?"

"No, Grey, I don't want to dance. Not yet."

"What *do* you want?"

"You." I lay a hand on his chest, the section that's bared by his half-open shirt, and tease his skin with my fingertips. When his lips fall open a touch, I skim that hand down his torso to the leather belt that encircles his waist. Pushing two fingers inside the waistband, I give it a light tug. "Let me share a few things I've learned."

"About what?"

I smile in a way I hope looks sexy and mysterious, and I think it works since he starts breathing more heavily. God, I love getting him turned on. Watching his reactions gets me hotter too, and when I slowly undo his belt, I love the way his gaze is nailed to what I'm doing.

He rests his palms on the wall at either side of my shoulders. "Jessica, you don't have to—"

"Not doing this because I feel obligated. I want to do this for you. So shut up and let me do it."

"You've never been bossy before. I like it."

"Guess I have a thing for pirates, and it makes me bossy." I unhook the button on his pants, then take hold of the zipper pull and drag it down inch by inch until I've exposed his dick. And he's given me a surprise too. Grey Dixon is naked under all that leather. No boxers. No briefs. Nothing but skin. "Wow, thank you so much for ditching the underwear."

"These leather trousers are so tight I couldn't fit any pants on under them, not even briefs."

Yeah, I've known Grey long enough to have learned most of the Britishisms. I know that to him, "pants" means underwear. What I call pants, he calls trousers. But right now, none of that matters. I've gotten so excited it'll take all my willpower to keep going slow. I know exactly what I want, and I decide to tell him everything. "Grey baby, I want to work you into a lather with my hands on your cock until you're out of your head with the need to come. I want to feel your dick in my hands and rub you in places no one has ever touched you before, and only when you beg will I wrap my lips around you."

To prove I mean it, I close my hand around his cock and flick my finger across the underside of the crown.

He gasps. "Jess—"

"Shh. You don't need to talk. Just relax and enjoy it."

I keep one hand wrapped around his length while I slip my other hand under his shirt, gliding my palm over his skin. His abs feel even better than they look. I love touching him this way, like I've never touched him before even when we had sex, because it seems like such a naughty thing to do. I mean, he's my best friend. I'm not supposed to want to give him head. Maybe I've wanted to before tonight—like, a hundred times—but I always dismissed that as passing thoughts. Except they weren't "passing" anything. And I decide to tell him the naked truth.

Skating my hand up his chest, I pinch one nipple, then the other, loving the way he hisses in a breath. "I have a confession. I've fantasized about you so many times while I was getting off by myself. I've done that for years, off and on."

His eyes widen.

"Used to think it made me a bad person," I say, "wanting you while I was with other guys. But I couldn't stop those fantasies. Sometimes when I was alone, late at night, I would imagine you fucking me while I made myself come. I never could accept I'm really attracted to you, brushed it off as nothing, but I'm not brushing it off anymore."

I rake my nails down his chest while I flick my thumb across that sensitive spot on the underside of his crown.

He sucks in a breath, and his dick jumps.

My panties are damp. Drenched, actually. Talking to Grey about sex, about all the things I want to do to him and with him, it gets me so turned on I'm breathing harder too.

I slither down his body until my face hovers in front of his groin. The sight of his dick so close to my face mesmerizes me. I've never really seen him naked before. The first time we had sex, I'd asked Grey to turn off the overhead light and the lamp on my bedside table, which left only a night-light. Maybe I'd been nervous too. So yeah, I hadn't gotten a great look at his equipment. Now I have an up-close view.

His cock is thick and sleek—and I want it. With his length in my hand, I can't remember any of the reasons why we shouldn't do this, all those things that used to seem so important. All I know at this moment is that never in my life have I wanted to do this for a man as much as I want to do it for Grey.

"Jessica..." Grey's voice has gotten huskier, softer, like he's stunned by what I plan to do to him, like maybe he thought I wouldn't go all the way.

But I will. Right now.

Moisture beads on the head of his cock, and I drag my tongue across it to lick up the salty, delicious flavor of him. I moan too because damn, I'm getting tingly all over but especially between my thighs. Instinct takes over as I rub my cheek against his shaft and cup his sac with my free hand. The second he gasps, I take his balls in my mouth and suck.

"Fuck," he hisses while his entire body stiffens. He's breathing so hard his chest heaves.

I curl my tongue around his length and slide it down to the base then back up to the crown. More moisture has beaded there, so I lap it up.

He's breathing so hard he almost hyperventilates.

Yeah, I've teased him enough. I'd love to keep going like this, but I don't want to risk making him go off too soon. He'll be humiliated if that happens. I've had my appetizer, and it's time for the main course.

I open wide and take him into my mouth.

Chapter Twelve

Grey

JESSICA O'CONNOR IS GIVING ME HEAD. SHE HAS MY cock in her mouth. And the things she said to me... Hearing all that makes me want to describe to her in detail every last thing I want to do to her. That book gave me so many ideas. It had also gotten me so turned on I'd needed to beat off after I read it. I fantasized about Jess while I did that, and not for the first time. I've wanted her since the day we met.

And now I know she's wanted me too, for longer than a few days. Years, she said. She was in denial about it, but I never have been.

My muscles are as stiff as my cock. The only thing keeping me from falling down is my hands on the wall, and when she took me into her mouth, my fingers curled and my nails scraped on the wall. No woman has ever wanted to do anything like this to me. My hips want to thrust, but I fight back the impulse for as long as I can, not wanting to hurt her. I can't fight it for long, not with her tongue flicking over my skin and her teeth, covered by her lips, gliding up and down. She sucks gently at first, picking up the pace and the strength of it little by little. It feels so fucking amazing, and I can't stop watching the way her head moves and her hair spills over her face, brushing my skin. My pulse thunders in my ears, beating so fast that I can't think or control my own body. She sucks and licks, and fingers the skin behind my balls while her other hand pumps me, sliding up and down, moving in sync with her mouth. The sensation of her warm, wet, velvety tongue steals my breath, and I think my eyes literally roll back in my head.

I push a hand into her hair. "Fuck, Jess. Ah..."

There's no stopping it now. The pressure inside me seizes my entire body, and I know I won't last much longer. She'll pull her mouth away, won't she? Use her hand to finish me off. She won't want to swallow. But she doesn't stop. Jess tips her head back just enough to gaze up at me with hooded eyes, her lips tightening into the most erotic smile I've ever seen—and she keeps going.

That look on her face does me in. I clench her hair in my fist while I come inside her mouth, with her lips sealed around me, and feel every one of the rapid-fire spasms in my cock that force my body to spend everything I've got. The pleasure rockets up my spine, forcing my fingers to dig into the wall and my hips to thrust, pushing my length deeper into Jessica's mouth. She keeps working me until I'm done and so satisfied that I can barely catch my breath. What little strength I have left keeps me standing, braced with one palm on the wall, while I gaze down at the woman who's licking her lips and zipping up my trousers.

Once I recover some of my wits, I let go of her hair and cradle her cheek in my hand.

She turns her face up to me, her expression loving and lustful at the same time. Her cheeks are pink. Her lips look slightly swollen too and rosier than usual.

I grasp her upper arms and urge her to stand, then I push her back against the wall. "Thank you, Jess. That was...incredible. But I need to reciprocate."

Her lips curve into a sexy smile. "Only you could make the word reciprocate sound hot. I loved it when you said 'statistical certainty' too."

She loved that? Her statement gives me a brilliant idea that I'll need to flesh out later. Right now, the only flesh I want to work on is hers. That book she gave me had been very...illuminating. Thanks to what she just did to me, I feel relaxed and not at all anxious. To watch her come while I make it happen... Fuck, I want that. But I'm still not completely comfortable with the idea of describing to her what I plan to do. Next time I can try that. Tonight, I need to touch her.

I rest my hands on the wall again, then I bend my elbows to bring my body closer to hers. "I've learned a lot from that book. It's time for hands-on practice."

Her breasts rise and fall, pushed up by every labored breath she takes. Her pupils have dilated, making her eyes seem darker, and she catches her bottom lip between her teeth.

Did I look like that when she went down on me? Probably. Well, except for the lip-biting. Men don't do that as far as I know. But Jessica looks so bloody beautiful when she's aroused, and I can't wait another second to touch her.

I brush my lips over hers while I lay a hand on her hip, then glide it down until I can slide my palm under the open side of her skirt.

"Grey, you don't have to—"

"Yes, I do."

I love the way she said my name, her voice softer and throatier, but I'd loved it even more when she called me "Grey baby" a few minutes ago. Jessica has never called me that before. It's always Greybee. Maybe the new pet name means she doesn't think of me as just a mate anymore. Based on her confession that she's fantasized about me for years, she definitely doesn't think of me as asexual.

Jess bends her knee, turning it to the side, giving me access to the most intimate part of her.

I skate my hand down her inner thigh and back up until the hairs on her mound tickle my fingers. Those hairs are damp. Fuck, she's already wet and aroused. She must've liked giving me a blow job, right? Why else would she be so turned on after doing that?

Stop thinking, you idiot. Remember what the book said. Yes, I remember a particular bit of advice. "Don't overthink it," the author said, "and let yourself enjoy giving your partner pleasure as much as she enjoys receiving it."

All right, I can do that. I need to calm down first. Breathe, relax. Breathe, relax. My muscles slacken, and the thread of anxiety that tried to wind itself around me has disintegrated. Now I'm ready.

I comb my fingers through those damp hairs. They're softer than I expected, but then, I'd never touched Jess down there when we had sex. Tonight, I can explore her body like never before. She wriggles a little when I comb my fingers through her hairs again and cup her mound.

But I'm an idiot, so of course, I say something stupid. "If you don't want me to do this, I'll understand. I might cock it up like the last—"

She seizes my head and crushes her mouth to mine, holding our lips like that for several seconds. I still have my hand between her legs, but even when she peels her mouth away from mine, she keeps it so close that I feel her lips when she speaks. "Stop that, Grey. Our first sexual experience was bad because we both got nervous, so let's forget about that and start fresh. You read the book, so quit worrying and trust yourself the way I trust you."

All right. No more worrying.

While she grasps the back of my neck, I push two fingers between her folds, caressing them while I watch her face. Her juices make my fingers slick, like her flesh is. Slick and hot. The musky scent of her cream teases my senses, and I feel drugged by that aroma, drugged by her, by what she just did to me and what I want to do to her. Her eyes drift half-closed when I slide my entire hand between her folds, rubbing the heel against her clit and stroking her with my fingers. She likes this. I'm making her feel good.

Maybe I'm not rubbish at sex after all.

One finger slips, scraping her flesh.

She winces.

"Bollocks," I hiss. "Sorry, I—"

Jessica lays a finger on my lips and shakes her head. "Stop. It was an accident. Take a breath and keep going. I love what you're doing, Grey, really love it."

I love the sensual tone of her voice and the pinkness in her cheeks.

"Keep going," she says. "I want you to make me come. Please, Grey."

How can I say no to her? I can't, so I take a deep breath and let it out gradually. Then I start stroking her again and massaging that hard little nub in slow circles. She grips my nape harder, her nails pricking my skin, but I don't care about that. The slight pain barely registers in my mind because all I can focus on is her. Jess has her eyes half-closed again, her lips parted, and the pink tip of her tongue is just visible. I push my hand lower until I can thrust my longest finger inside her.

She gasps, squeezing her eyes shut. Her hips roll forward like she's trying to force my finger deeper inside her body.

Trust yourself the way I trust you, she'd told me.

I plunge two fingers into her channel, massaging the inner wall.

"Yes, Grey," she says, her voice half whisper, half moan.

The heel of my hand still grazes her clit, so I swirl it over that nub until her mouth falls open farther and her nails dig into my neck harder, then I push a third finger inside her.

Jessica's body goes rigid. She stops breathing, her entire face crimped.

Her channel tightens around my fingers.

A breath explodes out of her, and her body bows inward, seeming to collapse in on itself while she makes gasping, whimpering sounds.

I keep caressing her until she goes limp against me, her head on my shoulder. "Holy shit, Grey."

She came this time. Didn't she? Well, she must've done considering the look on her face and the way her inner muscles had pulsated around my fingers.

Jessica lifts her head to gaze at me with a dreamy smile.

I made her come. I put that look on her face. No, not rubbish after all. That book is bloody brilliant.

"Let's go back to our bungalow," I say, brushing hair away from her eyes. "I want to make love to you tonight."

Her dreamy expression makes me long to do exactly what I said—show Jessica how much she means to me by loving her body with every part of mine.

"That would be wonderful," she says. Then she flaps her hand like she's fanning herself. "Whew, Grey, that was intense and beyond mind-blowing. I feel kind of lightheaded and hot all over, and my heart is beating so fast. Oh God, that was the best sexual experience I've ever had."

I might possibly be smirking right now. So what? She called me the best ever, which means I've earned the right to feel a touch smug.

"That was intense for me too," I say. "Definitely my best sexual experience ever. Let's go back to our bungalow and make love all night."

She sags against the wall, fanning herself again. "Maybe we should wait. I mean, it was only yesterday that we kissed. Now, tonight..." She lays the back of one hand on her still-pink cheek. "Wow, I need time to recover before we do anything else. There's no need to rush."

I want to fuck her right here, right now. After years of dreaming about this moment, waiting another second seems like too long. But she might have a point.

Jessica cradles my face in her hands and kisses me. "Relax, Grey, I want to go all the way with you. Just not tonight. Let's go back to our bungalow and hang out on the sofa, watch some TV, whatever. I think we need more alone time, without the pressure of trying to change our relationship overnight. Okay?"

"Sure. That makes sense, I guess."

"I hope you're not too disappointed."

"No, I'm not. What you said sounds reasonable." I push away from the wall. "Why don't I steal some food from the buffet for us? You can head back to the bungalow and find a movie for us to watch."

"Perfect." She pecks a kiss on my lips. "See you in a few minutes."

Smiling, she trots toward the door and disappears into the hallway.

I steal food for us and sneak away carrying two dinner plates full of every sweet treat Jessica loves, plus a bit of nourishing stuff too. I'm rounding the corner of the guest house when a male voice chuckles behind me.

"You're pathetic, ye *cacan*."

I turn around and scowl. Naturally, it's Domhnall sodding Sterling. He's dressed like—what else?—a medieval Highland warrior, kilt and all.

"Are you stalking Jessica?" I ask.

"She doesn't want you, laddie. Jess wants a real man, not a wee shit who has his nose in a computer all day." Domhnall takes two steps closer, leaning in a touch to loom over me. "Since you aren't a Scot, let me explain. A *cacan* is a wee shit."

"Thank you so much for the Gaelic grammar lesson." Am I snarling those words? Not sure, but I don't care if I am. There's sarcasm in my voice, but that is intentional. "Sod off, Domhnall. My relationship with Jessica is none of your concern."

"You couldnae please her the first time you tried having a poke. And I'm fair certain you still can't make her happy, can you?"

Everything inside me freezes as if I've injected liquid nitrogen into my veins. For a second, I can't speak. How does he know about what happened between me and Jess two years ago? No one besides Jessica, Alex, and Jack knows, but they would never tell Domhnall. Maybe Jess mentioned it to him back when they were a couple. No, I can't believe that either.

"Who told you about that?"

Domhnall moves closer, leaning in more. "Doesn't matter how I know. She loves me, ye wee scunner. You are a flea running after her. I am a man, the sort a woman needs."

He called me a flea? That doesn't make sense in the context of his insults. Do fleas run after women? I thought they infested mongrels like him. I should say that out loud, but by the time I've formulated my response, Domhnall is walking away. Swaggering, in fact.

Should I run after him to lob my insult? No, the better man lets it go. I think. Christ, I am so bloody sick of being the better man.

Though I want to punch Domhnall, hard, I won't do it. Not tonight, at least.

Hurrying into the bungalow, I find Jessica on the sofa waiting for me. We settle in with our snacks and watch a terrible movie on the telly, cracking jokes about how awful it is. I haven't had this much fun in ages, and though I'd been disappointed when she suggested we wait to have sex, I can't feel anything but happy tonight. Later, I'll worry about what might happen when we finally have sex. Even if I cock it up again, I know one thing without any doubts. Jessica will not run away this time and take up with an obnoxious arse.

But she still thinks I can't beat Domhnall in the Highland games.

Can I? Soon enough, I'll find out.

Chapter Thirteen

LAST NIGHT, GREY CARRIED ME INTO MY ROOM AND TUCKED ME under the covers. Then he left. Yeah, he's an absolute gentleman, the kind every woman dreams of meeting. But I wasn't thinking about how sweet and considerate he is when he was giving me an earth-shattering climax last night. The way he'd touched me... God, it was incredible. Sure, he had one misstep, but that was an accident. I'd loved making him come, loved the look on his face and the way he'd seemed amazed that I wanted to do that for him.

When he said he wanted to make love to me, I'd wanted that too, so much. My body screamed for me to get naked with him right away, but my brain urged me to slow things down. Not forever. Not for more than a day or two. I know I can't hold out any longer than that. Grey is the hottest guy in the world, maybe the galaxy, potentially the universe. Who knew all he needed was the right sex manual? Sheesh, If I'd realized that, I would've bought him that book two years ago.

Of course, it was more than the book that changed everything. I finally admitted, to myself and to Grey, that I've fantasized about him for a long time. Two years ago, I hadn't been ready. Now, I am. Holy cow, am I ready.

We still have things to sort out, like one critical question. Do I love him as more than my best friend? Does he love me that way? Lust isn't the same thing. He's the most important person in my life. But is that love? The romantic kind?

I try to figure out the answer to those questions while I crawl out of bed and grab some clothes to wear today. I'd taken off my pirate wench outfit last night while Grey got our snacks, and I slept in my PJs. I feel a little weird about last night, and about seeing Grey this morning, but I know that's just nerves. Everything has changed between me and Grey. It'll take time to adjust.

I peek out the door to see if Grey is in the living room. He's not, so I head to our shared bathroom. Since it's across the hall from my room, I sprint into the bathroom with my clothes lumped up in my arms and kick the door shut, then I get naked and get in the shower.

Every time I think about last night, I wonder what it might be like to have a relationship with him—the serious kind, with hand-holding and kissing and everything else—and whether we can really make it work. I've known him for eight years, and aside from our bad-sex experience, we haven't behaved like anything more than the best of friends. I tell him things I would never tell anyone else, not even my boyfriends. Grey indulges my fascination with cheesy tourist attractions and taco trucks. He'll go anywhere with me just to keep me company. Domhnall hates road trips. He hates taco trucks too. He put up with the things I like, but he never really tried to enjoy it, not even a little just for me. Not that he's a total jerk. He simply couldn't understand why I like posing for a selfie in front of a giant statue of a hunk of cheese.

Maybe Grey and I are better suited to each other than Domhnall and I ever were. But do I love Grey? Like that? I still don't know.

Did I love Domhnall?

I'm shampooing my hair when that thought hits me, and I jerk my head, splashing suds in my eyes.

"Shit," I hiss as I rinse my eyes in the water, then I close them and let the spray sluice over me.

Had I ever loved Domhnall? I cared about him. For sure, I liked him. But love? I can't say for certain I felt that, at least not the way I should have considering I accepted his marriage proposal. Breaking up with him hadn't hurt as much as I expected. Maybe not as much as it should have. But if I get seriously involved with Grey and we fall apart...

That would wreck me.

Coldness washes through me, and I crank up the hot water until steam billows around me while I lean my head against the wall. What am I going to do? No frigging idea.

That means I need to talk to Grey. The thought makes me feel a touch queasy.

I stay in the shower doing nothing but staring at the tiles on the wall for several minutes. Then I straighten and haul in a deep breath, exhaling it slowly. What, am I going to hide in the shower forever? No way. I have a life to live and tons of shit to sort out. So I get dressed, blow-dry my hair, and put on some makeup because that's my war paint, then I walk out into the living room.

Grey is sitting on the sofa with his computer on his lap. He glances up when he notices me and fidgets like he can't get comfortable. He clears his throat. "Good morning, Jessica. Sleep well?"

"Yes, I did. How about you?"

"Fine, thanks."

I perch on the sofa's arm, at the end farthest from him. "About what happened last night..."

He shuts his laptop and sets it on the coffee table. Though he doesn't say anything, he angles toward me. His gaze flits around like he's looking for something, but I know him well enough to realize it's just nerves.

Though I get itchy thinking about what his answer might be, I have to ask. "Do you regret what we did at the party?"

"Regret it? No, not for one second."

"You seemed kind of anxious when you saw me a minute ago." I slide down onto the sofa, tucking my legs under me. "I'm nervous too. I mean, everything is different now between us. I don't know if we can ever go back to being just friends."

"Do you want to? I don't."

I hunch my shoulders. "I don't either, but I can't help worrying I'm ruining our friendship. You're the most important person in the world to me."

"And you're the most important person in my life."

"What if we can't work as a couple?"

"I know we can." He's looking at me in a way I've never seen before, not from him. He looks determined and genuinely concerned about helping me cope with our evolving relationship. "You admitted you've been masturbating while fantasizing about me, and you've been doing it for years. That's not what friends do. We mean more to each other than best mates."

"That's a good point."

"You always overthink and over-worry when anything in your life changes. What you're feeling is nothing more than natural anxiety. I'm feeling it too."

He's right, of course. But I want to do more than cope with our changing relationship. I want to get over these fears for good.

"I have an idea," I say. "We need some alone time, away from your brother, my ex, and all those other people."

"Thought you liked Alex."

"Yeah, I do. But you and I need a break from the crowd, time to get comfortable with each other again."

"How do you suggest we do that? The resort is packed with Dixons, MacTaggarts, and all their friends."

"I know." On my knees, I waddle closer to him. "Let's go on a road trip."

"Road trip? We only got here two days ago."

"Don't nix the idea until you've heard the rest." I slap my palms on my thighs. "Let's explore the area around the resort. There's a town nearby, and a state forest, and lots of other stuff that could be fun. Plus, we'll get a break from all this wedding craziness."

"Will there be giant balls of twine or enormous statues of cheese?"

"Maybe. I haven't researched the roadside attractions yet." I slant toward him until our noses almost touch, then I lower my voice and speak in a huskier tone. "But maybe you should do that. You're really good with search engines."

"You make the term search engines sound filthy."

"So do you."

He skims his fingertips along my jaw. "Were you joking when you said I make the words reciprocate and statistical certainty sound hot?"

"No. I love hearing you say all that technical jargon. Always have, but lately, I love it even more." I lay a hand on his thigh and squeeze. "It makes me wet."

The phone rings.

Oh damn. I was hoping he'd talk dirty jargon to me.

Instead, Grey gets up and answers the phone. He listens to whoever's on the other end for several seconds and rolls his eyes. "No, Alex, I don't want to enter the pie-eating contest. Jessica and I are taking a little road trip today—alone."

He listens to his brother again, and his brows shoot up. Then they descend. He grasps the back of his neck, head down, and turns his face to the side, away from me.

Are his cheeks turning pink? Grey is adorable when he blushes, but I'm wondering what his brother said that makes him avert his eyes from me. Well, Alex Thorne does have a super-naughty sense of humor.

"Yes, Alex, fine," Grey says in that slightly harried tone he often gets when his brother suggests some embarrassing activity like pie-eating. "I will be here tomorrow for the games. It's a day trip, that's all. But I am not stripping naked to play miniten."

He says goodbye and hangs up the phone, but he doesn't come back to the sofa. He keeps his head bowed and his face angled away.

I walk up to him. "What did Alex say that made you blush? And now you won't look at me. Come on, Grey, you know I can get you to tell me." I waggle my fingers. "I know every spot where you're ticklish."

He twists his mouth into something between a frown and a smirk. "I'd rather not tell you. Alex is shameless, I'm not."

"But you can tell me anything. Or has that changed since last night?"

"I'm not sure it was ever one hundred percent true." He finally looks at me. "You told me things I wished you hadn't told me, but I'm sure there are things we've kept secret from each other."

"Maybe it's time we shared all of it." I pull my head back. "What do you mean I told you things you wished I hadn't told you?"

"All that stuff about Domhnall. How fantastic he is at sex. You banged on about that at length, including sharing all your dirty pet names for him." He shoves his hands into his pants pockets. "Domhnallicious, the Gaelic God, King O. Didn't you think I could figure out O meant orgasm?"

My mouth opens, but I just stare at him. I said all that? Maybe I kind of sort of remember telling him that stuff. Jeez, what a jerk I've been. "Oh God, Grey, I'm so sorry. Can't believe I told you all those things. I mean, I know I did, but—Ugh. Why did I tell you that? How many times did I do it?"

"Three times." He shrugs. "I think it was always after you and Domhnall had a fight. You'd call me or text me, and I wanted to be there for you. That's why I didn't complain when you told me how bloody amazing he is."

"I meant those as sarcastic names for him."

"Yes, you were being sarcastic when you told me. But you also mentioned screaming those names when you had sex with him."

Oh. Dear. God. He's right. My hand flies to my mouth like my brain knows I should've kept my trap shut those three times I blabbed all that to Grey. But the impulse comes too late.

Hugging myself, I shake my head. "I'm such a horrible person."

"No, Jess, you're not." He takes hold of my upper arms, rubbing his hands up and down. "I was your best mate. Of course you thought it was acceptable to tell me things like that. Being your confidante never bothered me when you were with any other blokes. But it did get me to me when you were with Domhnall."

"Why only with him?"

"Because you loved him. Those others were boyfriends, not serious candidates for marriage."

"I never loved Domhnall." The words spill out before I bother to think about what I'm saying. Earlier, I'd wondered whether I ever loved

Domhnall. Grey thought I did. Domhnall must've thought so too. But suddenly, I know didn't. Not really. Not the way I should have if I'd wanted a future with him.

"But you—" Grey shakes his head the tiniest bit. "Why did you want to marry him, then?"

"He asked. Saying yes seemed like the thing to do."

"If he hadn't issued his ultimatum, would you have gone through with the wedding?"

"No. I was having doubts before he told me to get rid of you." I pull in a big breath and blow it out, my shoulders sagging. "To be honest, I think I might've picked Domhnall as a boyfriend because I knew I could never love him. I cared about him, but that's not enough."

"I don't understand. Why would you want to be with a man you couldn't love?"

Five minutes ago, I couldn't have explained why. I wouldn't have even said I got together with Domhnall because I could never love him. Talking to Grey about all of this, I'm experiencing a series of epiphanies. Maybe because of last night. The intimacy of what we'd done to each other. It triggered a seismic shift between us, and I can no longer deny the truth.

Though I don't want to, I force myself to meet his gaze. "I picked Domhnall because he's the polar opposite of you. He owns a gym, he used to be a wrestler, he's bossy and Scottish and not at all techie. I doubt Domhnall has ever spoken the phrase statistical certainty. He's not a bad person, deep down, but he has trouble with compromise and admitting when he's wrong."

"I see." Grey scrunches up his mouth. "I have a confession too. I never liked Domhnall because he was all the things I'm not. I thought you wanted a big, ripped he-man sort, and that's why you stayed with him longer than with any of your other boyfriends. I was jealous because I can't be like that."

"And I don't want you to be. You're so sexy, Grey, just the way you are." I can't resist skating my hands over his chest. "I do love your new and improved body, but I'd still want you even if you got pudgy."

"You can get pudgy too, and I'll still think you're the sexiest woman on earth." He hesitates, his lips flattening. "Domhnall knows we had sex once and it was a disaster."

"What? I never told him that."

"No, but someone did. I can't believe it was Alex or Jack, but I haven't told anyone else."

"I haven't told anyone, period. But I get why you told them. And I agree, they wouldn't blab to Domhnall."

"Doesn't matter, I guess." He kisses my forehead. "You were right about us needing time alone, but there's a problem. We don't have a car."

"I'll talk to Eve. I'm sure she can arrange something."

"All right." He winks and smirks, just the way Alex does. "I'll research tacky sculptures while you're gone."

"You do that, Greybee. Then you can tell me all about it, using lots of hot jargon about search engines."

"I will. And after that, I'll go to the guest house to get us breakfast."

He returns to the sofa and his laptop while I head for the caretaker's house.

But I get waylaid halfway there.

Domhnall steps in front of me and drops to one knee, grabbing my hand. "Give all to love. Obey thy heart. Friends, kindred, days, estate, good fame, plans, credit, and the muse; nothing refuse. 'Tis a brave master, let it have scope. Follow it utterly, hope beyond hope."

"Are you seriously quoting Ralph Waldo Emerson?" I ask.

Guests on the lawn stop whatever they've been doing to watch us.

I try to yank my hand away, but Domhnall holds it tight. "I mean those words with all my heart, Jess. I love you. Come back to me, please. I'm sorry for whatever I've done to make you unhappy, but I know we belong together."

"Do you think spouting poetry is the way to convince me? For heaven's sake, Domhnall, get up." I wave my free hand, indicating he should do just that. But he doesn't, so I scowl at him. "Let go of me, or I will make you do it."

"Ahmno letting go until you're mine again."

His. That's what he wants? Me to belong to him. No way in hell.

I kick him in the shin, and he winces. I yank my hand free when his grip loosens a smidgen. "We are finished, Domhnall. Get over it. Besides, if you love me so much, why did you wait so long to try to get me back?"

"Well, I..."

"Yeah, that's what I thought."

"I didnae answer your question."

"No need. I heard between the lines." I lean in only so I can whisper to him and no one else will hear. "How did you know Grey and I had sex once?"

"All that matters is the fact I can satisfy you. He can't."

"I want to know, Domhnall. Who told you?"

He glances around, his jaw working. "I overheard Alex Thorne and Jack MacTaggart talking about it."

I huff. "And you think eavesdropping will make me want you back? Gimme a break."

With that, I march to the caretaker's house.

Chapter Fourteen

Domhnall

I SPRING TO MY FEET AND HURRY AFTER JESSICA, DETER-mined to make her... Do what? See that I'm the right man for her and Grey Dixon is a slimy *cacan*? Aye, telling her we belong together convinced her, didn't it? I can't think about that right now, not until I've caught up to Jess and...done something.

She's knocking on the door to the caretaker's house when I reach her.

"Go away, Domhnall," she says, frowning at me.

"We're not done talking. I love you and—"

The door swings open. Val Silva glances at Jessica, then me. His brows lift, the expression aimed at me though he speaks to her. "What can I do for you, Jessica?"

"I'd rather not talk about it in front of *him*." She nods toward me.

Val waves for her to enter the house.

But when I try to follow, he blocks the door. "Why don't you have breakfast? The buffet is in the dining hall."

"I need to speak to Jessica."

"She doesn't want to speak to you right now." He sets a hand on my shoulder. "Have breakfast. It will make you feel better."

He shuts the door.

Mhac na galla. I don't want to eat. I want to see Jessica. Since I can't do that without breaking down the door, I lean back against the wall beside it and cross my arms while I wait for her to come out. She will have to eventually.

Now I'm a stalker? What the bloody hell is wrong with me?

I shut my eyes and groan.

"Having a good morning, are ye?"

When I open my eyes, the woman who spoke those cheerfully sardonic words is smiling at me. Fiona MacTaggart stands several feet away, wearing a bonnie flower-print dress with her hair piled on her head in a bonnie style that lets strands of it tumble down to kiss her cheeks. Aye, she's lovely. But I'm not interested in her. The dress reveals a hint of her cleavage, and her pink lipstick makes her mouth look enticing.

But I don't want her or anyone else. Only Jessica.

My eyes disagree, clearly, since I can't make them stop staring at Fiona.

She tips her head to the side a touch. "Well, are ye having a good morning? Since you stalked Jessica over here like a wolf tracking a deer, I'd say you aren't feeling particularly good today."

No, I feel like a wild beast. I've caught a scent and can't give up on capturing my prey.

Aye, that sounds like a romantic way to get Jess back in my life.

"Fuck," I hiss.

Gentle laughter bubbles out of Fiona. "You're head's mince for sure."

Even if I am a mess, I don't need her to tell me so. I grit my teeth, leaning forward to squeeze words out between them. "Away and boil yer head."

She laughs again with much more enthusiasm. "I have three brothers, and two of them can be very intimidating—to other people. If I can deal with them, I can handle you. Snarling doesnae work on me. Neither does a steely glare or Gaelic swearing. And honestly, I'd expect a mature man to do better than 'away and boil yer head' if he wants to offend me."

I gape at her. Christ, she must be off her head.

Fiona moves closer. "You're a braw man who could get any woman he wants. Why are you banging your head into a brick wall trying to make Jessica love you?"

Gazing into Fiona's warm brown eyes, I have trouble remembering why I'm doing any of the things I've done lately. Maybe I shouldn't be running after a woman who says she doesn't want me. Maybe there's another option.

Movement catches my eye past Fiona's shoulder. The guest-house door is opening.

Grey Dixon walks out carrying a tray of food. When he notices me, he lifts his chin and smirks.

That *cacan* is sharing a bungalow with Jessica. *My* Jessica.

In an instant, all my rational thoughts evaporate. I push away from the wall and tell Fiona, "Keep your bonnie wee nose out of my business."

She sighs and shakes her head. "If you want to keep banging your head on those bricks until your skull caves in, it's your choice."

Fiona sashays away from me, heading for the lawn where other Mac-Taggarts wait for her.

That woman is insane. I'm a growling beast, and she's trying to...do what? This isn't a fairy tale where the monster succumbs to a wee lassie's charms and becomes a decent human being.

I am not a beast, though. I'm saving Jess from that bleeding ersehole she calls her best friend.

The door to the caretaker's house opens, and Jessica emerges. When she sees me, she compresses her mouth. "Give it a rest, Domhnall. This is bordering on obsessive behavior."

"I love you, Jessica. I can't give up on us."

"There is no us. And you still haven't answered my question. If you love me so much, why did you wait four months before you tried to get me back?"

For a few seconds, I can't think of a thing to say. She wants an explanation, but I don't have one. So I make one up. "You needed time to think, that's what I assumed. I waited for what seemed like a reasonable length of time."

She laughs, the sound harsh. "A reasonable length of time? It was months, Domhnall. I may not be in love with you, but I can still tell when you're full of shit. Did you ever think that maybe you took so long because you don't love me as much as you want to think you do?"

My mouth drops open, but I have no idea what to say. Is she right? If I loved her as deeply as I keep telling myself I do, then I would have come for her sooner. Wouldn't I? But I cannae stand by while she lets that *sassenach* worm his way into her heart.

Aye, I love Jess. She belongs with me.

This wriggling itch under my skin is not a sign that I'm wrong.

"I shouldn't have ordered you to cut Grey Dixon out of your life," I say. "We should've talked about it."

"Talking wouldn't have changed anything. Unless you're claiming you would've given up that stupid idea." She plants her hands on her hips, fingers tapping, like she's waiting for me to agree with her. "No, I didn't think so."

"But you love me. Or you did once. Let me show you I can be that man again."

"I never loved you, Domhnall."

Her statement pierces me through the heart like a blade of solid ice. She never loved me? No, she's confused by whatever rot Grey Dixon is feeding her.

She closes her eyes, her shoulders sagging. "I'm sorry, Domhnall. I didn't mean to blurt that out, but it's true. I've realized that I never really loved you. I cared for you, I still do, but not the way I should feel about the man I planned to marry. I was having doubts before you gave me your ultimatum. Why do you think I never could commit to moving in with you?"

"Because you needed your independence. That's what you said, and I respected that." But we would've lived together once we were married. Why hadn't I wondered about her reasons for refusing to move in with me even after the engagement? "We had good times too. Didn't we?"

"Yes, we did. But that's not enough. Not for me, not anymore. It's over, for real and for good, so please move on. I have."

Jessica jogs off toward the bungalow behind the guest house. I can't see her once she rounds the corner of the building, but I know where she's going. Back to *him*.

I wander closer to the lawn where the MacTaggarts and the Dixons are playing volleyball. Fiona sits on a chaise nearby, watching the game. She grins and cheers when her brother Lachlan hits the ball, sending it sailing over the net. Fiona is bonnie. For reasons I can't understand, she's not afraid of me or put off by my surly behavior, toward her or toward Grey Dixon. Am I clinging to a relationship that died months ago? Should I give up and move on, like Jess suggested?

I have no fucking idea.

Chapter Fifteen

Grey

HOW CAN I IMPRESS JESSICA O'CONNOR? I NEED TO SHOW her I'm the kind of man who appreciates all that romantic bollocks and who wants to do whatever silly things she enjoys. I've already proved the second part to her over the past eight years. Haven't I? Anytime Jessica didn't have a boyfriend, she would enlist me to go with her on whatever barmy adventures she wanted.

We'd met on our first day at Bournemouth University when we were both confused by the large campus and all the students milling around there. I live in London now, but I'd grown up in Brockenhurst, a village far from the biggest cities. My father owned a farm on the outskirts of town, and I'd spent my childhood playing in the fields and watching the wildlife. Whenever it rained hard, the streets would flood, and cows would clog the roadway. I used to love sneaking into town to see that and to splash in the muddy water.

My father had insisted I should attend the best school he could afford to send me to, and I knew how long he'd counted his pennies to build my college fund. I couldn't say no. He wanted me to go to Bournemouth University, so I did. Adjusting to life in a city had been a challenge, but the university with its two campuses had left me dazed. I'd come from a small town, and there I was in the middle of a sprawling dual campus that had something like eighteen thousand students. Everyone else seemed at home there.

Well, everyone except for one beautiful girl.

I'd bumped into Jessica in front of the library, when we were both gawping at our surroundings and not paying attention to where we were going. I literally bumped into her. She almost tumbled over, but I caught her arm to halt her fall. I still remember the way she looked at me then, the memory as clear today as it was five minutes after we met. First, her eyes had been wide. Then she relaxed, and her lips gradually curved into the most beautiful smile I'd ever seen. Her eyes had sparkled in the sunshine. Her hair glistened too. She was stunning.

So of course, I couldn't manage to speak. Or move. Or let go of her arm.

Jessica laughed, and it was the most enchanting sound I'd ever heard. "You can let go now. I won't fall over, promise."

"Oh. Ah. Sorry." That's right, I stammered like a moron. It's no surprise why she didn't fall instantly in love with me. I remember jerking my hand away and scratching my arm. "Sorry. It's my fault for not keeping an eye on where I was going. Sorry."

She laughed again. "You said 'sorry' three times. Once was enough. Besides, I wasn't watching either. I grew up in Iowa, on a farm, so this place is a mega-metropolis to me. It's making me kind of dizzy."

"I grew up on a farm too. Here in England, not in America."

Yes, if I hadn't told her that, she wouldn't have known. Lots of American farm boys have British accents and wear England Rugby shirts like the one my cousin Reese had given me. I don't care for sports, but I didn't want to disappoint my younger cousin. He'd been sixteen at the time and a huge fan of rugby.

"The girls will love the shirt," he'd assured me a week before I left for Bournemouth, "and you'll have them clamoring to shag you."

His claim turned out to be bollocks. Girls did not clamor to shag me or to date me. But I did meet the woman of my dreams. And for about two minutes, I thought I might have a chance with her.

"We have to be friends," she'd told me. "Two farm kids stumbling around at a big university? I think we need to be best friends, don't you?"

"Ah, sure." I'd never had many mates, being quiet and having my nose glued to a computer screen most of the time. But this gorgeous girl wanted to be my friend. I held out my hand. "I'm Grey Dixon."

"Jessica O'Connor," she said as she shook my hand. "What town are you from? I mean, I doubt I'll know where it is since I'd never set foot in England until yesterday, but I can always look it up on Google Maps."

"I was born and raised in Brockenhurst. That's not far from here, to the northeast."

"Brockenhurst. What a cute name. I was born and raised in Eldora, Iowa, which is kind of halfway between Kansas City and Minneapolis, and Chicago is off to the east. I never went to the cities, though. I'm a country girl."

"Guess that makes me a country boy."

"Nothing wrong with that. I love the outdoors, and I love animals too."

"So do I." Did I fall in love with her right then and there? Maybe I had, but it didn't matter.

"Jessica, there you are!" shouted a man who was running up behind her. His American accent became obvious when he slung an arm around her shoulders and said, "Hey, looks like you made a friend already. Awesome."

"Yeah," Jessica told him. "This is Grey Dixon. Grey, this is my boyfriend, Kevin Reed. We both decided it would be a great adventure to move to the UK and go to college here, together."

She gazed up at Kevin sodding Reed like he was a god incarnate. She had adored the twat. Three months later, he cheated on Jessica with her favorite professor, a woman who taught sociology. Kevin moved in with that professor, though eventually, she would throw him over for another student and get fired for it. The twat begged Jess to take him back, but she refused. By then, I had a girlfriend. That relationship lasted only long enough for Jessica to take up with another bloke, then my girlfriend dumped me because I couldn't satisfy her in bed.

Thus began the vicious cycle. Whenever Jess was free, I wasn't. I couldn't dump my girlfriend because I hoped Jessica might want me.

We were best mates from the start, but our relationship changed during our third year at Bournemouth. That's when my father died, and the loss had been devastating. I'd never known my mother, and though my cousins wanted to be there for me, I avoided them. Selwyn Dixon had been the best father any child could've hoped for, and I'd been closer to him than most other people my age were with their parents. What was I meant to do? I'd become an orphan overnight. A heart attack had ripped my father away from me, and I hadn't even seen him in two months and had only rung him for a chat twice in that time, too busy with my new life at university to think about anything else. I started missing classes, sleeping half the day, not eating, beating myself up mentally for abandoning my father.

Jessica saved me from all of that. She made it her mission to nurse me through the worst of it, never leaving my side until I started to behave more normally. She would lie in bed with me, just holding me and stroking my hair. We both missed a lot of classes, but Jessica talked to the right people to make sure we wouldn't be expelled. She tried to get me to talk to a counselor, but all I needed was her. If I hadn't been in love with her already, I was after that. I'd fallen so deeply that I couldn't think about being with anyone else. Yes, I tried to date other women. But my sexual problem only got worse, and every day I fell a little deeper in love with Jessica.

The vicious cycle continued, though. It had begun with Kevin Reed, but it will end with Domhnall Sterling. It has to.

That's why I'm sitting on the sofa in our bungalow at a nudist resort trying to figure out how to impress Jessica with romantic gestures. Domhnall had recited poetry to her. She hadn't seemed to appreciate it. I can do better than that tosser. Jess loves personalized gifts, like when I'd bought her a coffee mug that had her name on it, but I'll need more than that to win her heart.

Maybe if I wrote a poem for her...

I've never written anything more personal than an essay about the Wars of the Roses, and that had been years ago at university. Can I be poetic? I spend most of my time staring at numbers on a computer screen and collating data so I can help my clients figure out how to get the better of their competition. That's what a business intelligence analyst does. But to woo Jessica, I'll need to tap into my creative side. I must have one of those, right? Somewhere, deep down.

Opening a new file on my computer, I hover my fingers over the keyboard. Poems need to rhyme, don't they? I think I've seen ones that don't, but rhyming sounds like the best option. I'm trying to make Jess love me, so haiku doesn't sound like the most romantic choice. All right, I'm writing a poem that rhymes. For Jessica. About how much I adore her.

I start typing. *Jessica, angel of America.* That's rubbish. Angel of America? That's got to be the bloody stupidest poem ever. I close my eyes and picture Jess. Her eyes. Her hair. Her smile. That look on her face when she came for me last night.

A flashback slams through my mind. Jessica's mouth on my cock. Her cheeks caving in while she sucked.

"Bloody hell," I snarl, thumping the heel of my hand on my forehead. I can't think about last night while I'm trying to write a romantic poem for Jessica. Fine, I'll stop thinking about it. No more picturing her lips around my—"Fuck!"

Think of her face, idiot. Remember how lovely and sweet she is?

I start typing again. She is the most beautiful woman in the world, and the sweetest too. She's also clever and funny and the best mate anyone could hope to have. Three years ago, she had invited me to go to

Disney World with her. I didn't expect to enjoy it, but I did, thanks to Jess. She can make anything, even a silly amusement park full of cartoon characters, seem like a wonderful adventure. So I write about all those things, not her body that I want to kiss and lick from head to toe.

Once I've written the poem, I wonder if it needs a little something more. Should I sing it to her? Turn the poem into song lyrics? I know nothing about composing music, but I could wing it. How hard can that be?

I've just shut down my laptop when Jessica comes through the door.

She flops down on the sofa beside me and snuggles up to me with her cheek on my upper arm. "I'm so glad I have you for a best friend."

"That's nice to hear, but why are you telling me now? It seems out of the blue."

I'd rather hear her say she's madly in love with me, but I'll take whatever I can get.

She lifts her head, propping her chin on my shoulder. "I had another run-in with Domhnall. No matter how many times I tell him it's absolutely positively over, he won't listen."

"I could tell Alex to evict him. He's only letting Domhnall stay because I asked him to."

"No, that would make Domhnall more determined to get me back. We need to show him that's never going to happen."

"How do we do that?"

She sits up and shrugs. "Don't know yet."

"Let's eat, then go on our road trip and worry about him later." I set my computer on the table. "I got your favorites—fried eggs, bacon, and raspberry danish. I got your coffee too, with three sugars and a dollop of cream."

"You know me so well." She pinches my cheek. "You're the best, Greybee."

Later today, I hope to prove to her I'm a lot more than that.

Chapter Sixteen

Jessica

AFTER BREAKFAST, WHICH WE EAT ON THE SOFA WHILE snuggled up together, Grey and I climb into a taxi that will take us to the car rental agency in town. We get the same creepy driver who brought us to the naturist resort, and he leers at us again like he did the first time. He doesn't make any comments about "weirdos" or "freaks" this time. At the rental agency, a nice middle-aged man takes us to our car, and he doesn't make a single comment about the place we came from, though he knows about the naturist resort because he gets a lot of business from there. Eve and Val have arranged a special discount for anyone who stays at Au Naturel.

Grey brought his computer bag, though it doesn't hold his computer right now. He put maps, snacks, and some pieces of paper in there. When I asked what those papers were, he told me I'd find out "shortly." Yeah, not many guys I've dated ever used that word. They'd say "in a sec" or "real soon."

We've rented a spiffy new Range Rover. It pays to have a best friend who's got money. Grey isn't rich like his brother, but he has more than enough spare cash to spoil me. He loves to do that, but only in low-key ways. He's never bought me a diamond necklace or anything. His splurging usually involves fun things like our road trip today or first-class airfare to fly to the UK for a visit.

Grey insists on driving. Keys in hand, he ambles to the right side of the car.

"That's the wrong side, Greybee."

He stops and looks at me with his brows furrowed. "What?"

I can't help laughing, though I'm not making fun of him. His confusion is just so darn cute.

"Wrong side," I repeat, pointing at the front passenger door. "You'll have trouble driving with no steering wheel and no gas pedal. You're in America, remember? The driver's side is on the left."

"Oh. Of course."

"Are you sure you want to drive? You'll have to remember to stay in the right lane."

He screws up his mouth, then rolls his eyes. "I can drive the American way, Jess. I've done it before."

"I know. But you were about to get in on the right side, so I'm guessing you're a little rusty with the American way of driving."

"Not rusty. I was thinking."

I walk up to him, leaning against the car. "What were you thinking about? Must've been fascinating to distract you that much."

He opens his mouth, then shuts it, then opens it again. "Never mind. Get in, Jess."

Grey stalks around the front of the car to the correct side for the man who insists on driving. He knows I love to drive, and he usually lets me, but today he's in a kind of bossy mood. And I've learned I like it when he gets all "man in control" on me. It's hot. Besides, I can enjoy the scenery better if I'm a passenger.

Once we're both seated and buckled up, Grey takes the maps out of his bag, then stows that on the backseat. He hands me the biggest map, a road atlas of Oregon. "You're the navigator."

"Thanks. I love having a spiffy title."

"I also have our itinerary printed out. The destinations are listed in order and marked on the map so we'll have the most efficient road trip possible."

"Efficient? It's supposed to be spontaneous and fun."

He reaches into the backseat to pull some papers out of his bag. Grey hands me the stapled sheets. "I wanted to make sure we could see as many attractions as possible today. That requires planning and attention to detail. Efficiency is key."

God, I love it when he talks that way. It makes me want to kiss him.

And I can do that now, right? We're sort of kind of dating or whatever.

I lean in and kiss him on the lips. "Thank you for planning this all out, Grey. Efficiency is so damn sexy."

"I'm glad you approve."

Relaxing into my seat, I study the itinerary. I clamp my teeth over both lips to keep from snickering. He's arranged the list of destinations with each one numbered and with bullet points that include the name of the place, the town or area where it's located, and the distance between each location. He also noted rest stops. Only Grey Dixon would think to include that to make sure we don't need to use bushes as bathrooms.

"You think my itinerary is funny," he says as he turns the key in the ignition.

"No, I think it's adorable how you typed this on your computer and used bullet points. You even have different fonts for the headers and the bulleted lists." I lay a hand on his thigh. "Wow, I'm so hot for you right now."

He squirms. "Maybe you should keep your hands to yourself while I'm driving."

"Okay. I'll wait until we get to our first destination, then I'll feel you up big time."

Grey pulls out of the parking lot onto the highway, and soon we're leaving the city behind, racing toward the first attraction on his list, a giant statue of Paul Bunyan. Most guys think it's dumb that I love hokey tourist traps, but Grey has never minded. He likes to tease me about it, though he does that with affection instead of annoyance, unlike Domhnall. My ex was all in for a weekend in Mexico, but not for a road trip. But all we did in Cancun was have sex.

We whiz past a speed limit sign.

I lean over to peer at the dial that shows how fast we're going. "Slow down, Grey. The speed limit is fifty-five."

He flicks his eyes to glance at me. "I'm going fifty-eight."

"Yeah, you're speeding."

"By three miles per hour. It doesn't count."

"That's still a violation of the speed laws."

He huffs. "And you think it's odd that I made a bullet-point list of our destinations."

"It's different. Driving too fast is dangerous." I lay my hand on his thigh. "Slow down, please, for me."

"All right," he says with a sigh.

He slows down to fifty-five precisely.

I kiss his cheek. "Thank you."

Maybe it is weird that I never exceed the posted speed limit and don't like other people to do it either. Everyone is allowed a few quirks. Grey certainly has his. I like his quirks, always have, and I think he likes mine too.

The road and the scenery unfurl head of us, mile after mile of green grass and green trees, with a gorgeous blue sky overhead and only a smattering of clouds. We couldn't have gotten a better day for our trip unless we could somehow special order the weather. After fifteen minutes, we approach a small town where we'll find the Paul Bunyan statue. I know from previous road trips there are Bunyan statues in quite a few states.

Up ahead, I see a four-way intersection with a stop sign.

Grey is barreling ahead at forty-five miles an hour. Okay, maybe forty-five isn't exactly "barreling."

"Stop!" I shout.

He whips his head left and right. "What? Am I about to hit something?"

"No, there's a stop sign ahead. You need to start braking."

"Bloody hell, Jess. You know I hate it when you do that. And I am braking, for your information."

"Good. Sorry I scared you."

"I'm used to the way you scream whenever there's a stop sign or a stoplight ahead. But sometimes you still get me with that trick."

He doesn't sound annoyed. Grey has known me longer than anybody else besides my parents, which means he's used to my quirks.

We pay our respects to Paul Bunyan, then visit a man-made geyser and a wooden statue of Bigfoot. Grey has me pose by the statue to take a picture of me, and I insist on snapping a pic of him too. I stand still and smile for my close-up with the Big Guy, but Grey pretends to be terrified when it's his turn. His way-overdone fear makes me laugh, but when he falls to the ground like Bigfoot has stomped on him and flails his arms and legs, I laugh so hard my eyes water.

"I'm texting that picture to Alex," I tell Grey.

He gets up and dusts himself off. "Why should I care? Alex wants to play that strange miniten game in the nude. He's the one who ought to feel embarrassed."

"Ooh, I'll get to see Alex naked again." I fan myself, then pretend to faint, though I don't drop to the ground.

Grey wraps an arm around my waist, pulling me close. "Afraid you won't get to see my brother naked. The miniten game is today."

"Yeah, but I think more games are on the itinerary."

"As long as you don't faint at his feet, I don't care if you do see him without any clothes on."

He kisses me in a way that's probably inappropriate in public. I love it, though. Damn, Grey Dixon knows how to kiss.

I feel wonderfully warm and soft by the time we jump in the car, and Grey lets me drive this time. He uses a map on his phone to tell me where to turn. I had used the actual map he gave me, but being a computer guy, he can't resist using the GPS thingy that's supposed to tell us exactly where to turn, down to the foot. Turns out GPS isn't perfect.

"Don't turn here," Grey says when I switch on the turn signal.

"But your GPS girlfriend just told me in her sexy voice to turn left in a hundred feet."

"Which is up there." He points to the next intersection. "And the GPS voice is not sexy. It gets rather annoying, actually."

"Maybe we should stick to the paper map. GPS Girl is confusing me with her 'turn left in a hundred feet' and 'take a slight right in fifty feet' stuff. What is a slight right, anyway?"

"Just drive, will you? And turn left at the next intersection."

"Yes, sir. Maybe if you gave me directions in your sexy voice, I wouldn't get confused."

"I'm saving my sexy voice for later."

Once I've steered the car around the correct corner, I glance at him sideways. "Are you saving that voice for when you tell me about that secret paper you've got in your bag?"

"Possibly."

"Come on, you have to tell me. What's that paper about?"

"You'll find out later."

Grey pulls out the mystery sheet and starts reading whatever's printed on it. Though I can tell there isn't much text on that page, he keeps reading it for several minutes. Is he memorizing it? I can't imagine why he would do that.

We explore a few more of the stops on our itinerary, then we have lunch at a restaurant, talking and laughing the whole time while we reflect on our road trip so far. Grey makes teasing comments about how silly these roadside attractions are, but he admits to having fun visiting all of them.

In the late afternoon, we take a break to relax in a state park. It's the one that borders the naturist resort, but we wanted to have some alone time before heading back to the wedding-week craziness. We're lying in the grass with birds twittering around us and wildflowers dotting the small clearing. I'm on my back while Grey lies on his side facing me.

He picks a flower and touches it to my lips. "We haven't been alone for this long since before you started dating Domhnall."

"Even after I broke up with him, you and I had trouble finding alone time because you've been getting to know your brother."

He skims the flower over my chin and down my throat. "I didn't mean to ignore you."

"That's wasn't a complaint. You should be spending time with Alex. He's your family." I shiver a little when he skates the flower down my chest, where the neckline of my shirt dips down, showing some of my cleavage. "I missed you, Grey, that's all."

"I missed you too." He feathers his lips over mine. "It's time for your surprise."

"Oh goodie."

"You should probably stand up for this. I have it planned out that way."

He stands and offers me his hands to help me up. I brush grass off my clothes while he grabs his water bottle and swigs the liquid. He drinks half the bottle before he sets it down again. I watch him shake his arms and swivel his head like he's loosening himself up for whatever he's about to do.

"Are you planning to dance?" I ask.

"No." He clears his throat. "This is for you, Jessica."

Chapter Seventeen

Grey

I'D MEMORIZED THE POEM I WROTE THIS MORNING, BUT SUD-
denly, I can't remember a single ruddy word of it. Jessica is
gazing at me with the sweetest expression on her face, a
mixture of excitement and affection that makes my throat go thick. Perfect. I can recite and/or sing poetry to her with my throat tightening up
like I'm having an allergic reaction to water. No problem.

Bollocks.

Two more gulps of water help with the dryness in my mouth and my
throat, though it still feels tighter than usual. I am not going to bugger
this up. Absolutely not.

I grab the paper from my bag, but my vision goes blurry when I try
to read the words typed on it.

"Relax, Grey," Jessica says. "Whatever you're about to do, I'm going to
love it, guaranteed."

Well, she might need to pretend to love it this time. I'm trying something I've never attempted before, and I'm doing it to show her how
much I love her. No pressure there, none at all.

After one more gulp of water, I do it.

"Jessica, sweet Jessica," I begin, trying to sing the lyrics by inventing a
tune on the fly, "your hair is like silk. Your skin, buttermilk. Your beautiful smile is so versatile, bright as the sun, it can't be outdone. And oh, you
are stunningly, perfectly, wondrously, expertly clever and sharp, with a

voice like a harp." My pitch rises during that line or stanza or whatever the fuck they call it, so I wind up sounding like a squeaky bird. Clearing my throat, I try to regain my normal voice. "You're never chilly, but often you're silly. And it's sweet, so upbeat. Oh Jessica, for you there is no replica. No one compares to you or dares to eschew your vivacity, for that would be a travesty." I suck in a deep breath, prepared to draw the final syllable out for as long as possible. Then I belt out, "Jessica, my sweet Jessica."

My voice dwindles into a rasping gasp at the end, and I start coughing.

Jessica is staring at me, biting her bottom lip so hard it's turning white. Her affectionate expression has mutated into a tightness that takes over her entire face.

"Uh, well," I say, "that's it. The whole surprise."

She keeps staring at me with that pained expression.

"I know it was rubbish," I tell her. "I'm not a writer. But I wanted to... I don't know. It seemed like a good idea this morning."

Jessica shuts her eyes for a second, then squares her shoulders and smiles. "That was very sweet, Grey. Thank you."

"You hated it. Go on, you can say it. That was the worst rot you've ever heard."

"No, it was very sweet." She studies me, her head tipped to the side. "Were you there when Domhnall recited an Emerson poem to me?"

"I was just going into the guest house when he did that. I heard and saw it."

"So, you were trying to outdo Domhnall."

"No, not specifically." I shove my hands into my trouser pockets, hunching my shoulders. "I wanted to give you something special. Maybe Domhnall's public display triggered the idea, but I wrote that poem for you, to express how wonderful I think you are. I should've done something else, shouldn't I? Like making dinner for you or...something."

"You manage to burn lettuce, so cooking probably would've resulted in a 911 call." She walks up to me and loops her arms around my neck. "You don't need to outdo anyone or put on a big show to tell me how you feel. Just be yourself. That's all I want." She raises onto her toes to place her mouth on my ear. "Remember, I think all your technical jargon is soooo hot."

"It's all right that you hated my poem-song whatsit."

"But I didn't hate it. That was the sweetest, most thoughtful thing any guy has ever done for me."

"My rhymes were bloody awful."

She tips her head back to look at me. "I loved it, Grey, bad rhymes and all."

Jessica loved my horrible poem-song. She loves my jargon too. And she wants me to be myself instead of trying to impress her. An idea I had last night at the fancy dress ball comes back to me now. I know exactly what I need to do—not to prove to her I'm better than Domhnall, but to show her how much I want her.

"I know we'd planned to have dinner in our bungalow," I say, "but I'd like to take you to a restaurant. Strictly to avoid the danger of starting a lettuce fire."

"Sounds perfect. The restaurant, not the flammable veggies."

It's dark by the time we get back to the resort, and the sky above us is clear and filled with more stars than I ever see in London. I remember the sky looking like that in Brockenhurst, but I haven't been back there in years, not since my father died. Tonight, I don't feel melancholy when I think of him. I'm sure Dad is up there watching me and Jess, and I know he's smiling because I'm finally with her as more than a mate. My father had encouraged me to let Jessica know how I feel, but I couldn't when she was always with some other bloke.

Not anymore. She's with me.

When I tell her to wait in the car so I can open her door for her, she says I'm "sweet" and "a real gentleman." That makes me want to kiss her. I hurry to the passenger side, and once she gets out, I shut the door. Then I sling an arm around Jessica and drag her in for a kiss with the full moon shining above us and crickets chirping all around. Maybe insects making noise shouldn't seem romantic, but it does tonight. Jessica wants me, despite my horrible poem and my horrible singing.

Inside the bungalow, I ask her to sit on the sofa with me. I have one more surprise for her, and this time I won't do an awful job of it. I'm relying on my strengths, not trying to outdo Domhnall.

Jessica sits down first, but when I settle in beside her, she tucks her legs under her and snuggles up against my side. "I'm ready for my next surprise."

I lay my arm across the sofa's back and turn partway toward her. "It's time I explained what exactly a business intelligence analyst does."

"You've told me before, twice, but I still don't get it. Do we have to talk about that tonight?"

I lean in until her lips are almost touching mine. "This time, I'll explain it better. With technical terminology."

Her face goes blank for a few seconds, then her mouth slides into a sensual smile. "Are you going to talk dirty jargon to me?"

"Yes."

She bites her lip, letting it slide free little by little. "Mm, yes, please lay some hot technical terminology on me."

God, I love her.

I try to channel my brother a little bit, not so much that I'm mimicking him, but just enough to inspire my attempt to arouse Jessica O'Connor with the sorts of things most women think are mind-numbingly dull. Alex knows how to titillate an audience, that's for sure. I decide to take a few pointers from him, from that lecture he gave earlier this year, the one about sex. Instead of showing pictures of archaeological artifacts or describing ancient sexual practices, I will make data and spreadsheets sound filthy. How hard can that be?

Lowering my voice the way Alex often does, I begin. "I am a fully certified business intelligence analyst with a degree in computer science. I have in-depth expertise in mining data as well as report development with SQL servers."

Does this sound ridiculous? I pause to study her expression.

Lips parted, she keeps her gaze locked on mine.

Am I imagining things, or is she breathing harder now?

"I'm also very skilled at presenting analytics via high-tech visualization tools," I tell her. "Did I mention I dive deep into the data to strip away the layers and expose the tantalizing secrets hidden within the architecture?" I'm not even sure that makes sense, but Jessica loves jargon so...onward I go. "I make the best dimension tables you'll ever see, and I always drill down to the naked numbers. My field transformations will leave you breathless."

Maybe I've never used the word naked when describing numbers before, but I can't help spicing up my explanations. When I said "naked," Jessica dragged her tongue across her bottom lip, then glided it up and over her top lip too. Her pupils have enlarged, and her breasts are heaving for sure.

Can't stop now. A little more... "I integrate my relational databases with the schema, and I always remember to keep my hands on the slowly changing dimensions. I never forget to massage the mobile analytics, but when I deliver the final metrics with all the key performance indicators, you'll get a full load thrust straight into your front end."

Jessica lays a hand on my thigh, her heavy breaths gusting over my lips. "Oh God, Grey, that was so hot. I want you right now."

I might have used some of those terms in a not-entirely-accurate way, but who gives a damn? Jess loved it.

"Time for a live data feed," I murmur against her lips.

"Yes, please, give me that."

I claim her mouth, pushing my tongue inside, groaning when she flings her arms around my neck and shifts onto my lap, straddling me. Fuck, she tastes good, feels good, smells incredible. Her breasts are mashed to my chest while she curls her tongue around mine and moans. With her legs straddling me, I feel the heat of her body pressed against my cock through our clothes. I spread my palms on her back, running them up and down while we keep kissing and I get harder with every passing second.

Tonight, I won't bollocks it up. Tonight, I will give her everything she deserves.

A phone rings. My mobile? Hers? The house phone? No idea, and I don't care.

Someone knocks on the door.

Jessica rips her mouth away from mine and makes a desperate noise, part whimper, part grumble.

"Piss off," I shout toward the door. "We're busy."

"It's me, Grey. Your older, wiser, and much better-looking brother."

"Didn't I just say piss off?"

"We need to discuss an urgent matter. It'll only take a second."

"Sorry," I tell Jess as I push her off my lap. "The only way to get rid of Alex is to talk to him. Thirty seconds, then I'm slamming the door in his face."

"Oh, fine," she says on a deep sigh, sinking into the sofa with her head falling backward. But her head pops up again, and she grins. "I'll undress while you're talking to Alex. Meet me in my room—and be naked."

She leaps off the sofa and runs down the hall.

I rush over to the door and tear it open. "What, Alex? Your urgent matter had better be apocalyptic."

He grabs my arm to haul me partway out the door, then pulls it half-way shut. "I saw you and Jessica snogging in the driveway and thought I should make sure you're prepared. Bought these in the resort gift shop."

Alex hands me a box of condoms.

This place has a gift shop? And it sells condoms?

"Why are you giving me these?" I ask.

"Aren't you planning to shag Jessica tonight?"

"Uh, well, yes. But—"

He slaps my arm. "Now you're prepared. And by the way, Domhnall won the pie-eating contest."

Alex walks away before I can ask why I should care that Domhnall Sterling shoved enough pie down his throat to win a contest for that.

To hell with the Scot. I'm about to shag Jessica.

And this time, I'll get it right.

I strip off my clothes right here in the living room, stumbling when I shove my trousers down because I forgot to remove my shoes first. With a hissed "bollocks," I get rid of the shoes and kick off my trousers, then I sprint for Jessica's room.

The door is open.

Alex's box of condoms tumbles from my hand.

Jessica is lying on the bed, naked, the bedside lamp bathing her in soft, golden light. Her hair is fanned out over the pillow with a few locks spilling over her shoulders.

I approach the bed, halting at the foot so I can enjoy the full view of Jess. I've never seen her naked, not really. The first time we had sex, she'd wanted the lights turned off with only a night-light to illuminate the room. Now, I can see every inch of her, from those gorgeous, round breasts and their stiff nipples to her flat belly and generous hips. My attention stalls at the curly hairs between her thighs. I've read every word of that sex manual she gave me, and I can't wait to make her come with my head between her legs and my mouth on her clit.

"You are so beautiful, Jess. Even more stunning than the most exquisite database architecture."

She arches her back, biting her lip. "You know how I love it when you get techie on me. I'm wet and ready for you, Grey baby."

Jessica spreads her legs.

And I can't stop myself from staring at the glistening flesh that's been revealed. Dusky pink, swollen flesh. Is this really happening?

"Come here, Grey," she says. "I want your body."

I crawl up the bed until I'm kneeling between her feet. "I won't cock it up this time. I'm not anxious, and I've memorized that book."

She nudges my arse with her foot. "I know you won't mess it up again. I've known that since the costume party. I loved the way you touched me then, but I need all of you tonight."

I lay down nestled between her legs and shimmy forward until my face is in front of her mound. With two fingers, I separate her lips and kiss her clitoris.

She gasps, then giggles. "Never been kissed there before."

While I skate my fingers down her folds, I curl my tongue around her hard nub. She gasps again, and I lift my head to look at her. "When it comes to your pleasure, I'm the right architect with the most agile analytics. You won't need a surrogate key. I've got multidimensional expressions."

She clenches the sheets in her fists.

I lick my way down her folds, swirling my tongue around the rim of her opening.

"Yes, Grey baby, yes."

Fuck, she's responsive. I love learning that, but I need to make her come, so she'll know without any doubts that I can give her everything she wants and needs. I drag my tongue up her flesh and seal my mouth around her clit, then I push two fingers inside her. She cries out, her back bowing. I suck, lick, and nip while plunging my fingers into her again and again until she's shouting my name and begging for more. She's getting wetter, the scent of it so arousing that I'm having trouble breathing. I push my fingers deeper and curl them toward her inner wall, massaging it while I suckle her nub harder.

She comes so fast that I don't even notice her body stiffening. Her muscles grip my fingers, but I keep rubbing that spot inside her and keep lapping at her clit until her last cry fades away and she goes limp. "Wow, Grey, that was amazing."

"Ready for more?"

She reaches down to tousle my hair. "I want everything—with you."

I hope she means "everything" literally. But for now, I'll settle for showing her how much I've learned, not only from that book, but from kissing and touching her too.

After grabbing a condom from the box I'd dropped on the floor, I roll it on and crawl up the bed to hover over her. My face is aligned with hers, though I hold myself up with my straight arms. My knees are wedged between her legs. I dip my head to kiss her, taking my time because I love kissing Jess, love the soft noises she makes and the way she mirrors the movements of my tongue with her own. I've kissed other women, but it never felt as right with them as it does with her.

I peel my lips away from hers. "Jessica, this is all for you. If I do something wrong, let me know and tell me what you need. Anything, and I'll give it to you."

She splays a hand on my cheek. "You are so sweet, but don't worry about it. Just make love to me, Grey. Take it slow, there's no rush."

Jessica bends her knees, bracketing my hips with them.

I slide into her body, experiencing every inch of her slick, hot flesh as it glides over my cock. Christ, this feels good. She grasps my biceps but never shifts her gaze away from mine, those beautiful eyes capturing my focus like I'm mesmerized. Maybe I am, because I've loved her and wanted her for so long, and now I'm inside her again, at last. When I begin to thrust with slow and gentle strokes, she rocks her hips up every time I push inside her. Her cream surrounds my cock, the warmth of it penetrating the condom, and the aroma of it inundates my senses.

"Our active cells are perfectly aligned in the spreadsheet," I say, not intending to mutter jargon. It just spills out of me while I draw my hips back and plunge inside her over and over. "I don't need a VLOOKUP to understand the data your body is giving me. The autosum—is—about to—ah, Jess, you feel so fucking perfect."

"Grey baby, you're making so wet, using all that jargon." She locks her legs behind my arse, bucking her hips into every thrust. "Oh God, Grey, click that autosum button, please."

I feel the heat of her body gripping me, and I hear the wet sound her body makes with every thrust. The need to come bears down on me, and I don't know how much longer I can hold off. "Are you close?"

"Oh yes, yes, yes, I am."

Though ninety-nine point nine percent of my brain has shut down, the fraction of a percent that's still functioning reminds me of something I read in that sex book. I reach down to massage her clitoris.

Her body goes rigid. Her mouth falls open on a silent cry, and she squeezes her eyes shut, clenching my biceps so hard her nails pinch my skin. I pump into her faster, deeper, consuming her like I can't live without her sheath wrapped around my cock. Her breasts bounce, and I rub her clit fiercely, desperate to make sure she hits that peak first.

She sucks in a shallow breath, her body bows inward, and the muscles inside her grip me in pulsating waves that steal my breath. "Grey, oh God, yes!"

I can't stop it. The climax rips through me like an electrical line has been jammed into my spine, the current hot and hard and so bloody incredible that I let out a hoarse shout, thrusting into her twice more before I collapse on top of her while still buried inside her body. My head lands on her shoulder, every inhalation sucking her hair into my mouth.

"Jess, that was..." I shut my eyes for a second, struggling to catch my breath. "I love you, Jessica."

Oh fuck. I said that out loud.

Chapter Eighteen

Jessica

GREY SAID THE L-WORD, AND I DON'T THINK HE MEANT IT IN an offhanded way, like he was saying "I love you as a friend." No, the tone of his voice and the look on his face convince me he meant that he *loves* me. I would've expected to be freaked out by his confession. Instead, I get a warm glow all over and a dull ache in my chest.

But I should make sure I'm interpreting his statement correctly. Shouldn't I?

My best friend rolls off my body to lie on his side, cuddled up against me. He nuzzles my cheek.

I swallow, but the lump in my throat won't go away. "What you said... Did you mean it?"

"Yes."

"In what way? Friend love or..."

He pushes up on one elbow to gaze down at me. "I am *in* love with you, Jess. Have been for a long time. You're the only woman I can imagine spending the rest of my life with."

I want to speak, but my vocal cords have decided to freeze up.

Grey smiles with such sweetness that my chest aches again. "I probably shouldn't have said that, not yet. Didn't mean to scare you. I know you're having trouble with the friends-becoming-lovers thing, so I'm sure you need time to figure out how you feel about me."

Maybe I should need time. I kept telling him I'm afraid of ruining our friendship with sex, but now that he's made love to me, I can't remember why I was so worried. Am I feeling this way because we just had fantastic sex? I don't know. But here, tonight, in this cozy little bungalow, I need to tell him the truth.

"I love you too, Grey. And I mean I'm *in* love with you."

"Does this mean you're not afraid anymore?"

"Yeah. But I can't guarantee I won't get anxious again. This is a big deal for us, saying the L-word and having amazing sex. Plus, there's Domhnall and his idiotic plan to win me back."

"But you don't want him."

"No, of course not." I take his face in my hands and kiss him. "You're the only man I want."

"Let's just spend time together and get used to being a couple. No pressure. I won't ask you to marry me tonight." He smirks. "I'll wait until at least tomorrow."

Would I mind if he asked me right now? No, I don't think I would.

And that's terrifying. But in an oddly good way.

Grey sits up. "Did you just say the sex was amazing?"

"Uh-huh." I sit up too and hook an arm around his neck. "You rocked the sex, Grey. Don't ever worry about that again."

"You didn't cry this time, so that's an improvement."

I wince. "Sorry I cried before. I wasn't upset because the sex wasn't great. I freaked out because we rushed into it and didn't stop to talk about whether we should be getting it on or what that meant. My anxiety infected you, and that's why things got screwed up. I'm sorry."

"Not your fault. I cocked it up."

"Let's forget about that other time. It doesn't matter anymore. We should focus on the present, not the past. Don't you think?"

"Absolutely."

"Would you mind standing up so I can admire your hot body?" I ask. "Didn't get a good look earlier since I was focused on making sure you weren't nervous."

"Sorry. You won't need to do that again."

"It wasn't a complaint, just an explanation." I wave my hands. "Get up. I want to drool over you, Grey baby."

"All right." He hops off the bed and backs away until I have a full view of his body. "Do you realize you've started to call me Grey baby instead of Greybee?"

No, I hadn't realized that. But yeah, I guess I have changed my pet name for him, though I still plan on calling him Greybee too. Unless he doesn't like that. "Do you mind if still sometimes call you Greybee? I should've asked if you like that nickname before I started using it, shouldn't I?"

"I like it, Jess. Maybe it's a little embarrassing when you use that pet name in public, but I don't want you to stop saying it."

"How do you feel about 'Grey baby'?"

"Love that one." He spreads his arms. "Look your fill, but do it fast. I need the bathroom."

"Me too."

I let my gaze travel over his body, starting with his face and those lips I've kissed and felt on my clitoris. Yesterday on the beach, I'd admired his new and improved physique, from his toned pecs and defined abs down to his strong thighs. He'd worn swim shorts yesterday, so I didn't see his package. I kind of saw it when I gave him a blow job last night, but the lighting wasn't great for ogling. Now, I fasten my gaze on that part of him, getting warmer the longer I examine his cock. Veins draw lines down his skin, and even though he's not aroused, his dick is impressive. Not enormous, but mouthwatering all the same.

Domhnall has an outrageously ripped body, but that's because he used to be an athlete and he owns a gym. Even when I was with Domhnall, though, I wished he didn't feel the need to be so muscled up. Maintaining that kind of physique took a lot of work, so he spent lots of time at the gym even outside his work hours.

Tonight, while I admire Grey's normal-guy hotness, I realize I don't want him to get ripped. I love his body the way it is. I'd thought he was sexy even before he started exercising more. Grey has always prioritized time with me over everything else.

And that's why I love him.

"You are so much sexier than Domhnall," I say. "And I mean more than your body. Everything about you is hot, especially your sweetness and the way you're always there for me when I need you."

"I always will be. And you do the same for me." He leans over the bed to kiss me. "Should we have a shower together? I'd love to rub soap all over your body."

"Oh yes, please. After I pee."

He leads me out of the room, giving me a fantastic view of his bare backside. Wow, he has an amazing ass. I'd love to nibble on it. Actually, I'd love to nibble on all of him.

After we relieve our needs, we get in the shower and do all sorts of naughty things to each other in the guise of getting clean. And yeah, our shower involves orgasms. After that, we go back into my room. Most guys don't want to turn sex into playtime, but Grey loves finding inventive ways to get me hot, and we both love silly role-playing fantasies. I pretend to be his intern who he needs to teach about that sexy jargon since I'm completely ignorant of all things tech. In real life, I'm not completely clueless. But when we're playing sex games, I'll be anything he wants me to be, and vice versa.

We fall asleep tangled up together under the covers.

I wake up in the morning lying on my back with Grey beside me, his arm draped over my belly, his head on my shoulder. He looks so adorably sweet when he's asleep. I've known that for years, though. In the days after his father passed away, I'd slept with Grey every night—in a clothes-on, platonic way. I stayed with him for weeks, getting special permission for both of us to skip our classes for a while and make it up in the summer term. We were both in our third year at Bournemouth, but I hadn't cared about school. All I cared about was taking care of Grey. I even went with him to Brockenhurst to help with the funeral arrangements and to attend the service by his side.

How could I not have realized until recently that I'm in love with him? Back in those awful days after Selwyn's death, I'd broken up with my boyfriend because he wanted me to go back to school instead of taking care of my best friend. I'd broken up with Domhnall because he wanted the same thing. I should've realized years ago that Grey means more to me than any friend should.

But I know it now. I love him, and I will do whatever it takes not to ruin things between us.

I lie here enjoying the feel of his body snuggled up to mine and wait for him to wake up. When he does, he yawns and looks up at me with sleepy eyes.

"Good morning," he says, his lips forming a lopsided smile.

"Morning, Greybee. How did you sleep?"

"Very well." He skates his palm over my belly. "I loved sleeping with you all night, in the nude."

"Me too." I turn onto my side, facing him. "Wanna make breakfast together, naked?"

"Aren't you afraid I'll start a veggie fire?"

"That only happened once, and you didn't set it on fire. You singed it."

"In that case, I'd love to cook with you." He screws up his face. "But I should check in with Alex first. He's probably arranging some sort of humiliating spectacle he'll coerce me into taking part in."

"Okay. I'll wash my face and stuff while you groan and roll your eyes at your brother's wacky ideas."

"All right."

He gets out of bed and stretches, yawning, then he wanders out of the room buck naked.

Will he get dressed before he calls Alex? I can't see why he'd bother since we plan to make breakfast while naked. Of course, it would be fun to undress him.

I pick out my clothes for the day but leave them on the bed, then I head for the bathroom. A few minutes later, I've finished my morning routine, except for the getting-dressed part. Grey hasn't come back. I haven't heard his voice in the living room, so I guess he hasn't talked to his brother yet. Maybe he wanted privacy, so he went into his bedroom and shut the door. After a few more minutes with no Grey, I wander through our bungalow to find him.

He's standing in the kitchenette staring at the wall—at a calendar, I realize. He has a blank expression, but he's rubbing his chest like it hurts.

"Are you okay?" I ask.

Grey shrugs but keeps staring at the calendar.

I come up beside him and rest my chin on his shoulder. "What's wrong?"

He stretches out a hand to touch the calendar on today's date. "I forgot."

"What did you forget?"

"It's my father's birthday."

"Oh, Grey." I wrap my arms around him. "It's okay that you forgot. You've had lots of other stuff on your mind lately."

"I know." He slips his arms around me. "But I've never forgotten before. And I'll still be here in America on Sunday."

"Selwyn won't mind if you aren't there this week to put flowers on his grave. He'd want you to be happy, not beat yourself up because you forgot today's his birthday."

"You're right, I know. But it's strange to realize I forgot, because it means I've moved on."

"Which you absolutely should do. Moving on doesn't mean you forget all about your father. It means you're living your life, and that's exactly what Selwyn would want for you."

He stares at the calendar for a moment longer, then he rubs his hands up and down my back and kisses my forehead, smiling a little. "I don't know what I'd do without you, Jess. You always know how to make me feel better, even in the worst times."

"You do the same for me. Remember when my mom had that cancer scare? You stayed with me twenty-four seven until we got the test results and found out it was nothing."

"I love you, Jess, love you so much."

"And I love you lots too."

He exhales a grumbly sigh. "I didn't get round to calling Alex. Guess I'd better do it now."

"After breakfast."

My best friend, the man I love with all my heart, grins and sweeps me up in his arms. "Can't wait to eat breakfast off your body, and I promise you will shout my name several times."

And he makes good on that promise. Grey Dixon never lets me down.

Chapter Nineteen

Grey

I COULD CALL MY BROTHER TO CHECK IN WITH HIM, BUT after Jess and I make breakfast together and eat every crumb of it, licking some of it off each other's bodies, I need exercise. She wants to ring her mate Carly to find out how her boyfriend is doing. I'd rather spend the entire day with Jessica, alone, but I can't do that. This is my brother's wedding extravaganza, so I need to be there for him too.

All the other guests are in the dining hall, but I don't see Alex there. I do find Catriona sharing a table with her two sisters and her sisters-in-law. Cat tells me Alex has gone to the entertainment room with Logan and Jack, so I head there. I find my brother sitting on a sofa with Logan while Jack relaxes in a big, puffy recliner chair. Alex has his feet on the table, but Logan sits up straight with his feet on the floor and his arms barred over his chest.

I'm hovering in the doorway when Alex notices me.

"Come in, wee brother," he says, waving for me to come closer. "We were discussing the ceremony."

"Would that be the opening ceremony or the closing ceremony?" I ask as I settle onto an armchair.

My brother clasps his hands behind his head. "I'm talking about the wedding ceremony."

"Oh, I see. It's hard to tell since you seem to have orchestrated so many ceremonies and games and whatnot. You're going a touch overboard, don't you think?"

"No, I do not. This is the wedding of the century, after all."

Logan shakes his head, almost smiling. "You're a bampot, Alex."

"Am I? Maybe I like everyone to think I'm insane."

"I'm dead sure you like everyone to think that." One side of Logan's mouth twitches upward, and he glances sideways at Alex. "Are ye ever going to choose your best man? Or should we arm wrestle for the honor?"

"Would you beat up Grey and Jack just to win the chance to be my best man?"

"No. I'd batter them to win the chance to batter you."

Alex sighs in his cheeky way. "And you think *I'm* a bampot."

"You *are* a lunatic, Alex. If you keep using the Scottish words for things, you'll need to adopt our accent too."

"Cat says my accent is much sexier than any Scotsman's."

Logan huffs, as cheekily as Alex had sighed. "Catriona is a bampot too."

Alex and Logan could take the piss out of each other for hours. Time to change the subject.

"What's going on today?" I ask. "More pie-eating contests?"

My brother closes his eyes and sighs again. "Honestly, Grey, you ought to know the answer to that question. You were provided with an itinerary of the wedding-week events."

"But I didn't memorize it." Was I meant to? No one told me that.

"Why don't you enlighten him, Logan? I might take a nap here on the sofa. Cat wears me out every night." He opens one eye to look at me. "You must be exhausted too since you shagged Jessica all night."

Yes, I absolutely did. But it's none of his business. "Sod off, Alex."

He chuckles. "So sensitive. Everyone could hear you two. I assume you've gotten over your sexual anxiety considering how loudly Jessica screamed your name."

She did cry out, multiple times, but I wouldn't have characterized it as screaming.

Logan chuckles now. "Aye, Serena and I heard it too."

"Aye, and so did I," Jack says. "But let's not embarrass the laddie. Don't want him bollocksing it up tonight when he's only just gotten it right."

I throw my head back and groan. "Could we please stop talking about my sex life?"

"See, Alex?" Jack says. "You've done it. The poor laddie is—"

"Not embarrassed," I almost snarl. "But it's private. Something I only want to discuss with Jessica."

Alex shuts his eyes again. "Have it your way. But you'll probably want to shag her again this morning in case you become…incapacitated after the Highland games this afternoon."

"Why would I be incapacitated?" I squint at my brother, but he can't see it. "What have you done now, Alex?"

"It wasn't me. Rory came up with the idea."

"Rory MacTaggart? Fine, what's *he* done?"

"He suggested you need the same sort of therapy Logan gave me last year, and that Rory gave Gavin Douglas before that."

"Which is what? I already had a therapy session with Jack."

Alex sits up and aims his most innocent, and completely false, look at me. "It's a simple test of your mettle. How hard can that be? I survived it, mostly."

Mostly? I think back on all the stories Alex has told me about the MacTaggarts. Last year would've been the time when Alex saw Catriona again after eleven years apart. What had he said about that? It happened at Dùndubhan, the castle Rory owns. And it had involved...

"Highland games?" I say. "I've already signed up for those, but I don't see why that would lead to me being incapacitated. Jess took me to Highland games in America when I visited her a few years ago. It didn't look dangerous."

Logan laughs, but it's a dark and somewhat menacing sound. "You've seen the American version. This is the MacTaggart clan's Highland games." He leans toward me, lowering his voice. "Do ye have medical coverage and life insurance?"

I stare at him for a long moment, trying to decide if he's serious or not. With Logan, it's hard to tell. He loves to pretend he's terrifying, and honestly, sometimes he *is* terrifying.

"You're winding me up," I say. "Why don't you lot just tell me what Rory has planned? I'm sure it's nothing hazardous."

"Are you?" Alex asks. "Well, I guess you can wait until the games this afternoon to find out, then. Since you're positive you can handle it."

"Come on, Alex. I know you're dying to tell me, so go on."

My brother lifts one brow. "What if I don't? That might be more en-tertaining."

"Have it your way." I stand up. "I'll see you later, Alex."

"We should tell him," Jack says. "Cannae let him walk into this battle blind."

Battle? He's exaggerating. Isn't he? Yes, of course he is.

"Have it your way," Alex says, pushing up off the sofa. He walks over to me and lays a hand on my shoulder. "The Highland games will have only two competitors—you and Domhnall Sterling."

"Why?"

"Because I said so. Rory suggested it, and I agreed." He pats my shoulder. "You need to prove to yourself that you can stand up to Domhnall."

"Don't see why. I have Jess, he doesn't."

"You seem to have a skewed perception of yourself and Domhnall. You are not a weakling, and he is not the Greek god Zeus."

"I know that."

"Compete in the games," Alex says, leaning in to stare into my eyes. "Prove to yourself that you can beat him. I was joking when I said you might be incapacitated. If Domhnall tries any dirty tricks, he will regret it. I'll make certain of that."

Alex declares that with a conviction that seems honest, not like a load of bollocks. Maybe he does care what happens to me after all.

"Fine," I say. "I'll compete."

"Good." He slaps my arm. "Now, go tell Jessica about this. Women love it when men battle for their affection. They pretend to hate it, but deep down, they adore watching blokes spill blood for them. It makes women randy."

I'm sure that's bullshit, but I don't see the point in contradicting him.

"One last thing," Alex tells me. "Rory has offered to tutor you in the Highland games this morning. He's waiting for you behind the bungalow. It will be a private session."

"Do I really need that?"

"It's your choice, but I would recommend it. Domhnall made a few special requests."

"What, exactly?"

Alex points toward the doorway. "Go ask Rory. He knows all about it."

More mystery. Alex excels at that sort of thing, but I'm comfortable with facts and numbers and computer systems. All this secretive rubbish makes me itchy from head to toe.

I will find Rory and see what he has to say about all this, but I go back to the bungalow first since I need to tell Jessica what's going on.

She's on the sofa watching a cooking show on the telly. When I walk in, she mutes the sound and rushes over to me, slipping her arms around my waist. "I'm so glad you're back."

"How is Carly's boyfriend doing?"

"Don't know yet. She wasn't answering her phone, so I left a message. But I'm sure he'll be okay. I mean, lots of people get appendicitis, right?" She hugs me tighter, crushing her entire body against me. "How was your talk with Alex?"

"Strange, as usual. Logan and Jack were there too." I link my hands behind her. "There's been a change of plans today, concerning the Highland games."

"You decided not to compete? Wow, that's a relief."

"Why is it a relief? I am competing, by the way."

"Oh. Well, I..." She bites her upper lip. "What's the change of plans, then? I assumed you meant you'd given up on the idea of taking part in the games."

"You assumed wrong. I am competing, but the only competitors will be me and Domhnall."

Her eyes bulge, and she shakes her head. It's more like she flaps it wildly. "No, Grey, you can't. He'll crush you."

Grasping her arms, I push her away until an arm's length separates us. "Do you honestly believe I can't beat Domhnall?"

"He was an Olympic-level wrestler, and he took up boxing last year, even won some amateur matches. He treats exercise like it's his second job, which it kind of is since he owns a gym. You..." Her whole face pinches into an agonized expression. "You're a computer expert."

"You honestly think I'm a weakling who doesn't stand a chance against a Gaelic god like Domhnall Sterling."

"No, that's not what I mean." She rubs her forehead, avoiding my gaze. "I don't want you to get hurt, Grey. Domhnall is obsessed with proving he's better than you, and these games are obviously his way of making sure you're humiliated."

"No wonder you couldn't admit you love me until last night. You think I'm a pathetic little orphan. Is sex all you care about?"

"You know that's not true. Why is it horrible for me to be worried about your safety?"

"Once again you're implying I'm no match for the amazing Domhnall. Do you want him back, is that it?"

Jessica throws her hands up. "Don't be ridiculous. I love you, but I don't want to watch you getting thrashed by my ex."

"Then don't watch." I release her arms and yank the door open. "Stay in here and stare at the telly. Because I am competing in the games—against Domhnall. Alex, Logan, and Jack believe I can do it. So does Rory, and he even offered to help me prepare. That's what I'll be doing."

I storm out, slamming the door behind me.

Chapter Twenty

Jessica

I STARE NUMBLY AT THE DOOR AFTER GREY LEAVES, IM-mobilized for seconds or minutes, I don't know. We never had a fight until this week, and now we've had two of them. Does this mean our new relationship will crash and burn? No, it can't mean that. I love Grey, and he loves me. We've been through hell together and survived it all. I thought nothing could break our friendship, but maybe becoming a couple has done it.

No, I don't believe that. We had fantastic sex for hours last night. I'd never felt as comfortable with any other man or as turned on or as free to explore all my desires. Grey wasn't shy once we got going. I loved being with him, and I know he loved being with me. So naturally, I implied he's a wimpy loser who could never outdo Domhnall in a physical competition. That wasn't how I meant it, but I'm starting to understand why Grey assumed it was.

While I try to figure out what to do, I drop onto the sofa and call Carly. She answers this time, so I ask how her boyfriend is doing.

"Troy's fine," she tells me. "The surgery went really well, and he's home now. I'm taking good care of him. How's the British cutie-pie?"

"Um, well, we had sex last night."

"How was it?"

"Amazing. We both said the L-word last night, and everything was going great until I accidentally implied he's a weak little loser compared to Domhnall."

"Why would you do that?"

"Because they're having Highland games today, and Domhnall wants to compete against Grey and nobody else. Just the two of them." I rest my elbow on the sofa's back and let my face fall into my raised palm. "Domhnall is a highly trained athlete. I don't want him to hurt Grey while he's trying to prove to me he's the better man. Grey stomped out. I tried to explain, but he's in stubborn mode. Honestly, I don't blame him. Can't believe I said that stuff. What is wrong with me?"

"Only you can figure that out. I know Grey is your go-to person, and I've never seen the two of you fight." She pauses. "Didn't I hear somebody say there's a psychologist in the wedding party? Maybe you could talk to him."

"Grey had a session with Jack MacTaggart. It did seem to help him."

"There you go. Nab that Jack guy and get some therapy."

"I'll think about it."

We chat for a few more minutes, then Carly says she wants to go check on Troy and we say goodbye. They're such a cute couple, and they're so good together. Are Grey and I like that? I know we are, and I can't explain why I panicked when Grey announced he's competing against Domhnall in a one-on-one version of the Highland games. I've been panicking off and on ever since Grey kissed me.

Maybe I do need a tiny bit of therapy. An itty-bitty session. A few minutes ought to do the trick.

When I go outside, I find lots of MacTaggarts and Dixons milling around on the lawn having conversations and telling jokes. Maddie Solberg tells me she saw Jack heading for the guest house, probably to grab some breakfast at the buffet in the dining hall. I start for the guest house, but Jack walks out the door just as I get there.

"Good morning, Jessica," he says, smiling. "If you're looking for Grey—"

"No, I was looking for you. I know you're on vacation, but you talked to Grey in a professional capacity, and I was wondering if, um…"

"You're wanting a session."

I nod. "Just a quick one."

"Let's take a walk to the horse pasture. That will be relaxing and private."

"Thank you, Jack. I really appreciate this."

He leads the way, since I have no idea where the horse pasture is. I used to ride when I was a kid, but I haven't seen a horse in years except at county fairs. We stroll down a dirt path through the woods until we come to a large, fenced field. Several horses graze in the pasture, but I don't see any other people here. Jack and I have the place to ourselves, like an outdoor office.

At least he won't ask me to lie down on a couch. There is no couch here.

Jack leans against the fence, turning toward me. "What's fashing you, Jessica?"

Luckily, I'd spent some time around the MacTaggarts before the wedding week began, so I know he's asking what's bothering me.

"Grey and I had a huge fight," I tell him. "It was my fault. I said things I didn't mean, or at least, I said them the wrong way so it sounded not like what I meant. Grey stormed out."

"Have you two never had an argument before?"

"No, not until this week. On Monday, we had a fight. Now it's happened again. Last night, we both said 'I love you,' and today we get in an argument." I hug myself, though I'm not cold. Not on the outside, at least. "We can't survive as a couple, can we? I mean, if we're arguing on the second day of our relationship..."

Jack chuckles, but it's so soft I almost don't hear it. "Did you never argue with your other boyfriends?"

"Well, no, of course we argued sometimes."

"And did those relationships end because of one fight?"

"We've had two, but no. Only my relationship with Domhnall ended because of an argument."

He studies me for a moment, his head tipped to the side. "Why did you break up with Domhnall?"

"Because he ordered me to cut Grey out of my life."

"Ah, I see." He smiles like he thinks he's figured me out. "Why are you ready to break it off with Grey because you had a disagreement?"

"I don't know. Grey and I have always gotten along. He never complained about my boyfriends, not even Domhnall, but now he's determined to prove he can beat Domhnall in the Highland games. I told him not to do it."

"Why?"

"I'm terrified he'll get hurt."

Jack raises his brows. "Is that the real reason?"

"You obviously have an opinion about it, so why don't you just tell me?"

"That's not how therapy works." He sighs and smiles again. "All right, I'll give you a wee bit of a clue. Couples argue, Jessica. If you were constantly bickering, I might worry. But you and Grey had two arguments, the first you've ever had in all the years you've known each other. Don't assume that's a bad thing."

"How can it be a good thing?"

"Because you two are behaving like a real couple now."

I start to tell him how stupid that sounds, but I stop before one syllable comes out of my mouth. Is he right? Grey and I have been best friends for eight years, but we never criticized each other's choice of boyfriends or girlfriends. Maybe we've had half of a relationship, wading into the shallow end of the pool, but now we're jumping headfirst into the deep end.

"How did you meet Domhnall?" Jack asks.

"At a hotel in Seattle. I was there for a dentistry conference, but Domhnall lives in Tacoma which is, like, right next to Seattle. He liked to eat lunch at the hotel restaurant, and I was escaping the dull workshops by ordering a gooey dessert." I can't help smiling when I think about what happened. "Domhnall was sitting at the table beside mine. We started talking, and we just clicked, so I moved over to share his table. We laughed a lot, but we didn't talk about anything super personal. That night, I slept with him. Two weeks later, I quit my job and moved to Seattle. Domhnall helped me get a new job."

"Why do you think you jumped into a relationship with Domhnall just weeks after you and Grey had sex?"

"Not sure. I don't love my job and taking off for a new city seemed exciting. Domhnall is definitely exciting—in bed."

"Was your relationship mostly about sex?"

My first impulse is to snap at Jack because he seems to be implying I'm a sex-obsessed moron. But I doubt that's what he means. I might be a little oversensitive about the Domhnall-sex thing. "I don't know, maybe. During sex, we never argued. We had good times, but his ultimatum was the last straw."

"Why do you think that is?"

I need to consider his question for a minute before I can answer. Maybe Grey was right, and all I care about is sex. No, that's not it. My mind circles back around to the idea that maybe I liked Domhnall because I knew I could never really love him. I took up with him right after Grey and I had bad sex because it was my way of escaping from the truth.

"You're beginning to understand, aren't you?" Jack says.

"Maybe. I've been so afraid of losing Grey if we decided to be more than friends that I panicked the minute we crossed that line. Now I'm panicking again, but I guess it's not because I'm worried Domhnall will beat the tar out of Grey. Is that right?"

"Sounds like you are seeing the light."

"And that probably means there's another reason I freaked out. It probably has more to do with suddenly realizing I'm in love with Grey than with worrying about what Domhnall might do to him. I stayed with Domhnall because I knew I couldn't love him, not all the way, but I do love Grey like that."

Jack points a finger at me. "I think you've got it now."

"I need to talk to Grey."

"Aye, you do."

I kiss his cheek. "Thank you, Jack, you're an amazing therapist."

He chuckles. "That's sweet, but I'm no psychology god. I'm the mirror, that's all. You recognized the truth on your own when it was reflected back at you."

Was that all I'd needed? To have someone else point me in the right direction? The second Jack told me the fight Grey and I had was the first time we'd behaved like a genuine couple, the truth had begun to dawn on me. I'd kept Grey trapped in the friend zone for so long while I kept myself in denial about my feelings for him. No wonder Domhnall and I hadn't worked out. He'd been hung up on his ex, and I'd been in love with Grey for all these years. Jeez, it took me a long time to realize that. Better late than never, though, right?

"Go on," Jack says. "Find Grey and tell him the truth."

"I will." Glancing around, I ask Jack, "Do you know where he is?"

"Behind the bungalow. There's an open area that Rory thought would be a good spot for training."

"Training? Oh yeah, Grey mentioned Rory would be helping him get ready for the games."

"I think it's more than a game this time. It's a battle for honor."

My mouth insists I should ask whose honor they're battling for, but I decide I don't really want to know yet. I'll find out soon enough, whether I want to or not.

Jack and I walk back to the lawn together, then I veer off behind the guest house, passing the bungalow, and find the small clearing Jack mentioned. The grass has been mowed, and piles of tree trunks with their branches stripped off lie in a pile on the far side of the clearing. Grey and Rory MacTaggart stand in the middle of the open area talking. Rory has his hand on Grey's shoulder. He points to the piled-up tree trunks, then gestures at a big rock that sits nearby. Grey nods like he's absorbing every word Rory says.

Those stripped trees must be cabers, and Rory must be advising Grey on how to play the Highland games. But it's no game this time. Domhnall will turn it into a battle royal.

Ugh. Why won't he give up and go home?

Rory notices me and nods. He says something to Grey, who glances at me over his shoulder. Grey nods too, then he strides toward me.

"He'll do fine," Rory calls out to me. "Donnae worry."

When Grey reaches me, I throw my arms around him. "I'm sorry. I know you're not a weakling, and I've never thought you were a poor little orphan."

"I know." He clasps his hands at the small of my back. "I'm sorry for running away like that."

"My fault, not yours." I pull my head back just enough to see his face. "I locked you up in the friend zone for too long. I've been in denial for years about what you mean to me, but last night, I couldn't deny it anymore. That terrified me. I had a talk with Jack, and he helped me realize that's all it was. Fear. I know you can beat Domhnall if you want to, but I also know it doesn't matter if you lose. You are the better man, no matter the outcome."

"I'm not doing this to make you love me. I need to prove to myself I can stand up to Domhnall."

"Yeah, I know. And I'll be there to cheer you on." I take his face in my hands, brushing my lips over his. "And if you get beat up, I'll be there to take care of you. I almost picked a sexy nurse costume for the party the other night."

"Find that costume. Even if I'm not trounced in the Highland games, I'll need a thorough physical afterward."

"That's what I'm here for." I touch my lips to his. "I love you so much, Grey."

"I love you just as much." He slides his hands down to my bottom. "Maybe you should give me a full physical now, as a baseline."

"Absolutely. Let's do that."

Grey leads me into our bungalow.

Chapter Twenty-One

Domhnall

HAVE I TURNED INTO A STARK-RAVING BAMPOT? I HAVE NO other explanation for why I march over to the bungalow Jessica is sharing with Grey Dixon. I'm about to bang on the door when I hear noises coming from inside. Is that panting? And moaning? I rest my ear on the door to listen. Now I can hear soft grunts and the slapping of flesh on flesh.

Mhac na galla. Now I'm spying on them with my ear pressed to the door, like a ruddy pervert.

"Yes, Grey," Jessica cries out. "Oh God, Grey, you're amazing. I love your cock."

I snarl a string of Gaelic curses under my breath, then I knock on the door. Jess never told me she loved my cock. She shouted those bloody silly nicknames for me and told me what she wanted me to do to her. Is Grey Dixon better at sex than I am?

No, that could never happen.

The door swings open.

Grey stands there naked, holding a dish towel over his groin. "What do you want? We're busy."

"I need to speak to Jessica."

"No, you don't."

He starts to shut the door, but I shove my foot onto the threshold to stop him. "I will see Jess whether you like it or not. Ye donnae speak for her."

"Actually, he does," Jessica says, approaching the doorway.

She's behind Grey, most of her body hidden behind his, but I can tell she's naked. Her cheeks are flushed, and pink dapples her upper chest too. Her skin always looks that way when she's being fucked.

"Go away," Jess tells me. "I have nothing else to say to you."

"But I—"

Grey glances at Jess, who nods, then he slams the door in my face.

Bod an Donais.

The noises start up again.

I growl and stalk back to the lawn, but I keep going, aiming for the nature trail. Get away from all these people, that's what I need to do. How did I lose Jess? To a bloody Brit? My ultimatum, as Jess calls it, tore us apart. Why had I demanded she give up Grey Dixon? My reasons had seemed rational and sensible at the time. Ever since I came to Oregon, I've kept convincing myself I am right to be here, that I need to fight for her even after she told me she never really loved me.

Maybe I should give up and go home.

But I love her. Even if she doesn't want me anymore, I cannae let her be taken in by that British scunner.

I don't know how far I walk before I finally stop and look around. Have I been down this path before? I'd made a turn or two, so I can't say for certain where I am. Not lost. I never get lost. If I turn around, I'll find my way back to the resort. Right now, I need a wee rest. Walking hasn't done me in. This exhaustion comes from struggling to keep a woman who says she doesn't want me.

With a whump, I drop onto the ground and lean back against a large tree. I let my head fall back, closing my eyes, and exhale a long, groaning sigh.

"Are you ill?"

The feminine voice sounds close.

I crack one eye open to peer up at the woman standing several feet away.

Fiona MacTaggart looks bonnier than ever in denim cut-offs and a short-sleeve shirt. She's tied her hair up in a ponytail, but strands fall over her ears.

"Well?" she says. "Are you ill? I can get help if you are."

"Not ill." Sick in the head, maybe. But not in the body, which I assume was what she meant. I open both eyes to squint at her. "Are you following me?"

"Arrogant, aren't you? Assuming I ran after you, like I'm a stalker or I'm smitten with you." She plants her hands on her hips. "I went for a hike on my own, and I saw you on my way back from the lake. Pardon me for stopping to make sure you're not dying."

"I'm fine. You can leave now."

She puckers her lips, tapping her fingers on her hips.

Groaning again, I wave a hand at her. "I said go."

Fiona settles onto the ground beside me, sitting cross-legged. "What have you done this time?"

"You're a bloody annoying woman. Do you know that?"

"Aye. Now tell me what's fashing you."

"Why do you care?" I push up to sit a little straighter. "I'm the *bod ceann* who's trying to split up Jessica O'Connor and Grey Dixon."

"You might be a dickhead. I can't speak to that. But like I told you before, I'm not put off by men who act like erseholes, not when I can tell they've got pain and tenderness underneath the prickly surface."

"We've spoken three times. Ye donnae know me. Maybe I am a *bod ceann*, a bastard, and an ersehole."

"It's been four times, not counting right now, that we've spoken." She wriggles until she's sitting alongside me with her back against the same tree. Her legs are still tucked under her. "Let's get to know each other, then I'll have all the facts to decide what sort of man you are."

Fiona is completely insane.

Maybe I am too, so maybe I should have a blether with her. What could it hurt? Things can't get much worse.

"Why don't you start?" I ask. "Tell me who the bloody hell you are."

"I'm Fiona MacTaggart. Have you forgotten already?"

"That's not what I meant."

She smiles and laughs. "I know, but it's fun to make uptight men squirm. Who am I? Well, I'm Scottish, female, and—"

"I know all that, you cheeky lass."

"You did seem to be a wee bit confused, so I figured I should start with the basics." She turns slightly toward me. "I'm thirty-nine years old, but I'll turn forty in eighteen days. I've never been married, though I've had serious boyfriends. Until recently, I owned a dress shop in Loch Fairbairn and shared a house with my sister Catriona. Now she lives with Alex, in a cottage not far from Loch Fairbairn. My shop closed down earlier this year, and I've been trying to decide what to do with my life."

"Why did your shop close?"

"Because it was hemorrhaging money. I didn't mismanage the finances, but sometimes things just happen. I created a lot of successful marketing campaigns, but it wasn't enough."

"I'm sorry to hear that."

She shrugs. "No need to feel bad for me. I'll find something else sooner or later. My cousin Evan offered me a job at his company, either in America or in Scotland. The global headquarters are at Inverness, but Evan lives in Carrefour, Utah, with his wife. Keely's lived there for a long time. Anyway, I could be the vice president of marketing at the global headquarters of Evanescent Security Technologies Limited, or I could become the general manager of the US headquarters. The Dixons know lots of people, and they've offered to help me find a job too. I'm still considering the options."

Maybe she's not a bampot after all. Any woman who ran her own business couldn't be completely off her head. She's unemployed but seems to keep a positive attitude about her life.

Should I be more like her? Look ahead rather than staring backward at a life that left me behind. Jessica left me behind.

"Tell me about you," Fiona says. "How old are you?"

"I'm thirty-six."

Her brows hike up. "You're eight years older than Jessica?"

"Aye. What does that matter?"

"Doesn't. So, I'm nearly four years older than you."

"Apparently."

She waves a hand. "Go on, keep talking."

This woman won't give up. I imagine she had to be tenacious to run a dress shop on her own. I don't want to tell her about myself, but I did start this by asking about her.

"I'm the co-owner of a gym in Tacoma, Washington. A college mate suggested we should start a gym together, and it seemed like a good idea. We'd both been athletes. I was an alternate on the UK Olympic wrestling team, and he'd competed in the games as a sprinter, though he didn't medal." I bend one knee to rest my arm on it, feeling oddly more relaxed now that I'm talking to Fiona. "Mick was born and raised in Tacoma, so he wanted to have the gym there. I moved to America ten years ago. Six months later, I was co-owner of a growing business and married to a beautiful American woman. I was with Sophie for six years until I found out she'd been cheating on me for most of our marriage."

"That's awful."

"Maybe I could've forgiven her if it had been a few flings. But she was shagging the same man for nearly five years, and I never knew about it. I thought she was unhappy because I worked long hours at the gym." I rub my eyes, remembering the day I found out Sophie had been involved with someone else. "I found them in bed together—in our bed, in our house. She said she loved him, and she was leaving me so she could marry him. I didn't hear from her after the divorce, but I saw a notice in the newspaper that she'd married a wealthy business-man. Then earlier this year, Sophie started calling me because he'd left her, and she wanted me back."

"You were with Jessica then. Weren't you?"

"Aye. And I told Sophie that. She left me alone for a while, but she started calling again while Jess and I were on holiday in Cancun. I took Sophie's calls, but I muted Jess's phone to keep her from talking to Grey Dixon." I look Fiona square in the eyes. "That's the sort of selfish *tolla-thon* I am."

Fiona shakes her head. "You are not an ersehole. But I think you have been very confused for a long time. Your wife betrayed you with another man, so now you see Grey as an interloper trying to steal your girlfriend. Do you think he and Jessica were having an affair while she was with you?"

"No, she wouldn't do that."

"Then why do you blame Grey for the failure of your relationship with Jessica?"

"Because he—I just know he's to blame. That damn Brit was always there, getting between me and Jess, even when he was in England."

Fiona folds her arms under her breasts, pushing them up a little, and studies me. "Maybe you should think about why you treat Grey like the enemy when he apparently never touched Jessica or told her how he feels while you were involved with her. You went through a bad marriage that involved betrayal. Think about all of that before you ruin Jessica's opin-ion of you forever."

"Ye donnae know what you're talking about."

"Maybe I don't, but maybe I do." She leans closer, fixing her gaze on me. "There might be another option, you know. It's not Jessica or no one."

I'd wondered yesterday if there might be another option. Can Fiona read my mind?

No, that's ridiculous.

"What are you havering about?" I ask. "If you start telling me there are plenty of fish in the sea—"

"I wouldn't say something as trite as that." She slants in a touch more, her breaths teasing my lips. "When was the last time you kissed someone other than Jessica or Sophie?"

"Too long, I'm fair certain." Why has my voice gotten hushed and deeper? My lips have started to tingle too, which is barmy. I'm not at-tracted to Fiona. I can't be. Jessica is the love of my life. But I find myself leaning closer to Fiona, relishing the sweet, feminine scent of her. "I've only kissed Sophie and Jessica since I moved to Washington."

"You should try kissing someone else, to see what it feels like. Call it exploring your options."

"Are you suggesting I should kiss you?"

"No, I'm suggesting *I* should kiss *you.*"

Fiona molds her lips to mine. Her mouth feels soft and warm, and I taste the faintest flavor of coffee and caramel. I shouldn't be kissing her, not when I've set my mind on winning Jessica back. But right now, I'm having trouble focusing on anything except Fiona's mouth and the way those stray hairs tickle my skin and her lips part a wee bit like she's asking me to deepen the kiss.

She pulls away. "How did that feel?"

Fucking wonderful. But I can't make myself say those words. I can't move, not even to blink.

"That's something to think about," Fiona says as she hops to her feet. "I'll see you later, Domhnall."

And she walks away.

I sit here for several minutes staring at nothing and reliving that kiss. Is Fiona working for Grey Dixon? Did he talk her into seducing me? No, that's too crackbrained even for me to believe. But I will not give up my plan because of one kiss from a woman I barely know.

Grey Dixon is going down.

Chapter Twenty-Two

Grey

JESSICA AND I EMERGE FROM OUR BUNGALOW AFTER lunch, which we enjoyed in private, and we wander out to the lawn to see what preparations are being made for the Highland games. I know Jess must still be worried about what Domhnall might do, but I also know she trusts me to handle whatever her ex throws at me. We had an argument this morning, but that's normal. Couples disagree once in a while. Since it's a new experience for us, we both overreacted.

That's over now, and we're good. Fantastic, actually. Ninety-three minutes of naked playtime with Jess has bolstered me better than any protein shake or performance-enhancing drug ever could.

I love her. She loves me. Domhnall is irrelevant.

Except that I'm about to compete against him. Even if I lose the games, I win big—because I have Jess.

We've just rounded the corner of the guest house, and the lawn has come into view. A lot of nude people have gathered there. Some are playing miniten, but most hang out on chaises and Adirondack chairs or stand in small groups chatting. My brother is, naturally, naked. So is Catriona, and so are her brothers and sisters as well as several of her cousins. My cousins don't seem to be here yet. They're probably still in the dining hall.

I do see Richard Hunter and Maddie Solberg, along with Nick Hunter. They've gone nude too.

Jessica whispers to me, "Is there any way I can talk you into trying naturism?"

Glancing at her sideways, I smirk. "I was almost naked at the beach the other day."

"But wouldn't it be fun to go all the way? Just for a little while. Alex is doing it."

"Alex is completely shameless and the biggest show-off in the world. He stripped naked in front of the entire MacTaggart clan when he proposed to Cat." I wasn't there on that day, but Logan showed me pictures. "I've never been naked in front of anyone other than medical professionals and my girlfriends."

"Okay. Never mind the naturism thing." She nudges me with her elbow. "You are super hot when you're naked, though. Well, you're super hot all the time, but without clothes, you're out-of-control-wild-fire hot."

"Thank you, but I can't see myself stripping..." My voice trails off because I've caught sight of Domhnall.

He is naked. One hundred percent free of anything that in any way resembles clothing. And he's strutting around like a peacock displaying his feathers for potential mates.

Domhnall sees Jess and waves at her. He stops walking, turning toward us—to make sure Jess gets a full view of his dangly bits, I'm sure. Though she waves, she barely glances at him.

Score two for the Brit.

Maybe it's more than two for me by now. I'd scored my first point on the beach when Jessica admired my body and virtually ignored Domhnall in his ridiculous swim briefs. But I've scored more points, haven't I? She loved my awful poem-song and hated it when Domhnall recited Emerson to her. So, I've got at least three points.

Not that this is a competition. I really shouldn't be counting, should I? All right. No more counting imaginary points.

But I'm about to compete in the Highland games against Domhnall, and I'm sure someone will keep track of who wins each round.

Domhnall struts up to us. "Jessica, you look as bonnie as the sunrise."

"Is that more Emerson you've plagiarized?" I ask.

His attention veers to me. "Get ready for a battering, *sassenach*."

"Ready whenever you are, Scots lout."

Why don't we Brits have our own language, like the Scots have Gaelic? Then *we* could spout unintelligible words to confuse *them*.

Maybe I do have my own language that will baffle the self-satisfied peacock.

I cross my arms over my chest. "I hope whoever's keeping score during our tournament will take into account the axioms of probability and the chi-square curve." I pretend to be concentrating intently, raising one hand to tap my chin. "Of course, there's also the issue of continuity correction. The minimax strategy might be the best option."

Domhnall stares at me blankly for a few seconds, then his entire face twists into a glower. "You're pulling that bollocks out of your erse."

"You're not familiar with statistics? I would've thought an athlete would appreciate the empirical law of averages."

"That's the best you can do, is it? Havering on about computer nonsense that you probably made up yourself."

I lean forward just a bit. "Look it up online, Domhnall. Maybe a small amount of real knowledge will penetrate that thick skull of yours."

Jessica tucks her arm under mine. "Let's go talk to Alex. Neither of us has anything to say to Domhnall."

We walk away, and Jessica does not look back at Domhnall. She didn't even get annoyed by his obnoxious behavior. I think she genuinely doesn't care anymore what Domhnall does.

Alex and Logan are exchanging sarcastic jibes when Jess and I reach them. My brother and the ex-MI6 agent are two of the strangest people on the planet, so of course, they get on well. I like Logan, but I don't think I'll ever understand him. Whenever my brother harasses Logan about something, the Scot jokes about assassinating Alex. At least, I think he's joking.

"There you are," Alex says when he sees me. "We've been discussing the dress code for the wedding."

"Dress code?" Visions of pink kilts and tiaras dance in my head. No, Alex wouldn't do that to me. He might dress that way for his wedding, but he won't force me to join in. I think. "Shouldn't we wear tuxedos? That's traditional."

"What about me gives you the impression I care about what's traditional?"

"Right. I forgot who I was talking to."

Alex gestures at his naked body. "Maybe the entire wedding party should go au naturel."

Catriona rolls her gaze heavenward and shakes her head.

Logan smirks.

Jessica grins. "I vote for that option. This is a nudist resort, after all."

Alex looks at me and tips his head toward Jessica. And then he smirks.

I have no ruddy idea what that's supposed to mean, but if he thinks I'll go naked at the wedding...

Cheers erupt not far from our group. Alex turns sideways to see what's going on over there, and so does Cat. The gap between them gives me a perfect view of the spectacle occurring across the lawn.

Domhnall Sterling is doing a headstand. In the nude. With all his dangly bits on display. He lifts one hand off the ground.

More cheers. It seems to be mostly women making a ruckus, and Fiona is the loudest one in the group.

Is Domhnall showing off for Fiona?

He gets out of his headstand by vaulting over backward, landing on his feet.

Fiona whistles and shouts, "Woo!"

That sort of bollocks actually works for Domhnall? Women like his strutting-peacock routine?

Alex lays an arm across my shoulders. "Maybe you should strip, just to show Domhnall how unintimidated you are."

"You're a terrible influence on me."

"Maybe that's what you've always needed. Someone to corrupt you."

I am the only person on this lawn, besides Jessica, who's wearing clothes. Maybe I should do what Alex suggested.

No, I can't. Can I?

Domhnall is doing cartwheels.

I kick off my shoes and shed my clothes.

Jessica gapes at me. "Grey, I can't believe you did that. In public."

"Felt like trying out the naturist lifestyle." I let my gaze travel over her entire body. "I wouldn't mind if you want to try it out too."

Her eyes flare wide, but then her lips curve into a sexy smile.

And she ditches her clothes.

I move toward her, about to put my arms around her.

Logan clears his throat. "Remember the rules."

Oh bugger. I forgot about Eve's speech on the first day, stuff about not touching each other when we're naked.

My cousin Reese and his wife approach us. They've just come out of the guest house, and they're fully clothed. When Reese notices me, he grins.

"Joining the party, eh?" he says. "Well, maybe Arden and I should too. Can't be outdone by my uptight cousin."

"I have never been uptight." Where do people get the idea I ever was?

"He's shy about his body," Jessica says. "Or he used to be. Now, he's as shameless as Alex."

"Brilliant!" Reese says, then he glances at his wife. "What do you say, Luscious?"

"Let's do it," Arden says.

They strip too. When Dane and Rika show up, I don't expect them to dive into the madness with us, but they do. Well, I'm not too surprised Rika's game, but when her husband sheds his clothes, I am shocked. Dane had gotten very uptight before he met Rika, but he's clearly overcome that.

I'm not as shameless as my brother, but I don't feel as strange about being naked in public as I expected I would.

Every woman in attendance stops by to tell me how wonderful it is that I've gone the naturist way. A disturbing number rove their gazes over me from head to toe. Isn't that breaking the resort rules? Not that I mind. I get kissed on the cheek by quite a few women. Alex's adoptive parents show up after a while and tell me how brave I am and how glad they are that I've come out of my shell.

If I had a shell, I wasn't aware of it.

Once everyone has stopped fussing over me because I'm naked, Alex and Logan ask me to go into the guest house with them.

"We need to get fitted for our wedding gear," Alex tells me. He glances at Jessica. "You don't mind if we borrow Grey for a bit, do you? We'll have him back in plenty of time for the games."

"Sure," Jessica says. "I'll hang out with the other ladies. They're a hoot."

I follow Alex and Logan into the guest house, down the long hallway, and upstairs to Alex and Cat's room on the third floor. When I see what my brother wants me to wear for the wedding, at first I don't want to do it, but I finally realize it's exactly right that we should dress this way.

And I can't wait for Jessica to see it. She might think it's silly, but I'm guessing she'll love it.

Chapter Twenty-Three

Jessica

WHEN ALEX AND LOGAN TAKE GREY INTO THE GUEST house, I decide it's time I settled things with Domhnall once and for all like a calm, rational adult. I've let him get to me, which is what he wants, and he probably thinks my anger implies I still love him. I don't. Though I told him that before, maybe I didn't say it clearly enough or with the right amount of conviction.

"Aye, you should do that," Catriona says when I tell her my plan. "Finality is essential. Men can be so bloody-minded, and sometimes they need to get bludgeoned with the truth. That's the only reason Alex and I are together now."

"Because you bludgeoned him?" I ask.

"Not literally, but aye. He has the thickest skull of any man I've met, even thicker than my brothers' heads, and they've got steel-reinforced skulls."

Yeah, I've heard the stories about her brothers, especially Rory. I'd rather not bludgeon Domhnall, but I will if I have to, and the bashing might not be metaphorical. Depends on what he says.

I say goodbye to Cat and hunt down Domhnall. He's talking to Jack MacTaggart, and I can't help hoping Jack is talking some sense into my ex.

"Mind if I steal Domhnall for a few minutes?" I ask Jack. "We need to settle things between us."

"Aye, you do," Jack says. He slaps Domhnall's arm. "Go on. And remember what I said."

Domhnall's lips turn down at the corners, but only for a second.

I gesture for him to follow me and take us to the little open area behind the guest house and the bungalow where Rory had tutored Grey in the art of the Highland games earlier today.

"Changed your mind, have ye?" Domhnall asks.

He doesn't look arrogantly certain or even hopeful. His expression is neutral, giving me no idea how he'll react to what I plan to tell him."

"No, I have not changed my mind," I say. "We need to talk, so I can make sure you understand we're over."

"I heard you the first time, but I still don't believe it."

"That's your problem, not mine." When he steps closer, I move back, holding up a hand. "That's close enough, Domhnall. Now listen up. I am in love with Grey, nothing you say will change my mind, and I will never get back together with you. I've loved Grey for as long as we've known each other, though I was in denial about that for a long time."

"But you loved me."

"I cared about you, and I won't deny we had good times. But it was never going to last. We both knew that." I sigh and shove my hands into my hip pockets. "You were still hung up on your ex-wife, and I was hung up on Grey. We each denied the truth for so long that we started to believe it, but now we can't deny it anymore. You know I'm right."

He stares at me, his face a mask that hides whatever he's feeling at this moment.

My feelings are crystal clear.

"I should never have gotten involved with you," I tell him. "Grey and I had our bad sexual experience just a few weeks before I met you. I was freaked out by that and couldn't acknowledge my feelings for him. You were a safe choice—the complete opposite of Grey, not the kind of guy I could seriously fall for. I think you probably picked me for a similar reason. Deep down, in our subconscious minds, we both knew our relationship wasn't the forever kind."

He rubs his jaw, gazing down at the ground, and exhales such a long sigh that it makes his shoulders sag. "Aye, maybe I did know you and I couldn't last."

Did he just admit to the truth? No bludgeoning required?

"I'm glad you've come to terms with things," I say. "Now you'll be free to explore other options."

"Other options? Someone else said that to me today."

"Good. Maybe you'll listen if somebody other than me tells you." I tap a finger on his chest. "And I've seen the way you look at Fiona MacTaggart. She looks at you the same way. You don't need to be looking for a wife or even a girlfriend, but you should get back out there and start dating."

"It's over between me and Sophie. As for Fiona... Donnae know. She can be very annoying."

"Uh-huh. I bet she's the one who suggested you should look for other options."

"She might've been." He gazes out at the woods, saying nothing for several seconds. Then he looks at me. "I'm sorry, Jessica. I've been a bastard about this Grey thing, and all I've managed to do is make you angry. I won't try to get between you two, but ahmno giving up on proving he's a scunner." He raises a hand when I start to speak. "Let me finish. I want to show you what sort of man Grey Dixon really is, but if after the Highland games you aren't convinced, I'll go away, and you will never see or hear from me again."

"Nothing is going to prove that to me because Grey is a wonderful man. Give up this stupid competition thing. It's not healthy."

"Are you afraid he cannae beat me?"

"I don't care either way." Giving him my sternest glare, I thump my fist on his chest. "But if you hurt Grey, even give him one tiny scratch, I will pummel you myself."

He chuckles. "You're bonnie when you try to be tough."

I thump his chest again. "No dirty tricks. Understand?"

"If Grey can't handle a real competition with a real man, he doesn't deserve a woman like you."

"Ugh." I throw my hands up. "What happened to 'I'll go away, and you'll never see or hear from me again'?"

"I meant that, but I also told you I aim to prove Grey's a scunner."

"So you lied when you said you've accepted that you and I are over and that I'm with Grey."

"No, I—" He screws up his mouth like he can't quite decide whether to frown, smirk, or sneer at me. "I know you're not coming back to me, but you need to see what that British *clag deireadh* is really like."

"This conversation is over."

I spin around and march back to the lawn. Did Domhnall seriously think calling Grey a jackass in Gaelic would win me over? If he wants to drive me to murder, he's doing a bang-up job of it. After the games, he'll have no choice but to give up and go away. He will never succeed in convincing me to dump Grey. Never.

Everyone on the lawn is dressed in casual outfits now. I guess Highland games are a clothes-on event. Since I don't see Grey, I wander toward the guest house. Halfway there, I stop.

The door to the guest house has just opened, and Grey walks out.

Wearing a kilt.

The plaid fabric is blue with slender orange lines through it, which I think is the MacTaggart clan tartan. He wears a black T-shirt too, one that clings to his torso and accentuates his muscles. I can't see his thighs, but big black boots cover most of his calves.

I want to crawl under that kilt and do dirty things to him. Wow, who knew a plaid skirt could be so damn hot? Grey is hot all the time, but in that kilt... Whew, somebody hose me down.

"What do you think?" Grey asks when he approaches me.

"You look amazing." I clasp his hand, threading our fingers, and lean in. "You wouldn't believe the filthy fantasies I've been dreaming up since the second you walked out in that kilt."

"Alex told me women love kilts, but I didn't believe him until right now. I'll be wearing the kilt at the wedding, but with a suit jacket and dress shirt."

"Can't wait to see that."

Logan and Alex amble out of the guest house. Alex comes over to us, but Logan holds the door open like he's waiting for someone else. I understand why a few seconds later when Lachlan and Rory haul a big portable chalkboard out of the guest house. It's the kind that swivels and has its own wooden stand so it can be used anywhere. They carry it out to the lawn's edge, then set it down. Rory pulls a box of chalk out of his pocket.

"What the heck is that about?" I ask.

"It's for the games," Alex answers. "You'll see."

"For pity's sake, Alex," Grey says. "What have you done this time?"

"Relax, wee brother. It's only a game, remember?"

Grey rolls his eyes.

Alex couldn't have done anything too outlandish. Could he? We're about to find out not only what lengths Alex will go to in his bizarre attempt to help Grey, but also how far Domhnall will push the boundaries in his quest to prove the man I love is unworthy.

Never. Going. To. Happen.

Chapter Twenty-Four

Grey

JESSICA LOVES ME IN A KILT. SHE LOVES ME, FULL stop. Whatever the outcome of my competition with Domhnall, I've won the only prize that matters. It's more like a gift, though, since Jess made the decision to be with me. Right now, I'm watching Rory MacTaggart write something on the chalkboard he and Lachlan brought out a minute ago. The board is facing away from me, toward the lawn. On the other side of the grassy area, cabers lie in a pile.

Alex cups his hands around his mouth like a megaphone and shouts, "Spectators off the lawn, please. Grab a folding chair if you need one. They're stacked along the south side of the guest house. The games are about to begin, so get a move on, would you? Scots are such a sluggish lot."

He says that with his patented breezy sarcasm, so no one gets annoyed about it. Only my brother could pull that off.

Alex leads me and Jessica out onto the lawn in front of the chalkboard, and I get my first good look at what Rory has written on it. Across the top, in colored chalk, he has scrawled, "Brit vs. Scot." The word Brit is in red, and the word Scot is in blue. Rory has also drawn a line down the center of the board, for marking off the points, I assume.

"What on earth is that?" I ask Alex.

"That's a chalkboard. Haven't you seen one before? I know you prefer computers, but we decided to go old school for this event."

"Of course I've seen a chalkboard before. But why is 'Brit vs. Scot' written across it in bloody great letters?"

"It's a scoreboard," he says like he's indulging a very stupid child by explaining the obvious. "How else can we know who wins? Competing in the games was your idea, after all. You volunteered for it."

"When I thought it would be all of us competing."

"Chin up, Grey. You have intellect on your side. Use it."

Jessica snuggles up to me. "Your brain is the sexiest thing about you. Well, your body is really hot too, but your mind is the hottest part." She stands on her tiptoes to whisper in my ear, "You know how I get when you talk to me in dirty jargon."

Oh yes, I know. And I love that about her.

"I don't care about the score," she tells me. "You'll be the winner no matter what. And I'll make sure you're rewarded later—with a sexy massage."

That sounds incredible. I've never gotten a massage of any kind, and I can't wait for Jessica to do that for me. Maybe I'll give her a massage too.

Domhnall Sterling saunters out of the guest house and onto the lawn. He's wearing a kilt, of course, made from what I assume is the Sterling clan tartan. It has mostly green, but also shades of blue and red lines with a dash of yellow too. Domhnall also wears a T-shirt with a lion on it along with the phrase "Scotland the Brave" and brown boots that go up to his knees.

He glances at the scoreboard and smirks at me, then looks at Rory. "Ye willnae need that, MacTaggart. I'll be winning every round."

I could say something macho about how I'll annihilate him, but I don't want to. Let everyone see what a blustering fool he is. I'll be the adult in the room—or rather, on the lawn.

Alex touches Jessica's arm. "You can wait on the sidelines if you like or join the other spectators."

She moves just past Rory to what would be the sidelines, I guess, if we had any lines drawn on the grass.

Domhnall surveys the crowd, smirks again, and whips his shirt off. He tosses it toward the spectators.

Fiona catches it.

He didn't plan that, did he? I thought he still wanted Jessica back. Not that he has a glacier's chance in the deepest, hottest furnace in Hell.

Domhnall faces me. "Taps off, *sassenach*."

I have no idea what that means.

"He's telling you to take your shirt off," Alex explains. "It's one of those incomprehensible Scottish phrases."

"Oh." I could refuse to do it, just to be contrary, but I don't see any advantage to that. If Domhnall thinks he can embarrass me this way, the Scots lout is as thick-headed as I thought. I take three steps toward Domhnall. "Taps off it is."

And I get rid of my shirt, hurling it toward Jessica.

She catches it, grins, and blows me a kiss.

Now I'm smirking at Domhnall.

He seems to be grinding his teeth.

Maybe I shouldn't feel triumphant about that—it's juvenile and insensitive, after all—but I do feel triumphant. The Gaelic God can't defeat me now, not even if he wins every round in these ruddy games.

Alex moves to stand beside the scoreboard, at the opposite end from Rory who's holding a thick piece of white chalk. My brother scans the crowd, then smiles in his devious way. "Shall we flip a lass to decide who goes first?"

"It's flip a coin, Alex," Logan shouts from the first row of spectators. "But I'd love to see you try to flip Catriona."

"They should flip Alex," Cat shouts from behind Logan.

My brother smiles again, at Catriona. "A coin it is, then. But thank you for the suggestion, love."

Alex flips a coin, and Domhnall wins the chance to start things off.

The damn Scot smirks.

Maybe I don't need to win this competition, but I want to win—to beat him and wipe that smug look off his face, preferably with a caber. I won't whack him with a tree trunk, but I do want to metaphorically smack him down.

If that makes me a petty, childish person, I can live with it.

"Fiona organized the games, but Rory and Lachlan have set the order of things," Alex announces. "You will start with the shot put, and Domhnall gets the first throw. If it's a tie, each competitor will throw again as many times as necessary to break the tie."

What's with these sodding rules? They sound like they're designed to make sure I get exhausted and lose. Did Domhnall have a hand in writing these guidelines?

As if he's read my mind, Alex tells us, "Rory and Lachlan set the rules of the competition. Good luck, and play fair."

He emphasizes "play fair" and aims his gaze at Domhnall when he says it.

The Scot gives me a look of mock disgust. At least I think it's mock. He shakes his head and says, "Need your brother to protect you, eh?"

No, I do not need Alex to protect me. And maybe I get mildly annoyed by what Domhnall said, so maybe I overreact a touch. "Do whatever you want, you kilt-wearing cretin. I can handle it."

He glances down at my kilt, his lip curling. "You're wearing a kilt too. I suppose that makes us both cretins."

"Let's get on with the games."

The spectators are spread out on the longest side of the lawn, but Lachlan leads Domhnall and me to the farthest end on the shortest side. That silly scoreboard is directly across from us, and Rory scrawled the words so big that I can read them from here. Lachlan hands Domhnall the stone, a smooth, grey, oval-shaped rock that's slightly wider than his hand. Lachlan pulls out a roll of duct tape and uses it to create a line in the grass in front of us.

"Take a running start," Lachlan says, "and throw when you reach the line. If your toe goes over the line, you forfeit that throw."

Lachlan moves to the side, out of our throwing trajectory and away from the duct-tape line. He's the referee, apparently, or whatever the Scots call the bloke who makes sure we stick to the rules.

Domhnall braces the stone against his neck, holding it in his palm. He runs forward and, when he reaches the line, he hurls the stone.

It flies a long ways before it whumps down.

The wanker struts past me wearing a self-satisfied expression.

Alex jogs out onto the lawn to measure the distance from the stone to the starting line. Then he calls out the distance. "Thirty-eight feet, two inches."

We're counting in imperial measures. My brother and most of the MacTaggarts think in feet and inches, though Alex switches to meters when he talks about archaeology. I got in the habit of using the metric system at school, like a lot of my younger mates have. Do imperial measures make it more or less likely I can win? I suddenly can't remember how to calculate the difference, as if my brain has decided to take a holiday. Inches are shorter than centimeters, and yards are shorter than meters, so... I have no fucking idea.

Lachlan hands me a stone.

It's my turn. I take the stone, hefting it to gauge how hard this is going to be. The stone is heavy, but not so weighty that I can't lift it or throw it. But can I land it farther away than Domhnall did? I brace the stone against my neck the way he'd done and take a deep breath. *Stay calm, you can do this.* So what if I've never participated in any sport? This can't be that hard.

After one more deep breath, I sprint to the line and hurl my stone.

It lands this side of Domhnall's throw.

My brother trots out to measure the distance, but it's so bloody obvious I've lost this round. "Thirty-seven feet, one inch."

"The winner of the stone put," Lachlan shouts, "is Domhnall Sterling."

Domhnall bars his arms over his chest, chin lifted.

Alex walks past me carrying both stones and the measuring tape. As he passes me, he whispers, "It's not over yet. Use your strengths."

Maybe it's not over, but I'm off to a smashing start, aren't I? Not even a tie, or almost a tie. I fell short by more than a foot. When I glance at Alex, who's standing beside Lachlan, he looks at me and taps his temple with one finger. Is he trying to tell me something?

Use your strengths, he'd said. Earlier, he'd told me I have intellect on my side. Is that what he's trying to say now? Use my intellect? I have no idea how that will help me in a battle of physical strength. I know how to calculate probabilities, analyze data, and collate results.

I swear I see an actual light bulb pop on above my head. Use my strengths. Domhnall is an experienced athlete, but I don't think he knows much, if anything, about probability distribution or Simpson's paradox.

Since Domhnall won the first round, he gets to go first in the hammer throw which involves a long wooden pole with a metal ball at one end. He takes hold of the opposite end, swings the whole thing around and around with the hammer circling from near the ground to high above his head, and then he releases it. The hammer flies across the lawn and thumps down.

Alex measures the distance. "Sixty-seven feet, nine inches."

I take my turn, picking up the hammer and testing its weight. The thing is heavy, and awkward to manage what with all the weight on the other end. Rory instructed me in the basics of these games, but it's different when a crowd is watching and my pride is at stake. Maybe I should concede since Domhnall is most likely going to beat me at every game.

"Go, Grey! You can do it, baby!"

That's Jessica's voice. I glance at her, and she blows me a kiss.

When I look at Domhnall, his mouth is pinched, and his eyes are narrowed.

I do a little trajectory calculation in my head and attempt to factor in the weight of the hammer plus the difference between my height and Domhnall's. This type of calculation isn't my strong suit, but I am good with numbers in general. I adjust my stance, firm up my hold on the hammer, and go for it, swinging the thing in a big circle, sort of like a cowboy does with his lasso. When I release the hammer, it soars over the lawn to crash down almost even with Domhnall's throw. Is mine slightly past his? It's too close to tell from this distance.

Alex rushes out to check. He measures the distance twice, running back to the starting line to drag that tape measure out again, then he stares at the tape measure and the two hammers that lie so close together. He squints, screws up his mouth, squints again.

Straightening, he winks at me. "Sixty-seven feet, ten inches. The Brit wins this round."

Domhnall gives me a smug look. "Ye squeaked by, *sassenach*, but ye havenae won yet."

Next, we do weight for height, which involves a rectangular stone with a ring-shaped metal handle attached to it. We each have to hurl the stone backward over our heads and get it over a bar set up behind us. Domhnall and I both get it over the bar on the first three tries. My arms are starting to ache, and sweat has broken out on my forehead. While he is sweaty, he doesn't seem in the least fatigued.

I lose the fourth round, though by a slim margin. The scoreboard announces the tally—Brit one, Scot two.

Time for the caber toss.

Domhnall gets the first throw, of course. He's in the lead, and this might be my last chance to overtake him. Domhnall grabs some dirt and wipes it on his hands the way an athlete might do with chalk. Then he hefts a caber, runs forward, and hurls it. The thing tumbles through the air end over end and smacks down.

"We're not measuring distance," my brother announces. "The winner will be selected based on the traditional method of determining whose throw is the straightest." He holds up a protractor and squints while attempting to measure the angle at which Domhnall's caber landed. "Looks like ten o'clock to me."

I roll my eyes. "A protractor measures degrees, not hours. It isn't a clock, Alex."

"Yes, I know that, Grey. I'm merely using it as a visual guide."

Domhnall has wandered back to the starting line, having run a good distance to make his toss. He kneels, seeming to fuss with his bootlaces, though he stares at the ground instead of his boot.

Lachlan declares, "Domhnall Sterling's first throw landed at ten o'clock. Your turn, Grey."

Are they measuring angles instead of distance because they think I can't win any other way? Alex had said this was the traditional method of determining a winner. He might be the king of obfuscation, but he wouldn't outright lie.

Taking a steadying breath, I approach the starting line. Lachlan helps me get the caber upright, just as he'd done with Domhnall, then I kneel to grasp the end and lift. Christ, it's heavy. Awkward too, what with most of the caber's length and weight above my head. I heft it up, ready to make my run.

I take one step and trip.

Though I don't fall down, the caber wobbles. I can't regain my equilibrium with all that weight swinging in my hands. Gritting my teeth, I struggle not to drop the ruddy thing, but the weight keeps shifting, the caber keeps gyrating, and my body can't adjust fast enough.

A shout erupts out of me, and the caber crashes down, sideways to me. Lachlan and Alex race to get out of the way, but luckily, no one else is in the trajectory of the falling caber.

Logan rushes toward us, checking on Alex and Lachlan on his way to me. They tell him they're fine. I'm lying flat on my face in the grass, one leg bent. Logan helps me get up.

"Are you injured?" he asks.

"No, I'm fine."

My pride might be seriously wounded, but I'll survive. Why did I trip? I'd been well-positioned with the weight balanced out. Then I took a step and...stumbled. Over what? My own feet?

Logan squats in the spot where I'd been standing when disaster struck. He runs his hand over the ground, intently focused on whatever he's examining. Suddenly, he freezes. His expression morphs into what Alex calls Logan's "deadly calm" look. The ex-spy plucks something out of the dirt, rises, and faces Domhnall.

"Someone planted this," Logan says, waving a small, dark rock at Domhnall. "It was pushed into the ground where anyone trying to run with a caber wouldn't be able to see it. Grey tripped on it. This was sabotage."

"It's a rock," Domhnall says, his tone scoffing. "Could've come from anywhere."

Logan holds the rock between his thumb and forefinger. "I've never known Mother Nature to polish her rocks."

Alex snatches the stone from Logan. "This came from the gift shop. I've seen an entire bin of rocks just like this."

Now Alex glares at Domhnall too, though he can't match Logan's menacingly calm stare.

"Since we can't prove definitively who sabotaged the caber toss," Logan says, "it's up to Grey to decide whether he wants to continue. If he does, we will void the first throw and start over."

Everyone looks at me.

"Let's start over," I say. "I want to continue."

Maybe I've gone somewhat insane, but I need to finish this.

I get the first throw this time, tossing the caber in a relatively straight trajectory, by my estimation.

Alex uses his protractor again. "Barely off twelve o'clock. I'd say it's twelve plus five minutes."

Domhnall makes his attempt.

My brother pretends to scrutinize his protractor, shutting one eye and then the other, tipping his head to the side and then straightening it.

I'm sure he's dragging this out for dramatic effect. Alex loves drama.

"Eleven o'clock," Alex announces. "Grey wins the caber toss."

"You cheated," Domhnall roars. "He's your brother, and magically, he wins the game. It's rot, Thorne, and you know it. The pair of you conspired to cheat."

Alex picks up the polished stone that mysteriously tripped me up. He waves it like a metronome—tick, tick, tick. "If you want to question my integrity, have at it. But do not insinuate that my brother would cheat."

Domhnall glances at the stone, then at me, his lip curling. "Fine. The result stands, which leaves us in a tie. There's one way to settle this."

I thought that was all they ever did in Highland games. Rory only gave me pointers for these four events. What else is there?

The damn Scot sneers. "It's time for the real battle—tug o' war."

"It's not on the agenda," Lachlan says. "We can do another round of caber tossing or—"

"Tug o' war," Domhnall says. He thumps his fist into the other palm, his gaze drilling into me. "And let's make this a genuine battle. Brits versus Scots."

Chapter Twenty-Five

Jessica

Silence descends on the lawn like someone has pressed the mute button on every person in attendance. Domhnall declared, loud enough for everyone to hear, that he wants a Brits versus Scots battle right here on the lawn of the nudist resort. What is he trying to do now? All the Scots here, except for him, like Grey and have known him for months. They just met Domhnall, and honestly, I don't think anyone here likes him much after the way he's behaved. They won't want to help a cheater.

This isn't the Domhnall I know. Cheating? No way, he never does that. He values fair play and sportsmanlike behavior, prides himself on always living up to those principles. Until today. What started out as a supposedly friendly game of Highland sports has become a real battle. Jeez, I'd been joking when I said I didn't want the Domhnall thing to turn into a reenactment of the Battle of Bannockburn. It's no joke now.

Grey throws his hands up. "This is ridiculous, Domhnall. All the other Scots here are my friends. You can't make them help you connive your way into winning a tug-of-war match with whatever other dirty tricks you've got up your sleeve."

That's a good point. The MacTaggarts won't cheat.

"Hey!" I shout, waving my arms until Grey and Domhnall look at me. Everyone else looks at me too, which is kind of unnerving. "I need to talk to Grey, Alex, and Lachlan. Please."

Everyone seems confused.

I keep waving my arms until the three men I've summoned finally amble over to me. Then I lead them over to the scoreboard, away from the crowd.

"What is it?" Grey asks.

"This is crazy," I say. "Domhnall cheated once, and he will do it again. He's obsessed with beating you, Grey."

"I know, but I won't give up because of that. I need to see this through to the end."

"Yeah, I get that, and I'm not trying to talk you out of this." I shut my eyes for a second and sigh, glancing at Alex and Lachlan. "I'm trusting you guys to make sure Domhnall doesn't do anything rash."

"He won't get away with cheating again," Lachlan says. "Not when MacTaggarts are on his team. We'll put Logan right behind Domhnall to keep him in line."

Alex chuckles. "Ah, yes, Logan. If Domhnall tries anything, James Bond MacTaggart will take him out so fast his head will literally spin."

"Head-spinning isn't necessary," I say. "Just keep this tug-of-war thing on the level."

"Relax, Jessica." Alex pats my arm. "I won't let a Scots thug hurt my wee brother."

"Stop calling me 'wee', Alex," Grey says, flashing his brother a scowl.

I resign myself to letting this craziness go on for a little longer. I know Grey needs to prove to himself he can stand up to Domhnall, but I love Grey too much to stand here praying my ex won't go postal on him. I did what I could. Now I need to take a step back.

So I haul him closer, planting a quick, firm kiss on his mouth. "Kick his ass, baby."

Grey smirks. Then he wraps an arm around my waist and kisses me. Really kisses me. By the time he steps away, I'm feeling deliciously soft and warm in ways that make me want to rip his clothes off. Since he's wearing only a kilt, I wouldn't need to rip his clothes off, though. I can just hike up his kilt.

He looks so damn hot in plaid.

I lunge forward, hopping up on my tiptoes, and whisper in his ear, "Are you wearing boxers or briefs under that kilt?"

"Neither. I'm 'swinging free' as Aidan likes to say."

Oh wow, that makes me even hotter for him.

"Time to gather the troops," Lachlan says.

He marches off toward the crowd of MacTaggarts, while Alex and Grey head for the Dixons and Hunters.

Fiona approaches Domhnall and starts talking to him. I can't hear what they're saying, but she keeps pointing a finger at him, her expression full of stern determination. He rolls his eyes and shakes his head, but it only spurs her to poke him in the chest with that finger, several times.

He bows his head, rubbing the back of his neck.

She lays a palm on his chest, her expression softening.

Domhnall raises his head, staring at her like she's said something that stunned him.

Fiona boosts herself up on her toes, slanting in to speak to him with their faces an inch apart. After a moment, she trots back to the crowd to rejoin her sisters and her sisters-in-law.

I wave at Domhnall until he notices, then gesture for him to come over here.

He scrunches his brows for a couple of seconds before he marches over to me. "What is it, Jess? Donnae feel like having another woman give me my head in my hands to play with."

Fiona reamed him? Good for her. But considering the way she touched his chest and leaned in to say something, I'm pretty sure she's attracted to him.

"Do you like Fiona?" I ask. "She's definitely into you."

His eyes go wide for half a second. "No, I—She's an annoying woman."

"Sounds like the old I-hate-you-because-I-want-you thing." I shove my hands in my pockets. "But that's not why I called you over here. Cheating, Domhnall? Seriously? I can't believe you did that."

"Couldn't stand to see that *cacan* win."

"Grey is not a wee shit or a large shit or even an in-between shit." I smack his chest. "You're the one who stinks of crap, Domhnall. You had better play fair this time or I will whup your ass myself."

I expect him to make a sarcastic comment about my ability to whup his ass, but he doesn't do that.

He bows his head and pushes a hand into his hair. "Christ, Jess, I've become the kind of man I always despised, haven't I?"

"You can still make things right. Fair play, no dirty tricks of any kind. Besides, I have it on good authority that Logan will kick your ass way worse than I ever could if you try something."

"No tricks. You have my word."

"Good."

He walks back out onto the lawn where eight MacTaggart men wait for him—Logan, Rory, Aidan, Lachlan, Evan, Iain, Jack, and the man

I've assumed is Jack's brother, Callum. The Brits saunter onto the playing field too, where Grey and Alex are joined by Chance and his two brothers, Reese and Dane, along with Richard and Nick Hunter.

"We need nine men on each team," Lachlan announces. "One stays on the sidelines as a coach. The Brits need two more to round out their team."

"I'll do it," a man shouts, though I can't see who it is. The man pushes his way through the crowd, and I realize it's someone I've seen but haven't met before. He has dark hair and olive skin, and he's wearing black jeans with a black shirt. "For anyone who doesn't know, I'm Damian Petrescu, the concierge at this resort. You Brits would be lucky to have a Ludar prince on your side."

"He means he's a gypsy," says a blonde woman who trails Damian out of the crowd. "My husband thinks he has supernatural powers, but just ignore him. He's completely full of shit."

"Come on, Heidi," Damian says to his wife. "You're wrecking my moment. I'm about to save their British asses with my Rom awesomeness."

Heidi kisses Damian, then waits at the edge of the crowd while he joins the Brits.

Another man saunters out onto the field too, and I realize it's Val Silva. "Damian can be the coach. I will pull on that rope along with Grey and his team."

Val Silva is on their team? Wow, that guy has ginormous muscles that will give the British team a serious advantage.

"Just so everyone knows," Nick Hunter hollers, "when Richard and Chance get too tired, Reese and I will take up the slack. We have more stamina than these old men."

"Like hell you do," Richard says. "You're the same age as me, Nick. Or have you forgotten we're twins?"

"I was born two minutes and thirty-eight seconds after you. I'm younger, sexier, and more fun."

Aidan, who stands beside Nick, chimes in. "I'm a lot younger than Lachie and Rory, but Logan put me at the back of the tug o' war line. Are ye wanting to lose, Logie?"

"Watch it, Don Juan," Logan says, giving his younger cousin a sarcastically threatening glare. "Call me Logie again and I'll tell your wife about all those lasses you shagged before you met Calli."

"There's a problem," Chance Dixon announces. "We don't have a rope."

Ollie Jackson emerges from the crowd, raising a hand. "Leave that to me. We've got ropes in the storage shed."

He and his wife, Mara, head out to get a rope.

Grey and his team are having an intense discussion by the looks of it, probably mapping out a strategy to defeat the Scots. Domhnall has joined the MacTaggarts for a discussion of their own, though that chat involves plenty of stern looks, especially from Logan, all of which are aimed at Domhnall.

Ollie and Mara return lugging a big, thick, rolled-up rope. Each of them carries half of the thing, and they manage to stay in perfect sync until the moment they dump the rope on the ground in the middle of the playing field.

"Here you go," Ollie says. "Get started whenever you want."

The battle is about to begin.

I feel a little nauseous, and suddenly, I realize I'm wringing my hands and gnawing on my lip. Domhnall won't hurt Grey. He promised to play fair. With all those MacTaggarts there to keep an eye on him, Domhnall can't do anything nasty.

The Brits will win. Grey will win, I know it.

Still, I clasp my hands, holding them under my chin, and I wait.

Chapter Twenty-Six

Grey

THIS IS IT. BRITS VERSUS SCOTS IN A BATTLE THE LIKES OF which I never imagined I would see, much less participate in. I need to beat Domhnall, even though that means beating my Scots mates. I like the MacTaggarts, but this is war.

Alex rushes into the guest house to get his kilt. Since there aren't enough kilts to go around, my cousins and the others on my team opt for removing their shirts but keep their trousers on.

When I glance at Jessica, she gives me the thumbs-up sign and blows me a kiss.

I wink at her.

Yes, I'm going to win this battle. My cousins have a lot more muscles than I do, almost as many as the average MacTaggart, and so do the Hunters. The American gypsy bloke who volunteered to fill out our team seems like he has plenty of muscles too, and Val Silva outdoes all of them.

"Coordination is key," Alex had proclaimed during our huddle, or whatever sports teams call it when they gather to talk strategy. I thought he meant "coordination" as in "balance," but no. He meant we need to work together as a "perfectly synchronized team, almost like we're a single organism."

That metaphor gave me a revolting vision of one giant amoeba with all our heads poking out of it. But I understand what Alex meant. We need to work together as one team.

After a vote, Damian the gypsy becomes our coach who will give us encouragement and advice from the sideline. We use the duct-tape starting line as our boundary for the tug-of-war. Whoever crosses it first loses the game. Everyone picks up the rope and gets ready. Domhnall and I are at the front of our respective teams, face to face, maybe four meters apart.

Catriona stands on the line, an arm's length from the rope, ready to start the battle. She waves her outstretched arm up and down in time with her countdown. "Three, two, one, go!"

She hurries out of the way while eight Scots and eight Brits start to pull as hard as we can. I lean back for better leverage, but Damian warns me not to lean back too far and to firm up my grip on the rope. He gives advice to my teammates too, and I hear Jack instructing the other team. Maybe I should feel weird about competing against the MacTaggarts since they've become my mates lately, but I'm laser-focused on Domhnall. Beat the bastard, my brain urges. Or maybe it's testosterone telling me that. All I know is I need to knock that cretin back on his arse.

I pull with everything I have, my arm muscles stretched to their limits, gritting my teeth and digging my heels into the earth. Behind me, Chance growls. Honestly, he does. Maybe he wants to win this as much as I do. I know Val Silva is right behind Chance, and I hear more feral noises that must be coming from Val.

Christ, my arms are burning, my legs too.

We gain a few centimeters, dragging the Scots closer to the line.

The crowd, which now consists of mainly women, starts shouting and cheering and clapping. Several female voices chant, "Go, Brits! Go, Brits!"

I glance in the direction of those chants and see Catriona among the women who keep shouting their support for us. Well, she is marrying my brother, so naturally, she supports our team. But the American Wives Club is also chanting for us.

The Scots suddenly make an enormous tug, hauling my team forward, my toes within a centimeter of the line.

"Fuck!" I shout and pull as hard as I can, every muscle in my body burning from the effort. My mates pull too, and we surge backward, dragging the Scots forward.

Domhnall leans back, teeth bared, snarling like a wild beast and glaring at me. "Ahmno letting a goddamn *sassenach* beat me. *Pòg mo thòin, ye cacan!*"

Kiss his arse? The bellend thinks I don't know the Gaelic phrase, but Alex explained it to me after I heard Logan say those words once. The phrase wasn't in Alex and Cat's burlesque show the other day.

"Sod off, Domhnall," I shout. "You're going down!"

More of the crowd joins in the chanting, all of it for my team. Someone whistles, and I can't help glancing toward the person who made that noise. Jessica is just removing her fingers from her mouth.

She gives me the thumbs-up sign with both hands. "Go, Greybee!"

We keep losing and gaining ground, over and over, our bodies covered in sweat. My eyes sting from the perspiration dribbling into them. It seeps between my gritted teeth too. I pull and pull and pull until I think I can't do it anymore, but every time I catch sight of Jessica, I get a surge of energy that bolsters me.

Men start to drop—away from the rope, not in the sense of passing out. Aidan MacTaggart drops first, then my cousin Reese goes. Rory trips and loses his grip, so he's out too. One by one, they fall, but the tug-of-war goes on and on until only Domhnall and I are left standing, left pulling like men possessed by wild demons.

"Give it up," Domhnall hisses. "Ye know ahm stronger."

"That's bollocks. This isn't about the size of your muscles, it's about strategy and stamina."

Domhnall's face has turned red, but though I might be covered in more sweat than I ever knew my body could produce, I don't feel on the verge of collapsing. The Scot is strong, but I will not concede.

A shout so loud it echoes off the trees explodes out of me.

My nemesis pulls so hard the rope is torn through my palms, scouring my skin. My hands burn like acid has been poured onto them, but I will not give up. I dig my heels in deeper, suck in a big breath, and pull with every iota of strength I have left inside me.

Domhnall bellows, loses his grip on the rope, and tumbles to the ground.

I stagger backward, the sudden release of pressure so disorienting that I stumble left and right with the rope still clutched in my raw palms. Why hadn't we worn gloves? We should've at least wrapped our palms in gauze or something, but none of us thought of that.

My legs give out, and I collapse onto my knees.

"The Brits have won, "Alex hollers, "so all you Scots can stop gloating about how superior you are. We just proved you're losers!"

He almost screams that last word like a crazed barbarian, though I know he's joking. Probably.

Jessica races over to me and drops to her knees, throwing her arms around me. "You won. I knew you would, but I was kind of worried Domhnall might try another dirty trick."

"He lost fair and square." I want to put my arms around her, but my palms are still burning. "I think I hurt my hands."

Jess pulls back just enough to look at my palms, turning them side to side to examine my abraded skin. "Poor Greybee, you got rope burns."

"Felt like all the skin got burnt off my hands."

"It's not that bad, but you do need some ointment or something." She brushes her fingers over my cheek. "And you definitely earned some of my special tender loving care."

That means sex. Lots of it.

"Uh, Jess, I think I might need a lie-down before you administer your TLC."

"Oh sure, yeah." She hugs me, kissing my cheek. "I'm so proud of you."

"For what?"

"Not giving up. Domhnall cheated, but you kept going anyway. At least this time he didn't pull any dirty tricks."

Over her shoulder, I see Domhnall still lying on the ground, flat on his Scottish arse. Jack, Rory, and Alex all offer to help him up, but he scowls and waves them away.

"There's something I need to do first," I tell Jessica. "To end the war once and for all."

She kisses me on the mouth. "Do whatever you need to do."

I get up and walk over to Domhnall. "Are you all right?"

"Aye, fine."

"Then why are you lying there like a cranky corpse?"

"Because you beat me. You, a scrawny wee British *tolla-thon*."

Maybe I'm not a behemoth like Domhnall, but I'm hardly scrawny or wee. There's no point in telling him that. The man just got trounced by a computer geek, so I decide he's earned a little self-pity. I would've expected I'd feel like gloating if I won, but I don't feel that way at all.

I offer him my hand. "Let's end the rivalry, once and for all. No hard feelings."

Domhnall stares at my hand for a moment, then he sighs and accepts the help. I lever him up off the grass.

Maybe I don't need to gloat, but I think I've earned the right to exact a small measure of payback.

I pull my arm back and punch him in the face.

He staggers backward, rubbing his jaw, but he doesn't glower. He almost smiles. "You should be a boxer, *sassenach*."

Scots are all off their rockers, aren't they?

"That's for cheating," I say, "and for harassing Jessica. We're even now."

"Aye, we're even. And I deserved that punch." He works his jaw like he's getting the joints realigned or something. "Maybe it is time we—*I* bury the hatchet. You won the games, and you won Jess, all without any underhanded tricks. You're the better man, Grey."

This might be the first time in history Domhnall has used my first name. Definitely the first time he has ever said anything remotely nice to me.

"You aren't a bad man," I say. "Just pigheaded."

"Aye, that's true." He holds out his hand to me. "Peace?"

"Yes, peace." I shake his hand. "I think there's someone who wants to see you."

I point toward Fiona, who's trotting toward us.

The second she reaches us, Fiona flings her arms around Domhnall's neck. "You didn't cheat this time. Congratulations, ye *cacan*."

"Are you trying to make me feel better?" he says. "You're bloody awful at it."

She pats his chest with both hands. "Donnae be grumpy. You get the consolation prize."

"What would that be?"

"You'll find out soon."

I leave the two barmy Scots to do whatever it is they're going to do. Ollie Jackson brings us ointment and bandages for my hands, but Jessica takes the task of tending to my wounds. My hands aren't as badly abraded as they'd felt at first. Once they're bandaged, they don't hurt at all. So Jess and I head over to the crowd where Alex and my cousins are chatting to a group of Scots.

Just as we reach them, Rory shakes his head at his wife. "Emery, you were cheering for the wrong side."

"Don't take it personally, Rory baby. My screams and clapping were a show of solidarity for a fellow geek."

Emery MacTaggart is an expert computer programmer, so to those of us who think "geek" is not an insult, she's a rock star.

"But why," Lachlan asks, "were Erica, Calli, Rae, Keely, and Serena all cheering for the Brits? My own wife rooted for the other side."

Serena, Logan's wife, speaks up to defend her sisters-in-law. "Come off it, Lachlan. You're not offended, and we all know it. You guys were aiding the enemy, so of course we rooted for the Brits."

"My sister was screaming for them too," Lachlan says, giving Catriona a sarcastically pointed look.

"No, she wasn't, actually," Alex says. "I've been made an honorary MacTaggart, remember? You lot voted on it. That means Cat was supporting both sides at once, Brits and Scots." My brother notices me and Jessica and slaps me on the shoulder. "Good show, Grey. You've brought honor to our family, which is quite a feat considering Mummy is an incarcerated grifter."

Whenever Alex says things like that, I ignore it because that seems like the wisest choice. He might say something bizarre and embarrassing otherwise.

Jess and I tell everyone we're going to our bungalow, with my injured hands as the excuse. I need TLC, you know. Lots and lots of that. But I wasn't joking when I said I might need a lie-down first.

Just as we exit the lawn, Domhnall approaches us.

"How are you?" Jessica asks him. "You were flat on the ground for several minutes."

"Not because I couldn't get up. I was...humiliated." He holds up a hand when I open my mouth to speak. "I deserved to be humiliated. And I meant it when we shook hands and agreed to end the rivalry. It's over, just like Jess and I have been over for months. I realize now I was being a *bod ceann*, trying to hang on to something I'd ruined a long time ago. I'm sorry, Jessica. I'm sorry, Grey. It's all over now."

He walks away.

Fiona MacTaggart accompanies him into the guest house. They're holding hands.

I glance at Jessica. "Do you think Domhnall and Fiona..."

"Yeah," she says with a snicker, "I absolutely think that. About damn time he got over his obsession and turned into a normal human being again. Whether or not his thing with Fiona works out, I think Domhnall will be better off for trying."

"Domhnall wasn't really obsessed with you, was he? It was the idea of losing to someone like me."

"Exactly. A computer geek and a Brit? You're like the antithesis of everything Domhnall thinks matters in life." She leads me around the guest house, heading for our bungalow. "Domhnall can't accept that techie jargon is way hotter than ginormous muscles. Brains beat brawn every time."

"I'm suddenly not feeling exhausted anymore." Randy as hell is more like it. As I shut the bungalow door behind us, I sling an arm around Jess and tug her into me. "Ready to hear about the correlation coefficient, multinomial distribution, and SQL server integration services? I can demonstrate all of those concepts with hands-on examples."

"Ooh, yes, please."

I pick her up and carry her into the bedroom.

Chapter Twenty-Seven

Jessica

GREY AND I SPEND THE REST OF THE DAY IN OUR LITTLE BUN-galow—having sex, yes, but also talking. Domhnall and I never talked the way I do with Grey. Being best friends for years taught us how to have real conversations, something that in my experience a lot of couples don't really know how to do. Maybe I wish I'd realized how I feel about Grey years ago, so we could've had this amazing intimacy for all that time, but I can't regret anything.

This was the journey we needed to take.

After the best night's sleep of our lives, we decide to join everyone else in the dining hall for breakfast. Domhnall is there, with Fiona, and her three brothers are sharing a table with them, along with their wives. Grey and I sit with Alex and Cat plus Logan, Serena, Evan, and Keely. Evan, the billionaire tech mogul, has his daughter tucked into a baby carrier that's strapped to his chest. Little Joy is asleep, looking absolutely adorable.

I lean in to whisper to Grey, "That's one thing we've never talked about."

"What?"

"Babies. Do you want them?"

His brows lower, cinching together over his nose. "Is this the right place to be talking about that?"

"It's a simple question. Yes or no, do you want kids?"

Grey's mouth falls, open but he doesn't speak.

"What have you said to my brother, Jessica?" Alex asks. "He looks stunned. But then, he is easily shocked, being an innocent who was shielded from the big, bad world until he met me." Alex pops a silver-dollar-size hash brown into his mouth and eats it. "So, Jessica, what salacious thing did you tell my brother?"

"It wasn't salacious. But it's private, so keep your big old nose out of it, okay?"

Alex chuckles. "I don't have a big nose. Mine is perfectly proportioned. But at least you insulted me cheerfully."

When breakfast is over, Grey and I decide to go for a walk down the nature trail to the hot spring. I haven't seen that yet. All the craziness involving Domhnall distracted me. Today, Domhnall is playing badminton with Fiona, Alex, and Cat, and he seems to be having a genuinely good time instead of pretending to in hopes of making me jealous. I believed it when he told me, after the Highland games, that he's decided to move on and stop obsessing over me, or rather, the relationship we once had.

Grey and I relax in the hot spring in the nude.

If anyone had asked me a week ago whether I'd want to strip naked in public, I would've said absolutely no way. But something about this resort, about the setting and the people, makes me feel comfortable going au naturel. I love getting naked with Grey anytime, anywhere, but lounging in the steamy waters of the hot spring with his arm around my shoulders has become my favorite moment ever. Well, maybe my favorite moment was when he beat Domhnall at tug-of-war. The look of sheer determination on Grey's face while he fought to drag Domhnall over that line... Wow, I'd wanted to jump him right there on the lawn in front of everyone. How could I not get horny? I mean, he was sweaty and determined, his biceps bulging.

Yeah, that was the single hottest thing I'd ever seen.

I love Grey the computer geek and Grey the kind of shy guy, and yeah, I even love Grey the horrible poet-slash-singer and especially Grey the badass Highland games champion.

"What are you thinking about?" Grey asks, stroking my arm with his fingertips.

"Lots of things, most of them about you."

"Anything you want to share?"

There are a few things we haven't talked about yet, and maybe it is time we do that. I turn partway toward him so I can gaze into his eyes. "What do we do now?"

"Get out of the water, dry off, and head back to the resort. We can also get dressed if you like."

"No, that's not what I mean. What do we do now, relationship-wise? You live in England, and I live in America. Bicoastal is one thing, but we're bicontinental."

"The UK is not a continent. It's an island."

I poke him in the side. "Stop that. I'm trying to have an adult conversation with you, my boyfriend, about where our relationship goes from here."

"Sorry. I'm not sure how to answer that question. I want to be with you, that's all I know, and having an ocean and half a continent between us isn't ideal. I didn't even like that when we were just mates."

"Hey, you complained when I called the UK a continent. Now you're doing it."

"No, I was referring to the United States."

"Oh. Right." I slide over to straddle him, linking my hands at his nape. "What are we going to do, Grey?"

"I work from home, so I can live anywhere. You might have heard of that barmy new invention called the internet that lets you send files and messages back and forth, and you can even make phone calls that way."

"Ha-ha." I wrap my arms around his neck, drawing myself closer to him. "You know I don't love my job. Being a dental assistant was a practical choice, not my life's passion. Maybe you can live anywhere, but your cousins are in England and your brother lives in Scotland. I don't want to tear you and Alex apart when you've only just found each other."

"I don't want to tear you away from your family either."

"Yeah, but I've known my parents since birth. You met Alex a few months ago."

He loops his arms around me and gets that crinkly thing between his eyebrows that I know means he's trying to untangle this mess. "Evan MacTaggart provided the jet that brought you and me to Oregon, and several of his cousins have jets too. I'm sure one of them would give us the same courtesy whenever we need it. That means we could fly your parents to England anytime they feel like visiting us."

"I'm sure Mom and Dad would love that. Mom retired two years ago, and Dad quit working a year after that. They've always wanted to see more of the world."

"We could send them on holiday too, anywhere they want to go." He slides his hands down to my bottom. "See? Everything will work out."

Can we do all of that? Can we actually pull this off? When Grey tells me everything will work out, I believe him. Grey Dixon always speaks the truth. Excitement shivers over my skin because I've just realized that I finally have everything I wanted and needed, though it took me eight years to figure out what that was. Better late than never, right?

"My cousins and my brother know lots of people," Grey says. "Maybe one of them can help you find a new career path. You always wanted to be a teacher, but you never could find a job doing that. This might be the perfect time to start looking into that option again. Believe me, when the Dixons and Alex Thorne are on your side, you can't lose. But there's no rush. You can take your time finding your new path since I make more than enough money to take care of both of us for quite a while."

I know Grey isn't rich like Alex, but I also know he's not financially strapped either. For years, ever since we graduated from college and I went home to America, we've often visited each other. Sometimes Grey came to America, and sometimes he paid for me to visit him in the UK. At first, we flew coach. But for the past three years, we've flown first class. His career as a business intelligence analyst took off faster than either of us expected, thanks in part to the support of his cousins. They believed in his skills and trusted his integrity, so they knew they could safely recommend him to their friends and business contacts.

"There's one more thing," I say. "About babies…"

"Yes, let's have loads of them."

I laugh. "Loads? Let's start with one and see how that goes."

"All right." His mouth crimps as he searches my face, though I don't know what he's looking for in my expression. "There's something else I've been thinking about, but…" He shakes his head. "Never mind. It can wait."

"You can't tell me there's something else, then refuse to share it with me."

"It's the wrong time and the wrong place. I'll tell you later, I promise."

We climb out of the hot spring and dry each other off, which gets us both hotter than the water in the spring. He tosses our towels onto the grass as a makeshift blanket, then lays me down and makes love to me slowly. Being with Grey feels so natural that I can't believe we wasted years being with other people when we should've been together. That's the past, though, and I want to focus on today, tomorrow, and every day after that for the rest of our lives.

But the thing he'd almost told me keeps niggling at my brain.

When we get back to the resort, a big, sky-blue bus sits parked in the driveway. I'd seen that bus parked behind the caretaker's house, and Eve mentioned they use it for ferrying guests to and from town for touristy outings. Now that I see the bus, I kind of remember an outing like that on the list of activities for this week. Since the itinerary described it as "a shopping excursion," I figure Catriona must have put that on the list. Alex doesn't seem like the shopaholic type.

Grey and I go back to our bungalow to change clothes, then everybody piles into the bus. It has plush seats with more padding than any bus I've ever ridden on. The inside has been decorated too, with painted images as well as fancy buttons sewn into the upholstery. Damian Petrescu drives the bus while his wife, Heidi, explains what the town has to offer in terms of shopping, but also in terms of historical sites.

I love history. That's an interest Grey and I have always shared. Maybe Grey's love of the distant past is genetic since Alex is an archaeologist.

Our tour group includes Alex, Catriona, all the Dixons, all the Hunters, and a few MacTaggarts. When the bus drops us off in the town square, everyone tumbles out and splits off into smaller groups. The group Grey and I wind up joining includes Alex, Cat, Logan, and Serena. Her son, Chase, decides to go with one of the MacTaggart groups that just happens to include Malina, the daughter of Iain and Rae MacTaggart. I'd seen Chase and Malina shyly flirting over the past few days, so I'm not at all surprised Chase wants to abandon his mom to go hang out with the girl he likes.

We stroll down the main drag, each couple holding hands.

This town has cute shops, everything from touristy gift shops to clothing stores and even places that make and sell sweets. Grey buys me a huge box of milk chocolate candies and feeds me a caramel. I love his playful side, but he'd kept that under wraps for a long time. Now, he's not shy at all about feeding me or holding my hand. He even slips an arm around my shoulders to hold me closer while we wander past more shops.

As we pass a jewelry store, Grey slows down. I have to slow down too, what with his arm around me. He gazes at the display of items in the window, everything from crystal stud earrings to diamond engagement rings.

The rest of the gang finally realizes they've lost us and comes back.

"Mesmerized by semiprecious stones?" Alex asks his brother.

Grey blinks rapidly, glancing at his brother for only a second before his attention returns to the display. "No, I'm not interested in those."

"What, then?" Alex moves up alongside Grey and bends forward, squinting at what lies behind the glass. His lips stretch little by little, easing into a sly, closed-mouth smile. He rotates his eyes to look at Grey. "Ah, of course. Maybe you and I should have a brother-to-brother mini-excursion while Logan takes the ladies down the street to the next gift shop."

Logan lifts one brow but then shrugs. "All right with me. But you'll need the lasses' permission."

Serena and Cat voice their agreement, so I chime in too. "Sure, it's cool with me."

"Excellent," Alex says. "Grey, it's time to release Jessica, though your arm seems to have become permanently attached to her. We might need a crowbar to separate you two."

Grey rolls his eyes, the way he often does when his brother is around. He kisses me, then I walk over to Logan and the other ladies.

Alex's sly smile returns. "Logan, you've acquired a harem, you lucky sod."

Serena, Cat, and I exchange sly smiles of our own. Before Logan knows what hit him, we swarm the poor man and peck kisses on his cheeks.

Logan looks shocked. I've known him for a while, and never before have I seen the former MI6 agent seem even mildly surprised. He wriggles away from us, grasps Serena's hand, and leads our group away.

When I glance over my shoulder, Alex and Grey are still admiring the jewelry shop's window display.

Chapter Twenty-Eight

Grey

I GAZE DOWN INTO THE GLASS CASE, MY HANDS RESTING on top of it, and chew on my bottom lip. I've never been a lip-chewer before, but what I plan to do—or might potentially, sometime in the not-too-distant future, think about doing—has me gnawing on my own flesh. I love Jessica. I want to be with her for the rest of my life, and we've worked out the geographic issues in our relationship. Well, mostly. The rest will sort itself out. But the hardest decision I've ever had to make confronts me now, here in this jewelry shop.

Which ring am I going to buy for Jessica? Engagement rings are vital, according to women. I want Jess to have the perfect one.

"Maybe Jessica should be here," I tell Alex, who's standing beside me wearing that faintly amused look he often gets around me. Well, around pretty much everyone. "She's the one who'll have to wear the ruddy thing forever after. Shouldn't she have a say in which ring I choose?"

"No, she wants it to be a surprise. Women always want that, even if they exchange the ring for a different one the next day." He pretends to scrutinize the items in the glass case. "You need to make a romantic gesture. The ring is only the beginning. You'll need a smashing proposal too, but I can help you organize that spectacle."

"Spectacle? No, Alex, you will not get anywhere near me or Jessica when I ask her to marry me. In fact, you should be on another continent when that happens."

"Whatever you want, wee brother."

Despite my every effort to change his mind, I can't convince Alex to stop calling me his "wee" brother. I've resigned myself to hearing that for the rest of my natural life and probably in whatever comes after that. I have no doubts Alex will haunt me if he snuffs it first. Not even death will stop my brother from harassing me and interfering in my life. But maybe I don't mind it as much as I used to, and maybe I've sort of, grudgingly, decided it's a sign that he cares about me.

All right, maybe I care about him too. I've never had a brother before, so it's taken time for me to adjust. It doesn't help that Alex is...Alex.

I focus on the display case again, scanning the rings inside it. One catches my eye, a rose-gold band with a central diamond surrounded by two curving lines of much smaller diamonds and two heart-shaped designs. Jessica loves pink, and rose gold is a lovely pinkish color. The ring costs a lot, but I can afford it—and Jess deserves the best.

"You've made your choice, haven't you?" Alex asks.

I point at the rose-gold ring. "That one."

"Brilliant choice. Now, go pay for the thing. Then we'll need to talk about how you're going to propose to Jessica, so you don't get nervous and cock it up the way you did with sex."

"Jess and I have amazing sex now, I'll have you know."

Alex chuckles. "Oh, everyone knows that. You two aren't exactly stealth lovers."

I'm sure he means that other people have heard the noise coming from our bungalow. I don't care. Jess doesn't care either. So what if all the MacTaggarts, the Dixons, and the resort employees heard us going at it? Let them listen and learn.

"I'm not going to cock up the proposal," I tell Alex. "And I don't need your help. Any plan you come up with would most likely involve things that you would do but that I would never in the entire lifespan of the universe do in public."

"You knew one day you'd try naturism, eh?"

"Well...no."

Alex chuckles again. "But that's something I would do. Have done, actually. Maybe you should try my kind of proposal and get your kit off in front of everyone."

"No, Alex."

I glance around until I see the bloke who showed me this case full of rings. When I wave, he comes over to help me buy the one I want. How should I ask Jess to marry me? I want to do it right because, after all the rubbish we've been through, I need to show her how much she means to me. I don't understand why my brother seems determined to "help" me propose. But then, I don't understand much about him. I keep wondering about that as we leave the shop.

Alex and I are walking down the street when an impulse hits me and I have to ask. "Why do you keep trying to help me? You hated it when the MacTaggarts interfered in your life."

"I had to put on a good show of not liking it, didn't I? My reputation as a bloody annoying bastard was at stake. But I realized even back then that Logan and his family were only harassing me because they wanted to help."

"But why are you doing the same thing to me? We haven't known each other long."

Alex stops walking and turns toward me. "You're my brother, Grey. It's my right to harass you, isn't it? That's what the MacTaggarts think siblings do, and apparently, the Dixons agree."

"You still haven't answered my question."

He bows his head, rubbing his chin.

"Come on, Alex," I say. "You've been hell-bent on getting me and Jessica together. Arranging a fancy dress party? Convincing me to let Domhnall stay? Competing with me in the tug-of-war? I can't see why you bothered to do any of that."

"It should be obvious, shouldn't it?" He lifts his head, sighs, and flaps his arms once. "You're going to make me say it, aren't you?"

"Of course I am. I won't have any idea what the reason is unless you tell me."

He groans, shutting his eyes for a moment. "You're my brother, Grey, and I love you. That's why I bother."

Alex swerves his gaze to the side, warping his mouth into a strange expression.

He can't be embarrassed. Nothing unnerves him. Or does it? He did just say he loves me. I should say something back, shouldn't I? But I don't tell other men I like them, much less...this.

My brother flicks his eyes to glance at me sideways—repeatedly.

He *is* anxious. If aliens landed and announced they're about to transform the Earth into a ball of candyfloss, I couldn't have been more shocked. For my brother to feel embarrassed and anxious must mean my entire perception of reality has been wrong.

"Uh, Alex," I begin, "I wasn't expecting you to say that. But, er, I...Well, I suppose I sort of... love you too."

He gives me a quick hug, thumping me on the back, then he steps away from me. "Let's never tell anyone we had this conversation."

"I'll need to tell Jess. We don't keep secrets from each other."

"Yes, and I suppose I'll have to tell Cat." He jabs a finger in my direction. "But no one else will ever know. Agreed?"

"Fine, yes."

"That means you can't tell Jack either."

"How many times do I have to promise not to tell anyone?"

Alex scratches the back of his neck. "Sorry. I've only spoken those words to one other person, and that's Catriona. But I've never had a brother before, so I've probably fucked that up in many ways."

"No, you haven't." His mention of Cat triggers a realization, and I groan now, not unlike the way he'd done a moment ago. "I can't propose to Jessica yet."

"Why not? Eight bloody years is long enough to wait. You don't want to tie my world record for Slowest Man Ever to Propose by waiting fourteen years, or worse, breaking my record."

"I won't wait that long. This is your wedding week, though. I don't want to steal your thunder."

Alex stares at me for several seconds, his face blank. Then he smacks my arm and gives me his favorite devious smile. "Do all the thunder-stealing you want. We can have a double wedding."

"What? I haven't even asked her yet."

"Get a move on, wee brother."

I grumble and throw my head back. "Alex, you're doing it again. Going overboard. There are licenses or whatever, aren't there? Might be a waiting period too. And her parents will want to be here."

He scoffs. "We have two lawyers in the wedding party, not to mention several chaps who own private jets. Trust me, we can get this done fast. If that's what you want."

"Let me propose before you start bribing county officials."

"Thank you for not assuming I would beat them into doing what I want. A slight bit of bribery isn't as bad as you think."

Slight bit of bribery? I can picture my brother tossing an enormous bag full of money onto the desk of whoever's in charge of issuing marriage licenses in this county.

"Maybe you're right," Alex says. "I should hold off to make sure Jessica says yes first."

"Are you implying she might say no?"

"Not at all. But I do believe in having contingency plans."

Logan and the women emerge from a shop one block down the street. Our conversation ends, thank heaven, as Alex and I jog up the street to meet the rest of our group. I have the ring box in my trouser pocket, and I've untucked my shirt so it covers the bulge at my hip.

Jessica eyes my shirt. "Did you forget to tuck that in after you went to the bathroom?"

"No, I—Alex's shirt is untucked. This way we match."

I might have gotten over my sex issues, but I still excel at coming up with asinine excuses to cover up whatever I'm trying to hide. Jess and I don't keep secrets, but I can't tell her there's a ring in my pocket, can I? That would spoil the surprise. Obfuscating Alex-style seems like my only option at this point.

Except I have no talent for that.

Alex aims his devious smile at Jessica. "I dared Grey to pull his shirt out and go untucked. He's too uptight about clothing."

Yes, he's much better at lying than I am. For the first time, I appreciate that quality in him.

"He used to be," Jessica says. "But these days, my Greybee is a relaxed, uninhibited sex god."

I can't help smirking. Didn't she just call me a sex god? I've earned the right to be smug about that. Domhnall might've been crowned the Gaelic God, but I'm the all-around sex god.

Alex eyes Logan and the three women who are still grouped around him. "Are you planning to give me back my fiancée? I think Grey wants his girl back too."

"But you gave me your harem," Logan says with a deadpan expression. "It would be rude to return a gift. Maybe I'll re-gift these three bonnie lasses and give them to Grey."

Alex crooks a finger at his fiancée. "Catriona darling, come here."

She flashes him a sassy look, then throws her arms around Logan and kisses his cheek. "Thank you for helping me pick out a wedding present for Alex."

Cat sashays up to Alex, wraps her arms around him, and kisses him passionately.

Jessica kisses Logan's cheek too. "Thanks for helping me with my shopping."

Then she rushes toward me, flinging her entire body at me.

I catch her, and we kiss as passionately as Alex and Cat are still doing.

"Don't want to be left out, do I?" Logan says. "*An toir thu dhomh pòg, Serena.*"

With Jessica's mouth sealed to mine, I can't think about what that Gaelic phrase means—or anything else in the entire universe.

Jess and I stop kissing first. Logan and Serena separate their mouths a few seconds later, but Alex and Cat keep kissing for a long time after the rest of us give it up, so long that passersby give them strange looks.

Finally, they peel their lips apart.

Our group starts back toward the town square, each couple holding hands.

When we get to the square, Alex takes me aside and whispers, "It will be a double wedding, mark my words. Maybe we should bet on that. A fiver?"

"You know I don't make wagers."

"But you want to, don't you? You are my brother, so the grifter gene is probably hidden deep down inside your jargon-filled DNA."

"Were you trying to bet me five dollars or five pounds? We're in America, but you live in Scotland, so I wasn't sure."

"Does it matter?"

"I suppose not."

He slips an arm around my shoulders. "Now, here's my advice for your wedding night..."

Yes, I let Alex give me his outrageous advice. But I don't need anyone else to tell me how to make Jessica feel good. All I need is our bodies and my business intelligence jargon.

Goodbye, sex cocker-upper. Hello, British sex god.

Chapter Twenty-Nine

Jessica

ONCE OUR TOUR GROUP GETS BACK TO THE RESORT, GREY and I return to our bungalow for some alone time. I loved hanging out with the MacTaggarts and with Alex, but I need a break from the crowd. I also need to snuggle up with my hot geek. Will he whisper more dirty jargon to me? God, I hope so. Maybe I love that stuff a little too much, but I don't care. If other women heard Grey explain spreadsheets and business intelligence whatsits, they'd go crazy for him too.

Since we had lunch in town, we settle onto the sofa so I can cuddle up to him. He drapes his arm around me. I rest my cheek on his shoulder, but I can't resist laying a hand on his thigh.

"You looked so hot in a kilt," I tell him. "Do you still have it?"

"The kilt? Yes, Alex gave it to me." He screws up his mouth. "I'm supposed to wear it for the wedding. Alex will wear a kilt too."

"Fabulous. I can drag you into a dark corner at the reception and shove my head under your skirt."

"I'd love that."

"Want to know what I'll be wearing?"

"Not just yet." He squirms and coughs. "I, ah, need to talk to you about something. Well, ask you something. Blimey, I'm already cocking it up."

"You haven't done anything or said anything that makes sense. How can you 'cock up' a thing you haven't done yet?"

"Right. Okay."

He gets up and drops to one knee. Then he freezes, like he's forgotten something, and mutters "bollocks" under his breath. He jumps up a little too quickly, stumbles into the coffee table, and falls backward onto his ass. After muttering "bollocks" again, this time with more vehemence, he scrambles to his feet and digs around in his pocket.

Grey brings out a small, rectangular box.

Is he about to... My tummy flutters, and my heart races. I think he *is* about to.

"Let me start over," Grey says, dropping to one knee again. "I love you, Jessica. After all these years, we're finally together, and I don't want to wait any longer for our shared life to begin in earnest." He opens the box, revealing the most beautiful diamond ring I've ever seen. "Will you marry me, Jessica?"

"Yes, of course I will."

He slips the ring onto my finger. "I got you a rose-gold ring because you love pink."

"Oh Grey, it's perfect. You always know exactly what I want."

I slide off the sofa to wrap my arms around his neck and kiss him. Our lips collide as he hugs me to him with his hands on my lower back, and our tongues curl around each other, diving deeper with every sensuous swipe. He moves his hands down to my ass, squeezing gently. God, he always tastes so damn good. I love the way he kisses me, and I wish we could do this forever. But I need more, and I can tell he does too since his dick is getting firmer and larger.

Giving up his lips, I pull my head back to look at him. "Let's do something different."

"Shouldn't we make love now? We just got engaged."

"I meant we could try something different when we have sex." I trace my fingertips over his bottom lip. "After what we did at the costume party, I know you've got a naughty streak. I want to take advantage of that."

"In what way?"

"There's a miniten game scheduled for right about now."

"But I don't want to play miniten. I want to shag you, Jess."

"Let me finish." I flick my tongue out to tease the seam of his mouth. "Let's find a shady spot at the edge of the woods to watch the miniten game, not too close to the lawn, but not too far away either. I want you to whisper filthy jargon to me while you fuck me where we might get caught."

His mouth opens. He stares at me, but he doesn't seem horrified. No, he looks aroused, based on the way his pupils have gotten bigger and his dick has gotten bigger. He's breathing harder too, and I bet if I felt for his pulse, I'd find it's racing.

Mine has sped up for sure.

I rake my tongue across his bottom lip. "What do you say?"

"Yes, Jessica, I want to fuck you where anyone might see us."

Oh God, I love the way his voice has gotten rougher.

Grey rushes to his room to grab condoms, then we race out of the bungalow. We slow to a fast walk as we round the corner of the guest house, so nobody will think we're running from a crazed bear or something. The miniten game is in full swing, with Logan and Rory competing against Domhnall and Jack. It's still kind of weird to see all these other people naked, especially men whose dicks flap every time they jump to hit the ball. It's also bizarre to watch people bat a tennis ball around using wooden boxes that cover their hands.

Maybe it's the miniten game, maybe it's the whole nudist thing, I don't know. But ever since I suggested this idea to Grey, I've felt giddy and almost lightheaded. Never have I done anything this brazen before, and I'm sure Grey hasn't either. This will make our encounter during the costume party seem tame in comparison.

Grey leads me past the miniten court, and the spectators gathered there, waving to people who shout hello, as he guides me to the edge of the woods at the far end of the lawn. He lets go of my hand, glancing around at the trees.

"Something wrong?" I ask.

"No. I need to find the right one. But first, we need to get naked."

The second he says that, I tear my clothes off. I love the way he devours me with his gaze, his tongue scraping across his lips, his hand stroking his cock through his pants.

He sheds his clothes too, then wanders from tree to tree, running his palms over the trunks until he finds one that seems to satisfy his mysterious requirements.

"This one will do," he says. "The bark is smooth."

"Why is that important?"

"You'll see. Come here, Jessica."

I approach him and the tree he's picked out.

He slaps a palm on the trunk. "Face the lawn and lean against this."

A thrill rushes through me, hot and tingly. And I do what he said. I plaster my body to the tree with my left cheek pressed against the bark. I can see the lawn from here. This tree stands at the very edge of it. Though the miniten game is taking place on the other side of the large grassy area, anyone might spot us. Only this tree and the shade of its leaves conceal us.

I hear a ripping sound, and I know Grey is rolling a condom on.

He glides his hands down my back, over my hips, and molds his palms to my buttocks, massaging them tenderly. It feels so damn good, but I want him inside me. I need it. When he slips his fingers under my ass, between my thighs, I can't help moaning. His fingers tease my slick flesh.

"You're ready for me, aren't you?" he says, his mouth grazing the shell of my ear. "I love how wet you are for me, Jess. And I want to lick up every bit of your cream, but I need something else first. I need you to watch all those people out there while I fuck you."

"Oh Gray baby, yes."

"I know what you want, and I'm about to give it to you." He pushes my feet apart with his, baring me to him in the most intimate way. With his lips covering my ear, he murmurs, "Are you ready for me to drill down into your field transformations?"

"Yes, please, yes."

He pushes inside me, inch by inch, filling me so deeply that I moan and clutch at the tree. My eyelids want to close, but Grey whispers to me, "Watch *them*, Jess."

I keep my eyes open, my gaze on the crowd gathered on the lawn. Grey moves slowly at first, grasping my hips and lifting them into every thrust while whispering jargon into my ear, his voice so rough and hot that it makes me burn from head to toe. I can barely breathe, but I don't care. What if I scream when I climax? Those people out there might hear it.

And the idea makes me hotter, wetter, even more desperate for Grey to make me come.

He mashes his chest to my back, his cheek against mine, and plunges in deeper, harder, increasing the pace with every inward lunge. God, it feels incredible, and I never want this to stop. I can't manage any words, only desperate moans and whimpers. I hug the tree tight because without it holding me up, I might crumple to the ground. But I need to touch him. Need it so badly. While he grunts with every thrust and drops his chin to my shoulder, I flail a hand backward to grasp the nape of his neck, gripping him like I'll die without the contact.

"Jessica," he growls against my neck. "Give me a full join on every column."

I have no idea what that means, but it doesn't matter. Just hearing him speak those techie words with his voice all rough and sexy pushes me over the edge. My entire body goes rigid, gluing me to the tree. My mouth falls open, my head slams backward, and I come. The power of it steals my breath, my voice, and consumes my focus until I wouldn't notice if a herd of buffalo stampeded around us. My body clenches Grey's cock, over and over, and the sensation of his hardness surrounded by my flesh makes me come even harder. I want to scream his name, but I have no voice. I tear my hands away from the tree to clutch his head, digging my nails into his scalp while he blows apart inside me.

"Jess!" he shouts, then he bites down on my shoulder.

I feel his release pulsing inside me. My climax keeps going, dwindling little by little, while he sags against me. He's still buried inside me, but I never want him to move. He squeezes a hand between my body and the tree, pushing one finger between my folds. Just when I think my orgasm is over, his expert finger toying with my clit sets off more waves of mind-blowing pleasure, my inner muscles milking him though he has nothing left to give. Grey keeps rubbing my nub until the very last spasm fades and I collapse. If it weren't for his body and this tree, I'd fall into a heap on the ground.

A moan is the only sound I can make. A long, throaty moan that conveys the fact I'm completely satisfied.

Grey pulls out of my body but keeps his head on my shoulder and his chest plastered to my back. He kisses his way up my shoulder to my throat, where he feathers his lips over the sensitive spot just under my jaw. "How would you feel about a double wedding?"

"Huh?" No one can expect me to be at full brainpower right now, not after that incredible climax.

My hot Brit chuckles, his breaths puffing against my throat. "You need a few minutes, don't you?"

"Uh...huh."

Grey picks me up and sits down with his back against the tree. I'm on his lap now, with his arms around me and my cheek resting against his. He combs his fingers through my hair, gliding his other hand up and down my arm.

After a few minutes, my brain starts to work again. Well, sort of. At least enough that I realize what those syllables he spoke earlier meant.

"Did you say double wedding?" I ask.

"Yes." He kisses the tip of my nose. "I love you so much, Jess, and I don't want to wait to get married. Do you?"

"I'll marry you right now, with grass for wedding bands." I lift my head to gaze at him. "What does a double wedding have to do with anything?"

"Alex helped me pick out an engagement ring, and he also suggested you and I could get married in the same ceremony with him and Catriona."

"Oh. But that's Saturday. We probably can't get a license that fast."

"My brother thinks we can. We have two lawyers on the premises, my cousin Chance and Rory MacTaggart. And I wouldn't put it past Alex to grease the wheels."

"You mean he'll pay someone off."

"It's best not to dwell on the things Alex might do. He's not a criminal, but he's also not above using his influence to get what he wants."

"And he wants the four of us to have a double wedding."

"Yes." Grey gets that tight, anxious look on his face, the one I know so well. "It's up to you."

I lay a hand on his cheek, stroking his skin with my fingertips. "We've waited a long time to be here, together, a real couple. Let's not wait any longer."

"What are you saying?"

"Yes, Grey baby, I'd love to marry you on Saturday."

He grins and whoops.

Chapter Thirty

Grey

JESS AND I ARE GETTING MARRIED. I DON'T WANT TO know how Alex did it, but somehow, we got our marriage license within thirty-six hours after we told my brother we want to do the double-wedding thing. Logan has become Alex's best man, and I've asked Jack to be mine. It seems appropriate since Jack not only helped Alex, but he helped me too. Would I have ever kissed Jessica, much less told her how I feel, if Jack hadn't encouraged me to do it?

The answer doesn't really matter. The result is all that counts.

Cat has her sister Fiona as her maid of honor, while Jessica will have her friend Carly standing at the altar with her. Carly's boyfriend is much better now but not up to traveling, though he encouraged Carly to come for the wedding. Jessica's parents have flown in too.

I will be the only one who doesn't have a mother or father there to watch me tie the knot. That fact makes me a little sad, but naturally, Jess notices and says exactly the right thing to make me feel better. We're curled up on the sofa in our little bungalow when I mention the bit about not having my dad around.

"You'll have your father there on our wedding day," she tells me. "Selwyn will be watching over you, smiling and cheering. And besides, you have a brother and cousins and a passel of Scots who all love you."

"I don't think Domhnall loves me. Not sure the other MacTaggarts do either. We don't know each other well enough for that."

"Don't be so literal about everything."

"Can't change that. I deal with facts and figures all day long, so 'literal' is my default position."

She snuggles closer to me. "Ooh, you know how I get when you speak jargon."

After that, we both forget about everything else for a long, long time. Yes, that means I shag her—repeatedly.

When Catriona and Carly take Jessica into town to shop for a wedding dress, Alex insists on accompanying me to that jewelry store again so I can buy wedding bands for me and Jess. He stares over my shoulder the entire time, shaking his head or making a disapproving face every time I point at a ring. Naturally, he wants me to spend an obscene amount of money on the wedding bands. We compromise on rings that are priced middle-of-the-road expensive instead of in-debt-for-all-eternity expensive. Alex wants to buy us the priciest rings available, but I put my foot down.

"I'm paying for my own wedding band," I tell him, "and Jessica's too. Do you think I want to think of you every time I glance at my left hand?"

"Why not? I'm wonderful to think about."

Only that twinkle in his eyes lets on that he's joking.

For once, Alex gives in. He pats my shoulder and says, "Have it your way. But you will wear a kilt."

"I'm not Scottish."

"You'll look foolish wearing a tuxedo when the rest of us are wearing kilts."

I smirk at him. "Maybe I'll go naked instead."

His expression goes blank. For several seconds, Alex Thorne says nothing at all, like he can't come up with a sarcastic response. Then he laughs. It's loud and boisterous and not at all like the way he usually laughs.

"You almost had me there," he says. "Every day, you get a bit more like me."

Maybe I should be insulted by that statement, but instead, I like the idea. Alex might be strange, and he might enjoy skirting the boundaries of what's strictly legal, but he's also a good person deep down. Peel back the layers of his who-gives-a-toss attitude and you'll find the soul of a loyal, compassionate man.

It's taken me months to realize that. And yes, I do love my brother. I admire him too, but don't tell Alex I said that.

Saturday arrives, and the lawn of Au Naturel Naturist Resort becomes an outdoor wedding venue. White chairs are lined up in rows bisected by an aisle that leads up to the altar. Alex hasn't gone overboard this time. The altar consists of a simple wooden arch, painted white and overflowing with flower garlands that wrap around it. The sky is a deep blue today without a cloud in sight, and the temperature is warm but not too warm, just right for a wedding in the wilderness.

I watch from the window of Jack's room in the guest house as the wedding guests take their seats.

"Time to go," Jack says.

Why do I feel slightly nauseous? I love Jessica, and I can't wait to marry her, so this must be excitement rather than anxiety.

Jack leads the way as we head downstairs and out onto the lawn.

Alex and Logan are already at the altar waiting for us. As soon as Jack and I take our positions, the music starts. A string quartet plays the introductory music while Lachlan and Erica's little boy carries the rings and Iain and Rae's daughter tosses flower petals onto the long carpet that leads up to the altar. The maids of honor march down the aisle next and take up their positions.

The string quartet switches to the wedding march.

Catriona walks down the aisle first. She smiles and winks at Alex as she moves into her assigned spot.

Then I see Jessica.

She's wearing an intricately beaded white gown with flowing skirts and more layers than I can count. The long sleeves hang off her shoulders, and the neckline shows just enough cleavage to look tastefully sexy. My God, she's beautiful. Her hair hangs in loose waves that kiss her shoulders, and her eyes glisten like she's overcome with emotion, though she's not crying. My throat goes thick, and I'm having trouble catching my breath. Jess is always stunning, but today, she's like an angel strolling down the aisle toward me.

That woman is about to marry me. How did I ever get so lucky? All those Martians will have to suffer with having worse luck than me because my fortunes have not only changed, they've realigned the stars.

I can't focus on the words the minister is saying. All I see is Jessica. We gaze at each other through the whole ceremony, and when I slip that gold band onto her finger, I can't breathe. My chest aches, but only in the best way. Tears trickle down Jessica's cheeks. Her lips quiver when she smiles, but even with red, puffy eyes, she's still the most beautiful woman I've ever seen.

When Alex and Cat exchange vows and rings, they both cry. Alex tries to hide it at first, turning his head to the side, but then he gives in and lets everyone see how deeply this moment affects him.

Once we've all said our vows and put those rings on, Alex and I kiss our brides. He wraps his arms around Cat and kisses her like a man who's waited fourteen years for this moment. He dips her backward, their mouths still fused, and then grabs her around the waist and lifts her off her feet, holding her above his head. They both grin and laugh, and the crowd erupts into cheering and clapping. Several people whistle.

I let Alex have his moment. He's earned it. Once he's set Catriona on her feet, I pull Jess into my arms and kiss her.

The cheering and clapping starts up again. Someone whoops.

Even though I have my eyes closed, I know it's Alex since he's standing a few feet away. When I finally peel my lips away from Jessica's, she smiles in the most beautiful, slightly dazed way.

And my brother whoops again. He slaps me on the back too.

I punch him in the arm and grin.

Then Alex strips naked and flings his kilt at the crowd. It lands on Rory MacTaggart's head. The man everyone calls the Steely Solicitor does the last thing I ever would have expected. He pulls the kilt off his head, grins at Alex, and shouts, "We're brothers now, whether ye like it or not. That means ye keep the kilt."

He tosses it at Alex.

Everything becomes a big blur after that. We all head into the guest house where the dining hall has become a party venue once again. There's no disco ball this time, and the lights stay on. I'm a little disappointed by that. I'd love the chance to shag Jessica in a dark corner again, but right now, it's time for our first dance as a married couple.

We don't even try to do a formal ballroom dancing whatsit. I hold Jess in my arms, her head on my chest, and we shuffle around the dance floor. She smells wonderful and feels even better. Her silky hair tickles my chin, but I don't care. Less than a week ago, I believed I had the worst luck in the universe. Today, I have everything I could ever have hoped for and more. I have the woman I adore, a brother I genuinely do love and respect, and more family than I could've imagined ever having. Not only do I have Alex and my cousins, but I have the MacTaggarts too. They might not be blood relations, but they've become like family to me.

After our first dance, Jack asks to "have a whirl" with Jessica.

I wander over to the spot where my cousins and the Hunters are having a conversation without their significant others present, though Nick isn't married, and I don't think he has a girlfriend either. Their conversation seems like a fun one. They're smiling and laughing.

"What's going on over here?" I ask as I reach them.

Reese points at Nick Hunter. "We were just harassing our mate about his lack of a womanly appendage."

"Womanly appendage?" Dane says, giving his brother a sarcastically offended look. "You are such a sexist twat, Reese. They're our life partners. And when was the last time you used the word appendage in a sentence?"

"A minute ago," Reese says. "You heard me say it, obviously. I thought Rika pulled that stick out of your arse, Dane. Must be sliding back in there. Better get a tune-up, mate." He claps a hand on his brother's shoulder. "That means go find Rika and get her to shag your brains out."

Nick looks at me. "You've left me all alone here, Grey. I don't have an unattached mate anymore."

"This reception is full of beautiful women," I tell him. "At least a few must be single."

Richard Hunter pretends to be horrified. "What are you saying, Grey? Never tell my brother to hunt for women. He'll leave a string of broken hearts in his wake."

"You're not funny," Nick says. "Honestly, Rick, only your fiancée thinks you're entertaining."

A chiming sound makes everyone check their mobiles.

"It's mine," Nick says. He squints at the screen on his mobile. His cheerful expression disintegrates, his eyes widen, and I swear his face pales half a shade. "What the bloody hell? The barmy cow..."

"What's wrong?" Richard asks.

Nick's lips work like he's trying to speak but can't quite manage it. He blinks several times, his focus on the mobile's screen. "She's trying to ruin me."

All of us, except Nick, exchange confused looks.

Richard speaks up first. "Ah, maybe you should give us the full story, Nick. What's happened?"

Nick tucks his mobile back into the inside pocket of his suit jacket. "Last week, a client made an unreasonable request, and I refused to do it. Now, the daft woman has started a nasty rumor about me. I got a text from a mate warning me that the rumor is spreading like wildfire, and I'd better get home and try to mitigate the damage."

"What rumor?" I ask.

"Yes, explain, please," Chance says. "And what was the unreasonable request?"

Nick rubs his jaw, averting his gaze to the floor. "She asked for a 'special' massage with a 'happy ending.' I don't do that sort of thing, not ever. I politely explained that's illegal, and she stormed out. Now she's telling everyone in town that I gave her that 'special' massage and that I do those all the time. She's making me sound like a gigolo."

I know Nick is a self-employed massage therapist, but I'm a bit confused by what he said. "What's a 'special' massage? I've heard the term happy ending, but I thought it referred to fairy tales and romance novels."

My cousins and the Hunters all stare at me like I'm daft.

"That's not what it means," Nick says. "The ruddy cow is saying I gave her a hand job. That means orgasms, Grey, not fairy tales."

"Oh. I see. What will you do?"

"Worry about it once I get home. She can't have done too much damage, can she?"

Everyone shrugs because none of us has a clue what to say.

Richard lays a hand on his brother's shoulder. "I'm sure it will all turn out fine. Don't worry about it today. Have a good time and leave all that rubbish for later."

"I'm sure you're right. The rumor will fade away."

After a few more minutes of chatting to my mates, I excuse myself to find Jessica. She's glad when I take her away from the American Wives Club because we both want the same thing—to hide in our bungalow and shag for hours. That's what wedding nights are for, isn't it?

The wives of the MacTaggart men have made Jessica the first member of the American Wives Club British Branch. Gavin Douglas became the Original American Husband back when he married Jamie, but now they've named Alex the Second American Husband and the Original British Branch Husband, thanks to his dual citizenship in the US and UK. They've also decided I'm the Second British Branch Husband.

This is all getting bloody confusing.

Jess and I hurry out of the dining hall and head for the kitchen. We need food to sustain us during our wedding night, don't we? A few meters from the kitchen doorway, we both stop. Strange noises are coming from inside there. We exchange glances, then edge closer to the doorway, peeking around the jamb to see what's going on.

Fiona MacTaggart sits on the island with Domhnall Sterling standing in front of her. His trousers are lumped around his ankles, and her dress is hiked up around her waist.

And they're shagging.

I back away from the door, dragging Jessica with me because she's grinning and staring at them.

"What are you doing?" I whisper.

"Same thing you were. Peeping."

"Yes, but I backed away as soon as I realized what I was seeing." I drag her further down the hallway. "Well, at least Domhnall isn't plotting to win you back anymore."

Jessica wraps her arms around me, pressing her whole body against mine. "Let's run back to our bungalow and make lots of noise."

"We'll show those two how it's done, won't we?"

"Absolutely."

I sweep her into my arms and run for the bungalow.

Chapter Thirty-One

Jessica

OUR WEDDING NIGHT IS BLISS. I NEVER WOULD'VE IMAGINED Grey could be so passionate and inventive, playful too, but every time we make love, he comes up with something new and exciting. Maybe sex with him is way better than it ever was with Domhnall because I love Grey so much, and we suit each other so well. Our week at the naturist resort changed everything, thanks in large part to Alex Thorne's meddling. Grey made me swear I would never tell Alex that. I'm also forbidden to mention, in the presence of anyone who's not Grey, that he and Alex admitted they love each other. Guys are so weird about anything related to their feelings. But I'm so glad Grey and Alex have gotten closer because they both need family—good family, not criminals.

Alex and Cat offer to send us on a whirlwind European honeymoon, but we decline their generous offer. Grey and I need to settle into our new life, and I need to find a new career. We rent an adorable cottage on the outskirts of Manchester because it turns out that city is almost exactly halfway between where Grey's cousins live in southeast England and where Alex and Cat live in the Scottish Highlands. With several well-connected Brits and Scots working to help us create our new life, Grey and I have things nailed down quickly. I've got a teaching position at a private school in Manchester, though I don't start my job there for another month.

That gives us plenty of time to visit Alex and Cat in Loch Fairbairn. They're just home from their honeymoon on a private island owned by a Nobel prize-winning author. Richard Hunter asked Sir Dexter Armstrong-Hill if he would host Alex and Cat, and Dexter said yes. Apparently, he loves having guests. Grey and I have a standing offer from Dexter to honeymoon on his island whenever we want.

Though multiple MacTaggarts offer to fly us to the Highlands, Grey and I prefer to turn our visit into a road trip. My husband—wow, I'm *married*—drives the last leg of our journey, so I use his phone to call Alex and Catriona and let them know we're almost there.

"You'll need to detour to Dùndubhan," Alex tells me. "The MacTaggarts insist on greeting you two in their unique way."

"Please tell me it's not Highland games."

"No, of course not. The games can wait until tomorrow."

I glance at Grey, who lifts his brows, and I ask Alex, "Do I even want to know what they've planned for today?"

"Come to Dùndubhan and see for yourselves."

"Okay, fine."

We say goodbye, and Grey gives me a suspicious sideways glance. "What is my brother plotting now?"

"Our presence is requested at Dùndubhan. Alex wouldn't say why, only that the MacTaggarts want to greet us."

"Alex loves to be cryptic."

Half an hour later, we drive through the gates of Dùndubhan, which is a genuine castle with a wall around it, big wooden gates, and even turrets. Other cars are already parked outside the walls and inside them too, but we find a spot in the driveway alongside the main doors to the medieval structure. Grey orders me to wait for him to open my door for me. He's such a gentleman. Just as I take his hand to get out of the car, Alex trots out of the walled garden and waves to us.

"Come on, you two," he hollers. "Leg it, would you? Everyone's waiting."

Hand in hand, we jog after him as he heads back into the garden, leading us to the far side where a wooden door hangs open. It leads out onto the green, aka the lawn, behind the castle compound. I've been here before, but not with all the mystery we've got today.

Alex disappears through an open door before we can catch up.

Grey and I rush through the garden doorway onto the green and freeze.

The MacTaggarts have gathered here, along with the Dixons and the Hunters, not to mention more people I can only glimpse through the crowd. Lachlan and Chance hold up opposite ends of a large banner that says, "Welcome, Grey and Jessica."

Alex and Cat stand in front of the horde.

We hurry over to them.

"Ready for your first surprise?" Alex asks.

First surprise? Oh jeez, what have these crazy, wonderful people cooked up this time?

Alex spreads an arm wide. The crowd separates to let two people pass.

My parents rush up to us and hug me, then Grey. My mom kisses his cheek.

"Why didn't you tell us you were coming for a visit?" I ask my parents.

"It's not a visit," Dad says. "Alex bought us a little house in Loch Fairbairn, so you guys can visit whenever you want, but we won't be in your hair all the time. Newlyweds don't want a couple of retirees fussing over them."

Grey looks at his brother, shaking his head the tiniest bit, smiling too despite his mouth hanging open. "Why did you do this?"

"Because you're my brother, and now Jessica is my sister. Get used to being lavished with gifts, Grey. Henry and Imogen have finally given in and let me spoil them, so you should too."

I spot Alex's adoptive parents in the crowd. Alex bought them a house a few months ago, and it's not far from where he and Cat live.

Now my parents will live in the UK too. Could life get more perfect?

"Here's your second surprise," Alex announces. "Look who else has moved to the Highlands."

He spreads his arm again, and two people walk out of the crowd, approaching us.

Domhnall and Fiona are holding hands, smiling as they reach me and Grey.

I can't speak or blink. Domhnall and Fiona had gotten cozy during the wedding-week extravaganza, and Grey and I saw them getting it on in the kitchen. But this looks like more than a vacation fling. Alex mentioned someone else had moved to the Highlands, but Fiona already lived here, so he must mean...Domhnall.

"Donnae worry," Domhnall says. "I'm not plotting to steal you away from Grey anymore. Fiona has shown me what an ersehole I was and taught me how to move on. I know that sounds like rubbish, but it's true." He gazes at Fiona with an expression I can only describe as loving. "Who knows if this will last, but we're giving it a go. Mick and I are opening our first branch location, here in Scotland, and I'm staying to run it. Fiona will be working for her cousin Evan at his company's headquarters in Inverness. That's where the new gym will be too."

"That's wonderful," I say. "I'm so happy for both of you."

"Yes, it's wonderful news," Grey says, offering Domhnall his hand to shake. "Congratulations. It sounds like everything worked out brilliantly for all of us."

"We'll see each other once in a while," Domhnall says, "since we're both connected to the MacTaggart clan now."

"Looking forward to it."

The battle of Brit versus Scot ends with not only a peace accord but also friendship. Life really is perfect.

Alex and the MacTaggarts have set up an outdoor party for us, and we spend the afternoon just hanging out with our friends and family. I've never seen Grey so happy before. He's gone from being an orphan to having a brother, in-laws, and a ton of other people who love him and treat him like family. He's got me too, and I've never been happier in my life.

"Is Jack here?" Grey asks while we're sharing a pitcher of lemonade with Alex, Catriona, Logan, and Serena. "I haven't seen him, but I'd like to say hello."

Alex gets that sneaky look on his face. "Jack is...otherwise engaged."

"What does that mean?"

Logan sighs and throws Alex a pointed look as he tells Grey, "Haven't you heard? The raging ersehole you call a brother connived to reunite Jack with his ex-wife. We know she's in the area, and she must be staying with Jack, but neither of them has left the house since she got here a few days ago. We have no idea if they're dead or alive."

Alex waves a hand to dismiss what Logan said. "Don't listen to him. I set up Jack and Autumn on a blind date two months ago, but it apparently turned into quite a mess. I didn't connive to bring her back here. Lachlan was driving past Jack's home and saw Autumn walk through the door, but I've no idea why she's in Loch Fairbairn again. Since Jack isn't answering his phone, none of us can say what's happening inside that house."

"A mystery?" I say. "How exciting. Has anyone tried knocking on Jack's door?"

"Yes, but no one answers."

"Maybe we should go over there and try again. Jack really helped me and Grey, so we owe it to him to make sure he's okay. Don't you think?"

Grey clasps my hand. "Tomorrow, love. I'm sure they'll survive until then, and I'm exhausted."

"Okay, tomorrow."

Alex clears his throat. "I hope you don't mind, but we arranged for you two to stay at Dùndubhan tonight. Choose whichever bedroom appeals to you."

Sleeping in a castle? That sounds like a great adventure. The biggest adventure yet is still unfolding, though. My life with Grey has just begun, but I know it will be amazing. Sometimes the last person you expected to fall for is the only one in the world you ever needed. I believe in second chances and true love, so I'm rooting for Jack and Autumn to get both of those. I am a member of the American Wives Club now, so maybe a teeny bit of meddling is in order.

Grey leans close to whisper in my ear, "I know what you're thinking. Don't do it."

"But Grey baby, meddling worked for us, and for Alex, and for Logan, Rory, Lachlan—"

"All right, I surrender." He kisses that sweet spot just below my ear, and warmth tingles over my skin. "But maybe I can distract you with erotic jargon."

"Give it your best shot, Greybee. I'm all in—for a lifetime."

Want more of Jack and Nick? Experience their stories in *Devastating in a Kilt* (Hot Scots, Book 9) and *One Hot Rumor* (Hot Brits, Book 5).

ANNA DURAND IS A BESTSELLING, MULTI-AWARD-winning author of contemporary and paranormal romance. Her books have earned bestseller status on every major retailer and wonderful reviews from readers around the world. But that's the boring spiel. Here are the really cool things you want to know about Anna!

Born on Lachland Air Force Base in Texas, Anna grew up moving here, there, and everywhere thanks to her dad's job as an instructor pilot. She's lived in Texas (twice), Mississippi, California (twice), Michigan (twice), and Alaska—and now Ohio.

As for her writing, Anna has always made up stories in her head, but she didn't write them down until her teen years. Those first awful books went into the trash can a few years later, though she learned a lot from those stories. Eventually, she would pen her first romance novel, the paranormal romance *Willpower*, and she's never looked back since.

Want even more details about Anna? Get access to her extended bio when you subscribe to her newsletter and download the free bonus ebook, *Hot Scots Confidential*. You'll also get hot deleted scenes, character interviews, fun facts, and more! Plus you'll receive the short story *Tempted by a Kiss*, two bonus chapters for *One Hot Chance*, and audio bonus chapters too!

Visit AnnaDurand.com to sign up.